"You would do well to watch your tongue, my girl, for one who speaks so crudely to her betters only begs to have her shapely bottom beaten soundly!"

Lord Bradford's arm shot out, wrapping around her slim waist. His dark, angry face descended toward her own.

"Release me at once, sir!" Genevieve demanded furiously, wrenching her neck to one side.

Lord Bradford smiled dangerously. "I shall, my dear, but not until you have apologized properly." Undaunted by her thrashing body, his free hand gripped the back of Genevieve's head and turned her face toward him.

His mouth covered hers completely. His lips were warm and firm. Genevieve was astounded by the chaos that surged through her body like molten lava.

To Genevieve's horror her lips began to move beneath his, and when he finally released her, it was her lips, not Bradford's, which clung and begged for more.

Other **Regency Romances**
from Avon Books

BELLE OF THE BALL *by Joan Overfield*
CLARISSA *by Cathleen Clare*
GEORGINA'S CAMPAIGN *by Barbara Reeves*
LORD FORTUNE'S PRIZE *by Nancy Richards-Akers*
MISS GABRIEL'S GAMBIT *by Rita Boucher*
SWEET BARGAIN *by Kate Moore*

Coming Soon

THE MUCH MALIGNED LORD *by Barbara Reeves*

The Mischievous Maid

REBECCA ROBBINS

AVON BOOKS ◆ NEW YORK

THE MISCHIEVOUS MAID is an original publication of Avon Books. This work has never before appeared in book form. This work is a novel. Any similarity to actual persons or events is purely coincidental.

AVON BOOKS
A division of
The Hearst Corporation
1350 Avenue of the Americas
New York, New York 10019

Copyright © 1993 by Robin Hacking
Published by arrangement with the author
Library of Congress Catalog Card Number: 93-90118
ISBN: 0-380-77336-8

First Avon Books Printing: August 1993

AVON TRADEMARK REG. U.S. PAT. OFF. AND IN OTHER COUNTRIES, MARCA REGISTRADA, HECHO EN U.S.A.

Printed in the U.S.A.

RA 10 9 8 7 6 5 4 3 2 1

Prologue

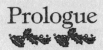

Miles, Lord Bradford, reminisced six months later that he probably should have been warned the first time he laid eyes on the Honorable Genevieve Quince that something about her was not quite as it seemed.

It was not the trim figure, covered innocently enough by an outdated riding habit of pale-green kerseymere, that he should have found peculiar. Nor was it the lustrous red-gold chignon peeking from beneath her pert cork bonnet, with its gauzy veil of spring-green net, that spoke of unusual things to come.

Lord Bradford had no reason to believe that there was anything amiss in the pale-tan gloves that encased her small hands. And why should the riding boots, with their gleaming brass buttons, wrapped around the girl's slender ankles, have aroused suspicion?

Now that he thought on it, he could not possibly have been alerted by the sedate pace at which she rode the dapple-gray mare beside a carriage piled high with trunks and boxes. It was quite natural for a young woman of spirit to ride outside the coach rather than within its stuffy confines even on as chill a day as that one had been.

1

The thing that should have alerted him was, rather, the angry, almost rebellious tilt to her head, and the way she seemed to lean forward on the mare as if riding into battle. However, those indications of the fiery nature that lay beneath her calm exterior, those telltale signs that should have led him to understand that the Honorable Genevieve Quince was made for mischief, merely caused him to smile and think what an uncommonly pretty girl she was.

If he had known that the modestly coquettish habit had been made by none other than its wearer herself, and that the demure chignon was threatening to pour russet flames over her slender shoulders and past her narrow waist at any moment, so loose were its pins, that the carriage was not her own but a hired public conveyance, and that her slender form was more a product of deprivation than of the fashionable miss's habit of eating sparingly, perhaps Lord Bradford's bland gaze would have turned speculative, and he would have been forewarned that to become acquainted with the young woman in question would bring nothing but trouble.

But he did not think on these telling details. He did not even notice them. For his lordship had one major failing. He was proud—so proud that very little occupied his concern except himself. And that is exactly why disaster, in the form of a single strawberry-haired, blue-eyed girl, chose Lord Bradford's head to fall upon.

1

It was mere chance, on that fateful early-spring morning, that Lord Bradford happened to throw an unconcerned glance out the side window of the breakfast room of his London town house in St. James Square as he helped himself to a third cup of tea and a second crumpet smothered in freshly made raspberry jam. Absently he watched the attractive young female riding down the narrow road that led to the outskirts of London. Nothing more pressing demanded his attention than that it was spring, the crumpets were slightly burned, and his best friend, Tony Ashleigh, the Earl of Glenworthy, had gotten leg-shackled the previous night.

Tony Ashleigh and Miles Bradford had grown up together. They had bloodied each other's noses over village maidens, tangled their horses while fox hunting, and nearly been expelled from Eton together when they were boys. This last event had come about when Lord Bradford, not the kowtowing type, had challenged to a duel an upperclassman who insisted that Miles play errand boy for him. With Tony as his second, Lord Bradford had nearly killed the older boy by running him through with his sword. Needless to say all the upperclassmen left both boys alone after that.

Lord Bradford smiled, remembering. But just as rapidly the smile disappeared, replaced with a bleak frown as he realized that time had passed more swiftly than even those two mischievous young boys could have imagined.

"Damnation!" he muttered darkly.

It was not that Miles disliked quiet, enchantingly lovely Lady Anne Farquahr, the young woman Tony had chosen from last year's crop of dewy debutantes to take to wife. It was simply that he and Tony had always sworn never to become entrapped by one of the more devious sex.

But ever since yesterday morning, when Tony, the same young rapscallion who used to drop frogs down little girls' bodices and yank their pigtails, had repeated his vows while staring with rapt adoration into Lady Anne's eyes, Miles's own mind had turned to the question of wedlock. No doubt the new countess would produce a future earl without delay—a disconcerting thought for Lord Bradford, since he had always cherished the idea that the Bradford and Ashleigh sons would grow up together. He had even contemplated matrimony between their two houses, if their respective wives had provided offspring of a gender suitable for such a match.

Now he sighed. If Tony, a year younger than Lord Bradford, thought it necessary to set up his nursery, then it was undoubtedly time for Miles to do so as well. If only there were some way to get himself a legitimate heir without having to wed! The thought of being chained to a shrieking, shrewish female for the rest of his days, rather than simply enjoying a string of charming, eager-to-please mistresses, turned the crumpets in his belly to sharp-edged stones.

Although he had known, deep inside, that this unhappy eventuality could not be avoided forever, he had not expected it to arrive quite so soon. With a grimace he began to contemplate candidates to share his future.

A debutante? Too inexperienced. The very idea of day after day with no conversation but "Yes, my lord" or "No, my lord" or "As you say, my lord" turned his stomach. Besides, this Season's crop seemed even more gauche and homely than last year's.

A widow? Too old. Spending one's days with a wrinkled hag would be worse than suffering the inane conversation of a green girl and would rule out any possibility of heirs—not to mention that most widows were already encumbered with brats of their own eager to claim fame and fortune without benefit of blood ties.

A female who had been out for a few years? No, no, a hundred times no! Although her dialogue would be better than a debutante's, and her face less wizened than a widow's, she would be, beyond a doubt, quite unforgivably ugly, since she had not yet been snatched up by some available bachelor. Or, worse, God forbid, she might be a bluestocking, who would assail his ears at every opportunity with her caterwauling about "women's rights."

Lord Bradford cursed with exasperation and hurled his butter knife down on the table, then groaned as the offending utensil crashed into his juice glass, tipping it and sending a sticky yellow stream over the pristine white-lace tablecloth.

Well known for his resolution in difficult situations, his lordship now found himself floundering helplessly as he considered how to find a suitable bride. One who would keep her mouth shut and her homely face out of his sight except during those brief, unpleasant periods of heir-getting, which could not be avoided. When she had provided him with a son, he thought with a decisive nod, she would be packed off to one of his country estates, out of the way so that he could continue enjoying his freedom, as was a gentleman's due. But how best to find her in the first place?

He half-rose from his chair, then fell back heavily, hastily discarding his half-formed intention of riding over to Tony's for an intelligent discussion on the matter. It was the morning after the chap's wedding night, after all. If Tony showed the same appreciation for his wife that he had been known, prior to his marriage, to show for his mistresses— and he undoubtedly would, since Lady Anne was a dashed attractive woman—the newlyweds would not be rising for several more hours today, if at all.

Lord Bradford sat for a very long time at the table near the window, watching the carriages rattle by and feeling most sorry for himself. With his long, slender, aristocratic fingers he shoved back his glossy black hair, ruining his valet's careful arrangement of the Windswept. He stroked his recently shaven chin. And between narrowed lids his shadow-dark eyes watched the young woman's caravan wind its way down the road.

At that moment one presumptuous ray of sunlight shone in through the window, flowed over the table, and lighted on the signet ring on his index finger, making it glint.

Lord Bradford suddenly smiled. He promptly called for the butler to bring paper, quill, ink, and sealing wax, and then began to write. Then he sat back, folded the sheets of thick parchment now covered with his bold, slanted script, dripped molten red onto the fold, and pressed his seal into the quickly hardening liquid with his signet ring.

He paused as he sealed the second letter, addressed to his mistress, remembering that he was promised to take Madame Devereux to the ballet in two days. Mimi was not known for her patience at being jilted. He would have to visit her briefly before leaving town, to explain that, although he intended to take a wife, she would still be the principle object of his passion. He smiled fleetingly at the thought of the coming pleasure in her arms, then dismissed her casually from his mind. He quickly sealed the third missive.

The peace and quiet of the country, he mused. Yes. It would do him good to get some well-earned rest. City life was picking up with the commencement of the new Season, and he was in dire need of a little respite and relaxation before it got too far under way. And he would be killing two birds with one stone—a prospect his businesslike mind found appealing. For what better place to find a wife than among the estates neighboring Bradford Hall? Not only would he gain a bride, but he would extend his landholdings in the area at the same time! Why, the thought almost made marriage palatable. Almost.

He wiped the wax off the signet ring and replaced it on his finger. With his mind thus occupied Lord Bradford caught his last glimpse of the unknown female as her horse disappeared around a bend. He picked up the three letters with a jaunty grin.

"Benson!" Lord Bradford shouted imperiously.

"Yes, my lord?" The ancient man, whose visage was nearly as wrinkled as his clothing, silently reappeared as if he had been waiting just outside the door.

Lord Bradford jumped back a step and glared at his elderly valet, who, refusing all offers to lighten his workload, had insisted on doubling as butler and gentleman's gentleman since old Trilby, the previous butler, had retired to the country to live with his two spinster sisters and take up his one true love, the breeding of pedigreed swine.

"Damn it all, man," Lord Bradford snapped. "Must you behave like a ghostly jack-in-the-box? You nearly gave me heart failure."

"Do forgive me, my lord," intoned the valet in his familiar doleful voice.

Lord Bradford sighed. He had long since grown used to Benson's odd ways, from his abrupt appearances to his constant apologizing to his wrinkled clothing, and he was ashamed of his snappish reply. Harsh words from him always sent the manservant into a decline. As long as Miles's own clothing was clean and pressed and in the height of taste and fashion, let the man dress and behave as he pleased, and devil take the opinion of Society.

Benson had, after all, been with Miles's father before him, and was loyal to a fault. His huge, limpid eyes, resembling so closely those of a King Charles spaniel, were now trained sorrowfully on his master's face, and Miles felt a stabbing pang of remorse.

"No, Benson, it is I who should apologize. I am not feeling quite the thing this morning. A bit blue-deviled from overindulging at Lord Ashleigh's nuptial fête, I fear. I shall be thirty-five in a few months, you know. I suppose that at my advanced age I should learn to restrain both my habits *and* my temper." Then, realizing that he was rambling in a manner he despised in others, Lord Bradford forced himself back to the matter at hand.

"Pack my things. We leave for Bradford Hall tomorrow. My nerves are as frayed as a horse's tail caught in a stable gate. I want to spent a few weeks in the peace of the country before the Season is too far gone. And just between the two of us," he said with a conspiratorial wink (he had the satisfaction of seeing the hang-dog expression leave Benson's eyes, to be replaced with joy at being taken into his master's confidence), "I intend to investigate the matrimonial prospects on the surrounding estates, and shall, if all goes as planned, return with a bride before the middle of the Season."

Benson beamed, his face cracking into an unholy grimace. "Yes, my lord. Very good, my lord. My, my. What a delightful surprise. May I offer my heartfelt congratulations on the happy event?"

"Hmmph," Miles grunted. "How can you look so pleased at such a hateful idea, Benson? Do you wish me so ill that you would see me leg-shackled already?"

Benson's expression once more hovered near dismay and Miles hurried on. "At any rate, I have written Dobbins, my solicitor, instructing him to choose the most likely eligible women he can find from among my class on the neighboring estates—considering, of course, pedigree, fortune, the quality of the landholdings, and, lastly, appearance. I shall choose my bride from amongst these maidens after a suitable period of wooing—perhaps a week or two.

"The fortunate lady's appearance matters least, I suppose," Lord Bradford murmured sadly, more to himself than to his valet, "as I can always come to her room only when it is in pitch-darkness. The other points are, naturally, of far more consequence."

He lifted an inquiring eyebrow at the astounded valet, whose mouth hung open slackly, unable, due to his ever-respectful tongue, to issue whatever questions were forming in his aged mind.

Unlike the rest of the household servants, Benson was not particularly put off by Lord Bradford's piercing gray-black eyes, although they did at times tend to make his master look disturbingly like a demon stepped up from the depths of hell. The valet was brimming with a curiosity so intense that it nearly overstepped the bounds of both propriety and containment. He managed at last to swallow the myriad questions threatening to burst forth from his thin lips and, remembering his place, merely bowed stiffly.

"It shall be as you require, my lord."

"Good. See to it. Oh, and please take this note to my solicitor this afternoon,"—he handed Benson one of the three letters he held—"this one to Madame Devereux,"—he handed the second missive to his servant, who was unable to contain the tiny, pleased quirk of his lips at the glorious news that his master was to take a wife, never mind the odd circumstances—"and this one to the post."

Then Miles hesitated. "No, better give Mimi's letter back to me. I shall deliver it myself. If memory serves, the last time you were called upon to give her such a message, she nearly brained you with a Ming vase. You were shedding shards of porcelain all over the house for a week." He took the note, grimacing knowingly at Benson's relieved expression.

The valet's attention returned once again to his master's forthcoming marriage, and he smiled. "Yes, my lord."

"Oh, and Benson?"

"Yes, my lord?"

"Wipe that smug grin off your face before I remove it for you."

"Yes, my lord." The valet straightened his lips much in the manner that he would one of his master's intricately tied cravats, and paced sedately from the room.

Lord Bradford grinned. Indispensable man, Benson.

2

The Honorable Genevieve Quince gripped the leather reins tightly in her small fist, trying, without success, to ignore the prickling sensation of the chill, damp morning air that easily penetrated her too-tight riding habit. While it had appeared merely outdated to Lord Bradford, it was also several sizes too small, having been made two years ago when Genevieve was only sixteen and a good deal smaller in the female sections of her anatomy than now.

The rage that had boiled over yesterday had finally slowed to a simmer, although Genevieve still snorted with disgust every few minutes as she thought about Cousins Marybelle and Augustus's latest connivance.

If only Father had not died two years ago, she thought, more with anger than self-pity. But then, it had been just like him to leave her penniless and at the mercy of his second cousin, that old hag Marybelle and her fat husband (there was no nicer way to put it, for in truth he was as large as a Jersey bull), Lord Merriweather, who, although getting on in years, still had his eye on a political appointment of great respect.

It was his political yearnings, not to mention his

carnal urges, that had led to Genevieve's flight from London. The despicable scene of two evenings before flashed through her mind.

Genevieve had stood at the kitchen counter, chopping an onion into tiny pieces for the butter-basted quail she was preparing for her cousins' dinner. The tears that streamed down her cheeks were not solely due to the pungent fumes, although she never would have admitted as much to anyone. She slid the last bit of diced onion from the cracked-stoneware saucer into the pan of plump birds just as the front doors of the town house on St. James Street opened, heralding her cousins' return home from their most recent entertainment.

Genevieve hurriedly rubbed a bit of dry mustard into her hands to rid them of the distasteful odor of onion, brushed it off on her apron, and turned swiftly toward the window so that her back was toward the kitchen door as Marybelle entered the room. Furtively Genevieve took a swipe at her streaming face with one corner of her worn gingham apron then winced as a stray bit of mustard stung her eyes.

"Genevieve," crooned Cousin Marybelle in a falsely affectionate voice.

Genevieve did not know why her cousin bothered to feign friendliness just now, since there was no love lost between them. Indeed, they were barely civil most of the time, Genevieve managing only with difficulty to keep a respectful tongue in her head so that she would not be thrown out into the streets. She turned suspiciously, taking in the excited flush on her cousin's cheeks and the sharp glint in her tiny reptilian eyes.

"My lady?"

Lady Merriweather had done away with any references to their familial relationship during the first week of Genevieve's arrival at their abode. How would it look, after all, Cousin Marybelle had asked, if a guest happened to hear a servant addressing her ladyship as Cousin?

"Come into the parlor, Genevieve dear. Augustus and I have something we wish to discuss with you."

Her cousin turned and left the kitchen before Genevieve could unwisely reply that she was too busy with dinner preparations. As she walked behind her cousin's thick form, she glanced down at her hands with disgust. They looked just like a servant's now—red and chapped, fingernails cracked and ragged.

Upon reaching the parlor, Marybelle seated herself in a Baltimore roll-back side chair with pawed feet, one of a group of pieces she had had imported especially from America. The remainder of the furniture was Duncan Phyfe. She settled the hem of her gem-encrusted crushed maroon velvet gown over her outsized feet and clasped her hands in her lap, a queen preparing to bestow a favor on her subject.

Although instinctively dreading whatever new imposition was coming, Genevieve grew increasingly curious. Ordinarily Cousin Marybelle changed from her gaudy evening gowns immediately upon returning to the house. Whatever she had to say must be of great import indeed.

Nearby, Cousin Augustus loitered beside a long, exquisite sideboard, perusing his selection of fine liquors. The sideboard was another American piece, its figured mahogany panels, fine inlay, and urn-shaped ivory key scutcheons proclaiming it to be the work of Seymour.

At last her portly cousin plucked one cut-crystal decanter from among the plethora of bottles and poured a generous dollop of fluid into a huge goblet. Only after swallowing the entire portion in a single gulp did he turn to gaze at the two women.

"Now then, Genevieve," Cousin Marybelle crooned. "Lord Merriweather and I have decided to take a trip to Paris. As you know, with the war finally over and that dastardly Napoleon safe at last on St. Helena, almost the whole of the Beau Monde is rushing to France. Why, there is scarcely anyone left in Town for the beginning of the Season! We cannot risk having someone else beat us to the newest fashions, and if we dash to Paris now, we can be back before the Season is half over."

Genevieve waited silently.

"How do you like your home here, Genevieve?" the woman asked, her tone leading her young cousin to the correct answer.

"It is very comfortable, my lady."

"Of course," said Marybelle with a confident laugh. "It was, I am sure you will agree, most kind of dear Augustus and me to take you in when your father died."

"Yes, my lady," Genevieve said through clenched teeth.

"Would you not agree that we have been everything that is generous to you, my girl?"

"Yes, my lady," Genevieve replied, praying that her cousin would not notice the anger blazing in her eyes or hear the sound of her teeth grinding together.

"As we have been so kind to you, would not you agree that you owe us a favor?"

"A favor?" Genevieve said, bracing herself.

"Indeed, my girl. Open your ears! We have given you a home and asked nothing in return!"

Genevieve bit back a sharp retort and forced herself to reply calmly. "I assure you, ma'am, that

I feel I have more than paid my ticket in your household."

Her cousin's face went an angry scarlet. "Paid your ticket? What a vulgar expression, my girl. And it is just as crude of you to intimate that by doing a few simple tasks around the house you are now fully absolved of your debt to us! Surely you cannot expect to live here free and clear forever without repaying us somehow, Genevieve! Why, it would be cruel of us to allow you to demean yourself by becoming overly beholden to us!" Marybelle cried. She half-rose from the chair and then fell back, clutching her chest as if exhausted by the exertion of needfully scolding her ungrateful kinswoman.

Genevieve felt a rush of distaste and wished for the hundredth time she had remained at Quince House, her derelict family estate which she'd been unable to bring herself to sell. Surely she could have eked out a living for herself somehow. Just now anything seemed more appealing then remaining with her demanding cousins. "Do not strain youself, my lady. Is there some way you have thought of that I could repay your kindness?"

The look of fatigue was replaced by a triumphant smile. Cousin Marybelle's hand dropped from her chest to her lap, and she sat forward, beaming with greedy anticipation. "Fortunately for your suffering self-respect, yes! It has occurred to me that you will probably never marry, since you are not possessed of a portion to snag yourself a husband. Still, it would not do for me to allow you to rot away on the shelf, seeing how I am your cousin, after all." She paused significantly. "Augustus and I have agreed that you must be seen by men of your class."

Genevieve gasped, and her eyes widened in surprise. They were going to give her a Season! She would make her come-out! She would dance at Almack's and have new gowns and take part in the promenade at Hyde Park!

Her cousin's next words brought her back to earth with a crash.

"There is a way that you can meet such men *and* repay Augustus and me for our benevolence. We have decided that, rather than send you to your grave a virgin, we will allow you to partake of pleasure with Augustus's political friends when they visit us. Who knows! Perhaps one of them will even suit you for marriage."

Genevieve felt the blood in her head rush to her feet and then surge back again. "Are you suggesting that I compromise myself with your guests, and by so doing snare a husband? A keeper, more like! You cannot be serious! What kind of man would have me if I ruined myself with a veritable multitude before him! No, Cousin Marybelle—"

"My lady," Marybelle snapped, her false expression of goodwill replaced abruptly with one of unconcealed fury.

"*My lady*," Genevieve corrected herself through gritted teeth. "I cannot do as you suggest. I would rather die!" She was breathing hard, trembling with horror. "Are you so desperate to please your high-and-mighty guests so that your husband's sluggish career will prosper at this late date that you would freely compromise your own kinswoman? Ah!" she cried as Marybelle flushed guiltily. "That is it, isn't it? Well, I tell you, I will not do it! It is beyond me how you ever came up with such a disgusting plot—much less how you managed to speak the words! That you could even suggest such a thing is revolting! Such a notion would embarrass even a charwoman!"

Lady Merriweather paled and drew herself to

her feet slowly. When she spoke her voice trembled with rage. "You will do as I say, my girl, or you will be out of my home and living in the street, where you will be forced to do exactly as I have suggested just to survive—but with filthy commoners rather than peers of the realm!" She took a deep breath, her massive breasts heaving. "I have simply offered you a chance to snare yourself a rich protector, which is more or less the same as a husband. Besides, any woman without a penny to her name should be honored by such an opportunity to meet the lords of London."

Genevieve saw that her cousin was not to be swayed. She stalled for time, hoping to come up with a suitable solution—something, anything— that would turn Cousin Marybelle's mercenary mind from trading Genevieve's body for favors. "But I—I have nothing to wear! How can you expect me to dine and converse with your honorable guests in the rags I possess, much less procure one's goodwill?"

Her cousin smiled, a nasty, satisfied smile, sure that the girl was going to submit. "No need to fret. Since you will continue to cook, you will be servicing their lordships *after* dinner. Besides, as you say, you have nothing suitable in which to be seen. This way, no one will see you until after supper. And you will not need to be seen *in* anything."

She chuckled evilly. "Now then, Augustus and I leave for France on the morrow. We will be gone for approximately six weeks. By the time we return, I trust you will be more pliant and willing to show your gratitude for our unbounded kindness. You are dismissed." She turned away imperiously, walked over to Augustus, took the newly filled glass from his hand just as it was rising to his lips, and tossed it back.

Genevieve shot a disbelieving look toward Augustus, but he ignored her, merely glaring at his spouse as he poured another brandy. Without a backward glance Genevieve fled the room and ran up the great stairs, down a corridor, and up yet another rickety flight of steps to the tiny window-less attic room that had belonged to one of the maids who had been dismissed upon Genevieve's arrival.

She forced several deep breaths, trying, unsuc-cessfully, to calm herself as she sank slowly onto the edge of the narrow bed, wringing her cold, white, bloodless hands. *Oh, God!* she thought hopelessly. *What am I to do? Why did Papa have to die? And penniless, at that.*

Barely a week after Leonardo Quince, baronet, died in a drunken attempt to jump his last unsold hunter, a ratchety hack that was not up to the en-deavor, over an impossible gate during a fox hunt, Genevieve had had a visit from Papa's hitherto unknown cousins Marybelle and Augustus, Lord Merriweather. They had kindly offered to give their young kinswoman a home and, as Genevieve found herself without funds to maintain her an-cestral residence, she accepted their offer grate-fully, leaving Quince House unoccupied until the day she could return and restore it to its former grandeur.

The very day Genevieve arrived on their door-step she was greeted with the sight of departing servants, from the lowliest chambermaids to the housekeeper and cook. The only duties Genevieve was not responsible for were the butler's, and those only because it was not *comme il faut* to have a female butler. There was no task too dirty or de-meaning for her, and she found herself flung into the distasteful situation in which she cooked sumptuous meals, emptied chamber pots, and narrowly escaped Cousin Augustus's grasping hands all within the same hour.

But what choice had she? Too young to be a governess, too well-spoken to be hired as a chambermaid, and too amply endowed to be trusted in a household as a lady's companion—she had tried to find work in all these avenues and failed—she was forced to suffer the "charity" of those two beasts downstairs.

At last Genevieve fell into an exhausted sleep, and her cousins, wisely leaving her alone to ponder their request, said nothing about the spoilt quail.

The next morning Cousin Marybelle patted Genevieve's hand, smiling confidently before turning on the glittering limestone steps of the town house and climbing into the plush landau. Cousin Augustus turned toward Genevieve with a leer, swept her into his meaty arms, and fondled her backside as he whispered how happy he was with the new arrangement and how fortunate she was to have found such a good home.

As if this new turn of events were not bad enough, no sooner had they departed than Genevieve went back indoors to discover that the butler had been given a holiday, there was no money for household expenses, and the pantry was as empty as a three-foot hole. Evidently her cousins intended to starve her into obedience.

Pushed beyond endurance, Genevieve kicked the pantry door violently, and an empty earthenware jar fell from a shelf and smashed on the floor at her feet. She stared at the shards rebelliously for a few moments, then mutinously turned away from the damage and walked with grim determination out of the kitchen and into the parlor. There she scooped up Cousin Augustus's discarded copy of the *Times* and hurriedly leafed through its contents until she came to the advertisement section.

Within a few moments Genevieve had scribbled two letters, one to the newspaper, the other to her father's former solicitor. She folded them quickly and, before she had a chance to think about it, hired a hackney cab with money purloined from Cousin Augustus's desk and delivered them to their destinations.

Task completed, Genevieve sat back in the conveyance, smiling. Now that she thought on it, she had a lot to thank Cousins Marybelle and Augustus for. Not only did she know how to keep house beautifully, but she could also cook like a dream and plan entertainments worthy of the best hostess in England. Unwittingly, Cousins Marybelle and Augustus had given her the skills to make her own way in what was potentially a lucrative business.

Genevieve spent the rest of the day making trips to various shops, where she used her status as housekeeper for Lord Merriweather as credit, purchasing whatever she thought she might need for her venture. The following morning, she hired a public conveyance under the same ruse and watched with a satisfied smile as her purchases were loaded upon the vehicle until it creaked under their weight.

Then she went to the stable behind the house where Cousin Marybelle kept her riding horse, a small gray mare named Storm, and saddled it. As she led the horse out of its stall, she thought furiously that her cousins had made certain that the horse had plenty of food—to be proffered by Genevieve after she mucked out the stall—while their servant had nothing but dust to eat. Well, she had to take the mare, she reasoned as she enjoyed the movement of the fine horse beneath her. If she left it, the poor beast would starve.

Thus, without a glimmer of guilt, Genevieve nudged the mare in the ribs and followed the slowly moving carriage down the street, across Westminster Bridge, and out toward the southeastern countryside. Not a single backward glance did she give the opulent town house; not a tremor of fear did she allow to shake her resolve. Her plan had to work. It just had to.

It was then that Lord Bradford glanced out his window and saw her ride past; for this reason her head was so stubbornly tilted, her body so rigidly poised. After two years of ill-usage, Genevieve Quince had had enough. And nothing would deter her from her plan of action. After all, anything was better than becoming her cousins' whore. Wasn't it?

3

If Lord Bradford had been thinking, he would
have realized that everyone who was anyone
was in London or Paris just now, rather than
awaiting his lordship's pleasure in a country bor-
ough. However, true to his lofty character, such a
thought did not enter his mind.

As usual, Lord Bradford thought smugly, he had
hit upon the perfect solution, as it would not only
protect him from the crowds of simpering green
misses and their calculating mamas already
swarming London, but would also negate the
need for all but the most cursory courtship rituals.

The marriage would, of course, in historical Bradford fashion, be solemnized at Bradford Hall. No
need to put off the inevitable once the lady was
won. The sooner the necessary heir was produced,
the sooner Miles could get on with his personal
entertainments—Mimi, for example. Although Society might frown at some other newlywed's haste,
no one would dare find fault with Lord Bradford.
He was one of the most powerful politicians and
one of the richest men in the country.

The unhappy thought that he might be refused
did not trouble his elevated mind, for such was

impossible. A woman would have to be mad to reject his offer. No, he amended silently, all women were mad. A woman would have to be a veritable nodcock to refuse such a matrimonial catch as he.

With his customary confidence Miles dismissed the entire matter from his mind, turned back to his tea, picked up his discarded knife, and buttered and ate another crumpet, absently making a mental note to discuss the faintly charred biscuits with his French chef, Antoine, who must be in a tiff to have let such shoddy work slip by.

Unaware of the catastrophe that was about to make a shambles of his well-ordered life, Lord Bradford brushed a few stray crumbs from the linen napkin at his neck and stood up. As he was wont to do in order to aid digestion, he went into the music room and relaxed for an hour by playing the pianoforte. His fingertips stroked the ivory keys with finesse, fondling them much as he would a woman's bosom. He was expertly skilled at both music and women, although he found the pianoforte infinitely more relaxing.

At last Lord Bradford stood with a satisfied sigh. He graciously allowed Benson to help him change into riding clothes and departed for his afternoon ride through Hyde Park.

When he returned home, exhilarated and perspiring, he felt decidedly charitable toward the world. After removing his damp linen shirt, he splashed water on his face and broad chest from the Sevres basin on the bedchamber washstand. Toilet completed, he contentedly perused his manly reflection in the cheval glass. There was a knock on the door.

"Enter!"

A liveried footman stepped into the room, looking tactfully away from his lordship's half-naked body. "Beg pardon, your lordship, but your lady mother awaits your pleasure in the blue drawing room."

"Tell her ladyship I'll be down directly," Miles ordered, and hurriedly began to mend his dishabille appearance as best he could without the aid of Benson, who had not yet returned from his mission.

Lord Bradford sighed. Had he dared mention that perhaps Benson should send a footman on the errand, the valet would have sulked for a week, and, as Miles knew from experience, *he* would have been forced to go without a decent cravat for the same period of time.

Within minutes he was as close to the picture of respectability as he was going to get without his manservant, satisfied that at least all traces of his excursion through the park had been erased. He wore a coat of claret superfine and tight buff chamois pantaloons; his cravat was restored to its usual waterfall of lace, tied somewhat successfully *en cascade*.

His mother smiled as he entered the drawing room. "Miles, darling!" she said, stretching out her arms to him. "It is so good to see you." As only a mother could, she looked right past the reparations he had so strenuously made. "But you look terrible. Haven't you been getting any sleep? At your age you should rest more, instead of continually gadding about like a young blade."

"And you, madam," he answered with a gallant if annoyed bow, "are looking as ravishing as ever, even if your tongue is a trifle more unkind." He bent to kiss the papery cheek she turned toward him. "But tell me, what brings you to Town? I thought you intended to remain in Bath for another month to partake of their famed health-giving waters. And are you still giving that charming admirer of yours, Lord Stanfield, the runaround? I don't know why you don't just marry the chap and put him out of his misery."

The elderly but still beautiful silver-haired woman gave him a scolding glance from beneath the rim of her intricately decorated wheat-straw leghorn. She smelled of lilacs, and her dress of fashionable lavender Circassian billowed around the almond brocade satin settee on which she reclined.

"Well, my dear, with the Season beginning, Bath became deadly dull—everyone rushing to London, you know." She sighed dramatically. "Besides, the waters were foul, and I felt worse after drinking them than I had before. As for Reggie, yes, he was there, too, and every bit as presumptuous as ever. If he were not such a convenient escort, I would not put up with him. He still insists that I shall marry him someday. As if I would take a husband at my age!"

Lord Bradford shook his head in disagreement. "My lady, who can blame his lordship for hankering after a woman as attractive as you? 'S truth, I think you lead him on dreadfully, yet he remains as besotted as ever."

His mother beamed but otherwise deflected his attempt to turn her up sweet. "As I sat there in the Pump Room, I found myself wondering if you intend to remain in London for the Season. I thought perhaps if you do, I might remain also—to chaperone any young ladies who capture your attention."

Lord Bradford narrowed his eyes at her attempt at guilelessness. Annoyed, he raised one hand to fend her off. "Mother, I will repeat what I have told you every year—even though it has done no good in the past and of a certainty will do no good again. I will have no meddling in my affairs." He frowned forbiddingly, remembering in excruciating detail all the simpering, stammering young debutantes she had thrown, one after another, into his path the Season before.

Lady Bradford slumped on the settee and looked up at him reproachfully. "Really, dear boy, as if I would meddle!" she retorted, irritated that he had found her out so soon. "Why must you be so suspicious? And of your own mother!" Removing pale-gray kidskin gloves, she held out one dainty hand to admire her nails while watching him out of the corner of her eye. The diamonds covering her slim fingers glittered in the sunlight that gleamed in through the long French windows.

"I say that, madam, because you have done so every year since I reached my majority," he said with a laugh, seating himself next to her.

Lady Bradford gazed at her son, pitying the many young beauties who had lost their hearts to him in the past. He was almost as good-looking as his late father. "Nonsense, you shameless cad," she reprimanded, shaking her finger at him. "You shouldn't talk that way to your elders. However," she said, managing to appear as if he had brought up the topic himself, "since you mention it, when *do* you plan to settle down and grace me with some grandchildren? I noticed in the *Times* that your nice young friend, the Earl of Glenworthy, was married yesterday. He is quite a bit younger than you, is he not?" She looked at Miles mistily. "While I, my dear, am rapidly getting old. I would so love to bounce my grandchildren on my knee before leaving this vale of tears." She drooped gracefully on the settee and raised one hand weakly to her forehead. "La, see how I fade. I feel quite faint. Have you any hartshorn, dear boy?"

"Certainly not. Your attempts to make me feel guilty will not work, my lady," he said, chuckling.

"Tony Ashleigh is barely a year my junior. And you—you are as spry as the day you were wed and could probably have babes even now if you chose to remarry. God knows you're still attractive enough to corner some poor unsuspecting lout. Just ask Reggie!"

Lady Bradford colored at this flattering if daring reply. "You will apologize at once, sir!" she demanded in mock anger, rapping his knuckles with the gold-tipped cane she affected but did not need, for she was, in truth, as spry as he had declared.

"Very well, madam," he replied in a slow drawl, "I apologize. As for me"—he paused momentarily—"I do not intend to wed for at least, oh, another ten years. If at all." He turned away at this, waiting for her fiery outburst. He was not disappointed.

Lady Bradford jumped to her feet. "Miles! How can you be so cruel? You are my only child and as such have a duty to me to marry and produce an heir! No doubt you take great pleasure in my discomfiture each time I take luncheon with my friends and they can all brag about their grandbabies, while I am cursed with an ingrate of a son who can't even appease my desire by *appearing* willing to marry!" She burst into tears and sank back to her seat. Miles's eyes widened in surprise.

"Why, Mother," he said softly, truly shocked, "I am sorry. I honestly had no idea you felt so strongly about the subject." He knelt at her feet and took her hands in his. "Indeed, I am even now giving the matter most serious consideration. I promise you."

His mother sniffed and looked at him, beseechingly. "Truly, Miles?" Extracting a lacy white handkerchief from her reticule, she dabbed at her eyes. They were the same peculiar shade of silver as

Miles's own but were fringed with slightly longer, sootier lashes. "Now see what you've done with your merciless teasing? You have ruined my face powder, and I was just on my way to take tea with my friends."

"Those old crones could never be as lovely as you, Mother, even after as torrential a cloudburst as this one," Lord Bradford declared. "And yes, really," he said, nodding in reference to her question. "Indeed, I am glad you chose to come to London just now, as I may inform you of my intentions and receive your blessing before embarking upon my endeavor."

"Oh? Of what endeavor do you speak?" Lady Bradford asked. "And since when do you feel compelled to ask my blessing on anything?"

Miles paced the Aubusson carpet nervously.

His mother frowned at her son's uncharacteristic lack of composure. "Miles?" she demanded with growing concern.

"I have decided to go to Bradford Hall for a few weeks. I know, I know," he said, waving a hand to stem any argument about his departing mid-Season. Three years previous he had installed his Aunt Hester, his late father's sister, a vacant, dull woman who had had nowhere else to go, on that very estate to act as caretaker in his absence, and since then he had not once visited the property. Now her presence would prove fortuitous.

"Aunt Hester is still there, which is fortunate, because while at the Hall I intend to make the acquaintance of the neighborhood ladies. Aunt Hester will be able to act as chaperone. I have already written informing our redoubtable kinswoman of my intention. At any rate, if one of said ladies is suitable, I shall marry her posthaste and give you all the grandchildren you can handle."

Lady Bradford stared at him, openmouthed.

Her son sighed irritably. "Have you nothing to say? I have decided to marry, Mother. You should be overjoyed, yet you sit there staring at me as if I have suddenly become a candidate for Bedlam!"

"May I have this in writing, Miles? Just to be sure this is not merely your idea of another very poor joke?"

"No, you may not. I am not in the habit of having my word questioned, Mother. I need a son, and you, as you repeatedly remind me, need grandchildren. So you needn't sit there looking so shocked!"

"I'm sorry, my dear, but, yes, I am shocked. And pleased," she bubbled delightedly, "as would be any mother who had long since given up hope of seeing her only child wed. All these years I have fought to see you married, and now, out of the blue, you drop this into my lap! It is beyond anything famous!" She laughed and rose to her feet, her skirts rustling as she threw her arms around her son's broad shoulders.

In an abnormally brusque gesture he shrugged her off. "You're as bad as Benson. The two of you act as if a bride will be my ticket through the pearly gates," he snapped testily. "At any rate, I trust I have your blessing."

Lady Bradford quelled her chuckles. "My son," she said in a grave tone belied by the sparkle in her eyes, "you know the answer to that question without even needing to ask it!" Then she turned and fairly skipped toward the double doors. "I shall hold you to your promise," she remarked, turning to eye him sharply as she pulled on her gloves. "Do not fail me now that you have finally given me hope. To do so would surely put me in my grave."

She turned to go, then glanced back. "Oh, I nearly forgot why I came! I am giving a come-out ball for old Lady Greysham's niece tonight. She was presented at Court recently, don't you know. A ridiculous chit, but family nonetheless. I will expect you. One dance with you and she will automatically be acknowledged a diamond of the first water." She paused, musing. "Why on earth cannot you just marry *her* without all this fuss?"

"Mother . . ."

At her son's ferocious glare, she huffed, "Oh, you never did do things the easy way." Without waiting for a reply, she fled the room while her luck still held.

Lord Bradford stalked into the library, a masculine room richly furnished in red leather with bookshelves stacked high to the ceiling. Matrimony. Fah! Little on this earth could be more distasteful. For the sake of legitimate heirs, one had to chain oneself to some homely little debutante, when otherwise one could have any number of delectable mistresses. It was quite unfair. Had not his search for a bride already been set in motion, Miles might have been inclined to forget the entire idea, no matter how much grandchildren meant to his mother.

The ball was a tepid affair to say the most. Lord Bradford, clad grandly in black velvet coat, white silk waistcoat, snug pantaloons slit up the sides and buttoned tightly, and elegant clocked silk stockings, stayed only long enough to gallant the green, tongue-tied chit for a single dance. Afterward he kissed his mother gently on the cheek, carefully avoiding her hopeful gaze as he whispered a swift good-bye. Then he headed off to enjoy a leisurely dinner and a hand of cards at White's following which he intended to make a last visit to Mimi to sate his desires in preparation for his absence.

"Ye gods, I wish my mother would find another gentleman to squire her debutantes," Lord Bradford growled to his whist playing companions. "I declare, their vapid company is enough to turn my stomach even for this fine Tokay." He swirled the liquid in the faceted crystal goblet he held, peering at the firelight refracted through the golden Hungarian wine.

He did not add that the thought of his upcoming bride search intensified his displeasure, for to do so would undoubtedly serve as a welcome diversion for his friends' customary ennui, sending them posthaste to the betting books of the very club in which they now sat. The last thing a man as high in the instep as Lord Bradford wanted was for his name to be bandied about humorously on the lips of everyone in London.

"Speaking of women, Bradford," Lord Fairly said with an exaggerated leer, "how is your lovely French *fille de joie* faring these days?"

Before responding, Miles casually laid down the winning hand in the high-stakes game, making his companions groan.

"God, Bradford, you have the devil's own luck at cards," Lord Fairly grumbled.

"And women," Lord Stanton quipped dryly.

"Mimi is as fetching as ever, I assure you, gentlemen," Miles drawled lazily. "Not that it's any of your concern." On this note he rose from the table, drawing his winnings into a black velvet satchel. "However, I shall be certain to relay your best wishes to Madam Devereux when I present her with this small token of my affection this evening." He waved the pouch at them with a grin and departed, leaving his noble companions to glare at his back before resuming their game and drowning their sorrows in another bottle of Tokay.

True to his word, after twice relieving his bore-

dom in Mimi's arms, Miles produced the velvet
bag with a flourish and poured a waterfall of
golden guineas over the delighted woman's naked
body. Noting that his mistress's exotic emerald
eyes lit up even more at the sight of the gold than
they had upon his arrival earlier, Miles frowned
moodily. With a growl he pulled the willing
woman back into his arms, letting the coins fall in
a shower of gold around their entwined bodies.

"You are too kind, my lord," she murmured
breathily into his mouth, tugging gently at his lips
and tongue with her white teeth as their bodies
became enmeshed for a third time.

Afterward, Lord Bradford lay back against the
pink satin pillows and watched Mimi brushing her
glossy golden curls at the Louis XV dressing table,
her upraised arms affording him a delectable view
of her generously rounded breasts.

"I really must be going, my dear," he said
lightly. "I leave tomorrow for Bradford Hall,
where I am soon to be wed."

Mimi's hands froze in mid-stroke, and Miles felt
mildly satisfied at her dismay, which went a ways
toward salving his earlier pique. He rose languidly
and began to pull on his clothing. "I will be returning in a few weeks with my new bride in tow.
Until then, I trust this will help ease your loneliness." From his coat pocket he plucked a long box
of black velvet and tossed it absently onto the table beside her.

Mimi's face darkened momentarily at the light-
ness of his tone, but she quickly hid her annoyance.
She was well aware that her generous protector did
not appreciate clinging, possessive women; only
through suppressing these unappealing traits had
she managed to maintain her hold on him for so
long.

She opened the box and gave a cry of genuine

delight. A necklace of diamond flowerets glittered in the candlelight. "Oh, Miles! It is lovely. Please stay a little longer, *mond amour*," she pleaded in a husky, seductive voice, her slender hand caressing his hairy chest where it was exposed between the folds of his white silk shirt. "Let me show you again how grateful I am to have a man such as you, and one so generous. How will I survive without your strong arms to hold me until you return?"

Lord Bradford gave her a bored smile and extricated himself from her grasping hands. "You were superb, as always, Mimi, but I truly must leave. The sooner I go, the sooner I will return." He finished dressing, ignoring the sulky look around the woman's mouth. With a final kiss he departed.

At once Mimi raced for the mirror, searching her face for signs of imminent decay. To be sure she was not so young as she used to be. In truth, she was five years older than Miles, not that she would have dreamed of telling him so. She sighed with relief to discover she was as dewy-looking as ever, thanks to her vigilance in protecting and pampering her skin.

Although it was very late, Mimi nonetheless called for her maid, who had long since gone to bed, to give her another facial. Then she spent an hour soaking in a tub of buttermilk, relieving the ache deep within her female parts caused by Lord Bradford's vigorous lovemaking. *Mon Dieu*—three times! The man was incredible.

At last she climbed out of the bath and allowed her sleepy maid to brush her hair until it shone like one of the guineas still strewn about the silk sheets on the enormous bed. Then, assured once again that she could pass for the twenty-eight years she claimed, rather than the forty she owned in reality, she crawled naked under the rumpled covers, luxuriating in the feel of the cold gold coins against her flesh as she fell into a deep, exhausted sleep.

4

Arising from some obscure slight or resentment dating at least ninety years prior to Miles's birth, a state of enmity existed between the houses Bradford and Quince, and their homes, built not a thousand yards apart, each situated atop a low hill, seemed to glare at each other across the road that ran from London to Hastings. Each strained to be the gaudiest and most impressive, from their twin lily-laden lakes to the huge white marble pillars supporting their balconies. With the passage of time, however, one house had definitely surpassed the other in elegance, as it had been at least a quarter century since a Quince had had either the finances or the desire to maintain the upkeep of the estate. Now the pillars of Quince House were dingy, the lake thickly strangled with lilies. All in all it looked to be an abandoned relic of a bygone era.

Like the house, the owners, too, had kept a distance, so that the current occupants had no acquaintance with one another. For some time Lord Bradford had attempted, through his solicitor, to purchase Quince House so that he might tear down the crumbling manor that obstructed Bradford Hall's view of the woods beyond. All offers had been summarily refused. Now he found himself standing at his library window staring out at the eyesore with a frown, wondering how he would explain its less than attractive presence to his prospective brides.

The opposing estate was a virtual wasteland, he thought with distaste as he examined the overgrown gardens and lawns, his brow creased in concentration as he watched for any sign of occupancy. After some time his attention was rewarded: a single figure wandered out the front doors and continued down toward one of the weed patches that had, many years ago, passed as a rose garden.

Lord Bradford spun on his heel, intending to visit Quince House in order to give his negligent neighbor both a piece of his mind and a final, excessively high offer for the property, an offer that could not possibly be refused. He walked swiftly down the hallway, emerged onto the steps of Bradford Hall, and proceeded around the side of the house toward the stables, where he demanded his huge bay stallion, Fury, saddled at once.

Minutes later the master of Bradford Hall cantered past the stooped form of Aunt Hester kneeling among the Hall's roses with her clippers. She did not acknowledge him. In truth, since he had arrived the day before, she had not said more than two words to her nephew, leaving Miles uncertain whether she was even aware of his presence. Of course, she had never been particularly quickwitted. Not that he minded. She would serve as a suitable chaperone; he did not require pleasantries.

Lord Bradford's stallion trotted up the illrepaired drive of Quince House, hooves crunching gravel, tail tossing spiritedly. Miles's eyes scanned the grounds like those of a hawk seeking its prey. When at last they rested upon the lone figure he had seen earlier from his window, they widened appreciatively. From the gown of faded blue muslin that she wore, to her pleasingly rounded backside, the woman presented such an attractive picture to Lord Bradford that it was some time before he could utter a syllable. Her rich, thick, redgold hair, which fell in a torrent of shining curls past her waist, captured his attention, making him forget his business momentarily and long to wrap the mass around his hands and inhale its fragrance, which, he had no doubt, would be like warm cinnamon.

With her backside negligently pointed skyward, the woman knelt on a blanket on the moist earth, digging furiously with spade and trowel, throwing clumps of winter-dead vegetation behind her, ignorant that several such clods were landing with dull splats upon a pair of champagne-polished Hessian boots.

Who the devil was she? Lord Bradford wondered. And what on earth was she doing grubbing around in a garden that for all intents and purposes appeared completely beyond hope? At last, more to quell a storm of rising desire and the flurry of questions forming in his mind than to save his ruined footgear, he spoke.

"Excuse me, miss, but may I inquire as to the whereabouts of your master?"

Genevieve whirled around to face her unseen inquisitor, strawberry curls flying, and her momentum sent a clump of mud sailing off her spade. Horrified, she watched as the clod flew through the air and landed with a thud on the broad chest of the handsome gentleman seated atop a large bay stallion, looking down at her with sheer amazement and not a little dismay.

"Oh, dear, I am so sorry!" she cried. Seizing the

blanket upon which she had been kneeling, Genevieve rushed forward.

Before Lord Bradford knew what she was about, the girl had begun to wipe his fine lawn shirt with the damp, dirty brown cloth, spreading the already horrid mess on his garment into an irreparable stain. So shocked was he that he merely stared down at the tiny, frenziedly scrubbing woman who stood on tiptoe, raking valiantly at his chest, tongue clenched between perfect white teeth as she concentrated on her work.

At last he recovered sufficiently to grasp her hand and bring her frantic movements to a halt. "Please stop, miss, or I shall have no flesh beneath the shirt that is already beyond hope of repair!" he begged with a chuckle, then fell quiet as a surge of recognition rushed through him. Did he know this pretty maid from somewhere? A past dalliance at an aquaintance's estate or somesuch? Then the fleeting notion passed as she spoke again.

Genevieve caught her breath. Was he laughing at her? "I do not think the situation amusing, sirrah," she declared.

"Ah, but I do, my dear. And as it is my shirt that has been ruined, it is very lucky that I am amused, rather than inclined to bend you over my knee and give you a good spanking. Come now, pretty maid," he said merrily, ignoring Genevieve's gasp of outrage, "a truce. I would sooner be friends than enemies. Now then," he said with a grin, taking her shocked silence for flattered acquiescence, "if you are finished abusing my poor chest, please be so good as to answer the question that led to this unfortunate state of affairs. Where is your master?"

Genevieve pulled her fingers from his grip. His touch had, much to her confusion, become gentle and caressing, his thumb softly massaging the palm of her hand as his storm-gray eyes drifted appreciatively over her flushed face. Backing up a few steps, she eyed him uncertainly.

"Do you always ogle maids so thoroughly, sir?" she asked haughtily in an attempt to mask her distress.

"Only when I have been presented with backsides as nicely rounded as yours, miss. Not, of course, that your front is not exceptionally rounded as well. Truly, a more delightfully rounded female anatomy I have never seen."

Genevieve's face went from flushed to flaming.

"Oh, dear, you are annoyed with me. Will you forgive me if I kneel down before you and beg your pardon?" he bantered irreverently. "Come now, if you will not give me the whereabouts of your master, will you at least tell me your name?"

Genevieve's eyes blazed. "I do not think I shall tell you my name, sir, as, were we to meet again in a more public place, you would feel obligated to wish me well, and I do not care for anyone to think that I associate with scum."

Lord Bradford's smile vanished abruptly. He slid from his mount's broad back and stepped forward, his tall, muscular form menacing.

Genevieve stepped back a few more paces, fearful that she had gone too far.

"You would do well to watch your tongue, my girl, for one who speaks so crudely to her betters begs to have her shapely bottom beaten soundly!"

Genevieve shrank back against the winter-worn rosebushes as her tormenter came closer.

Lord Bradford spoke again. "However, as I am a benevolent man and you are such a pretty, albeit ill-mannered, wench, I shall extract my penance in another form." He closed the distance between them with a single step.

Genevieve tried to scramble away, but the folds

of her gown caught in the thorns behind her, holding her captive as her assailant's arm shot out, wrapping around her slim waist. His dark, angry face descended toward her own.

"Release me at once, sir!" Genevieve demanded furiously, wrenching her head to one side.

Lord Bradford smiled dangerously. "I shall, my dear, but not until you have apologized properly." Undaunted by her thrashing, with his free hand he gripped the back of her head and turned her face toward him.

The leather of his glove chafed the tender flesh of her neck. His mouth covered hers. And Genevieve was astounded by the strange, quivering heat that surged through her body like molten lava at the touch of this rude stranger's warm, firm lips. When he finally released her, in an effort to hide her inner tumult, she flung out her palm wildly, catching him fully across the cheek.

Although his teeth clenched and his eyes narrowed to black slits, Lord Bradford did not lose his temper. "Now then," he said smoothly, as if nothing amiss had occurred, "run find your master and tell him that he has a caller. Then, if you are very, very quick about it, perhaps we shall take up where we left off when I have done my business." With a deft movement of his gloved fingers he plucked her faded muslin skirts from the thorns and pushed her toward the house, planting a well-aimed swat on her bottom.

Genevieve opened and closed her mouth rapidly several times like a stranded fish. Her senses were scrambled, her mind a complete blank. For she had returned his kiss every bit as warmly as some wanton country maid! Unable to utter a word to explain that she was her own mistress, she set out for the house at a run. Gripping her skirts in her fists, she took the stairs two at a time and slammed the double doors behind her, leaving Lord Bradford laughing at what he took to be the wench's eagerness for more of his kisses.

So she had slapped him, he thought with a broad grin. No matter. It meant nothing more than that she was fiery, spirited wench. Once she had learned the proper way to answer his embraces, the encounter that would inevitably follow his interview with the owner of Quince House would be all the more enjoyable. He thought, briefly, of how pleasurable it would be when *he*, after his purchase of this estate, was her master.

After waiting nearly ten minutes for the gentleman of the house to come out to greet him, Miles grunted with annoyance and strode toward the front doors. He climbed the stairs in two strides and rapped the knocker on the heavy wood portals. When no one answered his summons, he wiggled the latch to open the doors himself. To his irritation, the doors were bolted, and not a sound was to be heard. But the instincts that had been sharpened in battle with Napoleon on the Continent several years earlier made his lordship almost certain that another human being stood just on the other side of the great oak doors, listening. Thoroughly disgusted, he returned to his horse, mounted it, and rode angrily toward Bradford Hall.

No wonder his ancestors had always hated the Quinces, he thought savagely. The rude bunch of boorish cretins didn't even have the good grace to answer their front door. He reached the stables behind Bradford Hall and handed his mount to a groom. As he entered the house he was approached by Benson, who, although he did his best to hide it, was obviously brimming with curiosity. After his valet had hovered close behind him in a most disturbing manner for nearly twenty minutes, Miles finally turned on the man.

"What is it, Benson?" he snapped. "You're following me about like a bloodhound. Is there something on your mind? If there is, then out with it, man. If not, then please leave off trailing me like a lost puppy!"

Benson had the good grace to look shamefaced, but only for a moment. The sentiment quickly vanished and was replaced by rampant curiosity. "Well, sir," he murmured in an affectedly disinterested voice, "I was wondering if you had met Miss Genevieve Quince during your ride to Quince House. I happened to overhear one of the footmen saying that his cousin's sister's husband's brother-in-law drives a post chaise, and that Miss Quince had hired it to bring herself and a load of belongings to the estate. Odd thing, though. He said that she had absolutely no one with her. Don't you think that odd, sir? No maid? No chaperone? And her but a lass of no more than eighteen." Benson quirked his eyebrows expressively at his master, clucking his tongue.

Lord Bradford felt the blood drain from his face. "Alone, you say, Benson?" he rasped.

"Yes, sir," the valet replied sanctimoniously. "Almost as if she had come to the country for an . . . illicit tryst, shall we say. Not that it's my place to say, but what else would a young woman of Quality be doing at such a remote place all by herself?"

"Quite right, Benson."

The valet's shoulders rose importantly.

"It is not your place."

The shoulders drooped with disappointment.

"I would thank you not to mention this again—to anyone." On that rude note he turned from his dismayed servant and strode up the stairs toward his chambers.

"Well. I never," said Benson, even more amazed at his master's inexplicable rudeness than he had been at the news of the escapades of Miss Quince. Then he turned and wandered down to the kitchen to pass along this new tidbit. Perhaps Cook would be willing to trade some of her delicious fresh gingerbread, whose aroma was even now wafting through the corridor, for this provocative morsel of gossip.

Miles's hands were shaking as he opened the mahogany door to his bedchamber. He forced a deep breath and let it out slowly through pursed lips, cursing himself for a fool. Of course she had been no servant girl! Gentility was written all over her, from her lustrous red-gold hair to her enormous eyes of gentian-blue, from her tiny waist to her dimutive feet. Not to mention her voice. Definitely cultured. It was her less than elegant attire—and pose—that had put him off the mark.

Although it nearly killed him to do so, Lord Bradford quickly penned a note of apology and, along with a dozen of the gardener's most prized hothouse orchids, dispatched it to the house across the road.

When Genevieve received the delicate blooms and had scanned the piece of heavy parchment, she wrenched the heads off the flowers and dumped them unceremoniously onto the ground. Tipping her head back so that her chin was high, Genevieve thrust the beheaded stems back into the amazed footman's hands.

"Not bloody likely!" she said icily, slamming the door in his face.

However, once the astounded footman had disappeared down the drive, she opened the doors cautiously and gathered the lovely blossoms up in

her skirt, hurrying into the kitchen to place them
in a saucer of water.

Miles stood on the doorstep, anxiously awaiting
the footman's return, and confronted the servant
as he walked up the drive.

"Well? Speak up, man. What said she?"

The footman groped for words. "Well, my lord . . .
That is . . . You see, my lord . . ." The servant held
the stems behind his back, hoping his master would
not notice them and wishing he had had the foresight to dispose of them.

"Damn it all, man, spit it out! What did the
woman say? And what have you behind your
back?"

Agonized with fear that his master would turn
him off for failing at his task, the miserable footman thrust the bundle of decapitated blooms into
Lord Bradford's hands. "She said, 'Not bloody
likely,' my lord," he repeated in a terrified whisper.

"What was that? What did you say? Speak up,"
Miles snapped, gaping at the stems with horrified
disbelief.

" 'Not bloody likely'," the terrified footman
burst out loudly. Then, more softly, he added,
"That's what she said, my lord."

Lord Bradford's face paled, but he carefully controlled his tone of voice as he replied, "I see." He
turned, carrying the ruined flowers beneath one
arm, and walked with dignity into the house, the
only indication of his anger the resounding echo
of the door as he slammed it behind him.

5

Within days, much to the amazement of the unseen observer who gazed down on Genevieve's slender form in reluctant admiration from his library window at Bradford Hall, the rose gardens at Quince House were looking nearly perfect again. Huge piles of cuttings from the pruned plants scented the air with heady perfume.

Several early red and pink blooms had opened, and as Genevieve sat on her front steps cradling a cup of hot chocolate in her scratched fingers, she experienced a glow of satisfaction as she surveyed her handiwork.

Next she intended to row herself around the shallow lake in the small flat-bottomed dinghy that had turned up during her trampings among the outbuildings. Most of the overgrown lilies would have to be pulled out in order to restore the pond to its former beauty. She sighed as she stared morosely at the clogged waterway. Compared to the roses, this task seemed monumental.

Idly she wondered if the advertisement she had placed in the *Times* had been read by anyone yet. A quiver of excitement ran through her, and she smiled happily. Amazing as it seemed, even though she had worked very, very hard here at

Quince House, the days had flown by, and she had been happier than ever before in her life. Then she frowned, whispering her oft-repeated prayer that her cousins would not spot the advertisement or hear about her endeavor before she was able to reimburse them for the moneys she had borrowed to submit her advertisement to the *Times* to purchase supplies for her venture.

Still wearing the same faded dress of blue muslin in which she had met Lord Bradford, Genevieve wandered around to the back of the house, worked her way through the weeds strangling the outbuildings, and pushed open the door of the old shed that contained the decrepit dinghy.

It took considerable exertion to haul the vessel out of the shed, and when it finally lay on the gravel outside, Genevieve noticed a large hole in the prow. With a curse she dropped the end she was holding and eyed the boat with disgust. She had failed to notice the damage when she had discovered the tiny craft. Perhaps it could be mended.

Since there was very little light left in the day, Genevieve resignedly went back into the empty manor house and closed the doors behind her. They echoed dully, magnifying the loneliness that suddenly threatened to swallow her. She hurried down the hall and into the kitchen, where she started a blazing fire and put on a kettle for a pot of tea.

A knock on the front door startled her, and Genevieve jumped to her feet. *Drat that man!* she cursed silently. It had to be him, for no one else knew she was here! With a stubborn set to her full lips, she picked up a large wooden rolling pin and strode purposefully toward the front doors.

"Go away and leave me alone, you disreputable cur, or you'll get more than you reckoned for!" she said rudely, brandishing the makeshift weapon above her head as she flung wide the door and glared menacingly into the gathering darkness.

"Merciful heavens, child! I promise I have come to do you no harm!" squeaked a tall, gray-haired, gangly-looking female of fifty or thereabouts.

Genevieve stared at the woman in amazement and suddenly dropped the rolling pin with a clatter. "Pramble!" she cried happily. "Whatever are you doing here? It is so good to see you! Come in, please!" She threw her arms around the woman's neck and nearly strangled her before the slightly myopic lady could get a word out.

"There, there, my dear," the woman gasped, her wire-rimmed glasses pushed askew and resting precariously on the tip of her long, bony nose. "I'm very happy to see you, too." She stepped back and straightened her spectacles. "I was in London and stopped by your cousins' home to visit you. You can imagine my amazement at finding the house dark and not a soul in residence. I went straightaway to your father's old solicitor and asked if he knew where you had disappeared to. He told me that he had received a very peculiar missive in your own hand that informed him you were taking up residence in Quince House! Of course I knew that could not be possible, because Quince House has been closed up for years and could scarcely be habitable. Now I find that you truly *are* here, and I cannot decide whether to be more flabbergasted at your living arrangements or delighted to see you. My dear girl, what *can* you be thinking of?"

Genevieve laughed happily. "I shall explain all," she declared, and, taking her ex-governess by the elbow, led her down into the kitchen, where she seated the newcomer close to the fire and poured two cups of tea.

With many scandalized *ooh*'s and *aah*'s from the older woman, the lurid tale of life with Cousins Marybelle and Augustus and their sordid plans for Genevieve was soon made plain.

"So you see, I could not possibly have stayed there, Pramble, and, as no one would hire me, I had nowhere else to go. It was either return here or become my cousins' political bait."

"Well, I must admit that I never would have suspected your cousins of such evil intentions, Jenny, or I would have insisted that you come live with me. It seems so risky for you to be living here alone in this huge, empty old house! What would you do if someone broke in? Who would protect you?" She peered at Genevieve, her eyes magnified behind the lenses of her spectacles.

"I confess, Pramble, that I was so overwrought before I came here that I scarce gave any thought to the matter. Although you did give me a start knocking on the door just as it is getting dark outside. By the way, how did you get here?"

"Public coach, of course. But now, dear, back to the matter at hand. You cannot possibly stay here without some protection. Have you a gun?"

"Well, there is Papa's old revolver in the library, I suppose, but I should not have the first idea how to load the thing. I would probably shoot off my toe if I tried."

Genevieve laughed merrily, but Miss Pramble remained sober. "I had best come clean then, Jenny. Though I could scarcely believe what the solicitor told me, I have come prepared to stay with you until you decide what you are going to do with yourself. I cannot allow you, in good conscience, to live here in this great relic all alone. I would love to have you come live with me in Kettering, but I know you would never consent to do so." She peered at Genevieve hopefully but was not surprised when the girl shook her head. Her former ward was far too honorable to impose herself on another's tiny, meager household, no matter how desperate her own condition.

"At any rate," Miss Pramble continued, "I did think about this matter of protection before I left London. That is why I have brought you something. I left it outside." She nodded toward the front of the house, then gazed innocently at her teacup and took another sip of the brew.

"What on earth is it?" Genevieve demanded with a grin. "What have you done now?" She remembered some of the adventures she and the governess had embarked upon during her childhood, from collecting frogs to the ant farm they had constructed of glass tubing, which had, upon being dropped by a disgusted chambermaid, shattered on her father's library floor, resulting in an army of ants invading several of Sir Leonardo's favorite volumes.

"I shan't tell you. You shall have to find out for yourself. Go now, child. Run along and see what I have brought. It is out on the steps." She paused uncertainly. "I hope." Miss Pramble smiled at her former charge affectionately, once more nodding her head toward the front of the house.

Genevieve hesitated not a second longer but dashed out of the kitchen and down the hall. When she reached the set of double front doors, she pulled them open to peer out into the shadows. But no sooner had she stepped out than she was knocked on her backside by something huge and furry, which seemed determined to drown her with its enormous wet tongue. Sputtering, Genevieve clambered to her knees and gasped with delight at her new friend.

"Jasper, behave yourself!" cried Miss Pramble, who had just come down the hall. "He's a bit excited, you see, being cooped up in the carriage all the way from London. He's a mastiff, you must know."

"A mastiff?" said Genevieve with disbelief. "More like an elephant! He's enormous! Oh, Pramble, I do love him! Thank you so much!" She threw her arms around the beast's huge head and shoulders, hugging him while trying at the same time to evade the energetic, foot-long tongue and the thick tail that whipped furiously back and forth.

Miss Pramble beamed at the pair.

When Genevieve finally stood up, she discovered that Jasper's head reached nearly to her waist. He gazed up at her with adoring, limpid eyes of liquid black, evidently already prepared to do battle to the death, if need be, for his new mistress.

"I am glad, my dear. Now then, shall we go back into the kitchen? It's deathly chill out here." Miss Pramble turned back toward the warm room they had just vacated, and Genevieve watched, laughing, as Jasper bounded ahead to investigate the terrain so that it would be safe for his humans to enter. Happy tears welled in her eyes as she followed her two loving friends.

Once again seated near the warmth of the fire, Miss Pramble turned toward Genevieve, her eyes serious. "Now then, Jenny dear. What are you up to?"

Genevieve turned away and paced several feet before facing Miss Pramble. "I don't know that I should tell you. You will not approve."

"Nevertheless, tell me you must, if simply for the reason that I am not leaving until I know you are all right." The older woman raised her eyebrows at her former charge in challenge. "Now tell me, Jenny. What are you planning?"

Genevieve sighed and nodded. "Wait right here."

In an instant she was out the door and flying down the hall. She raced up the stairs and down a corridor until she reached her chambers. Grabbing a crumpled sheet of paper from her bureau, she pivoted and returned the way she had come. Gasping for breath by the time she reached the kitchen, Genevieve held out the paper toward Miss Pramble, who took a deep breath, and commenced reading.

TO WHOM IT MAY CONCERN:

Tired of being looked down on by those of a higher class? Is your blood not quite blue enough? Is your money tainted with manufacturer's smoke or Cit's germs? Not at Quince House. Come be my guest, live the good life, enjoy the ambience and style of the Beau Monde. For a modest fee, you, too, can live like kings and queens, being served by none other than bluebloods themselves. Respond to: Quince House, 203 Dunheath Road.

Miss Pramble gasped softly and looked intently at the printing on the paper as if she could not possibly have read it correctly. After a pregnant silence she looked up at Genevieve, her faded brown eyes filled with awe. "You cannot be serious, my dear. Why, all of Sussex will ostracize you forever. Will you not rethink this rash decision? What if you wish to marry someday? What gentleman will have you if you ruin your reputation through such a mad scheme?"

"Oh, but I *am* serious, Pramble," Genevieve declared. "More serious than I've ever been in my life. What have I to regret by giving those snooty-nosed tyrants some of their own back? What have they ever given me but slights because of the way my father lived and because he died penniless? Who offered to care for me when he died? No one except those who had use for first my hands and then my body. And when I had nothing of value left to give? God knows what would have become of me. No, Pramble, I am very serious. Didn't you notice how much better the house looks than you expected? I have worked hard weeding and pruning and trimming . . ." Tears filled her eyes.

Miss Pramble took her by the elbow and gently lowered her into her seat. Years of stifled emotions were suddenly overflowing, and Genevieve collapsed into her governess's arms, sobbing.

When she had finally cried herself out, she pulled away from Miss Pramble's embrace and looked at her solemnly, sniffing softly. "I am going to do this, Pramble," she whispered hoarsely. "And you can either help me or you can leave, but there is no place here for anyone who intends to stand in my way."

The two women looked at each other for a long moment. At last Miss Pramble nodded shakily, wondering as they walked up the stairs together to retire whether she would have cause to regret her course of action in the future.

Lord Bradford bent over his copy of the *Times,* idly glancing at the columns and reading whatever happened to catch his eye. Castlereagh was up in arms about something again . . . The Haut Ton was rushing to Paris now that the war was over and Napoleon safely incarcerated on the isle of St. Helena . . . Prinny had held a ball in honor of Lady Isabella Hertford's birthday . . . An elderly peeress had been found dead in Hyde Park and the Runners were searching for clues to her murder . . . Three thugs had hanged at Newgate . . .

Suddenly his eyes froze on a certain advertisement. His shoulders stiffened beneath his emerald-and-gold brocade dressing gown. He cursed vehemently and hurled the paper to the floor.

Striding to his dresser, he tossed off the dressing gown and, without even calling for Benson, threw on a coat of midnight-blue superfine and stepped into his gleaming Hessians. Glancing indifferently at his immaculate reflection in the cheval glass, Miles shoved his long fingers savagely through his black mane and stalked furiously out the door.

Benson, who had been coming down the hallway to prepare his master for bed, halted in his tracks.

His black brows forming an ebony wing of outrage across his forehead, Miles swept past the valet and stormed down the great staircase.

Aunt Hester, who had gone to the kitchen for her nightly mug of warm milk (she preferred to fetch it herself and sip it on the way to bed, for by the time a maid had walked the distance to her mistress's chambers, it was chilled), was nearly trampled at the foot of the stairs.

"Out of my way, woman!" Lord Bradford growled, so startling his aunt that the milk sloshed over the rim of the cup. Miles stalked out the front door, oblivious to his aunt's furious muttering. Down the stairs and across the lawn he streaked like an angry demon, intent on destroying that . . . that . . . *thing* that had caused him too much trouble to be allowed to live one second longer.

Skirting the lake, Lord Bradford crossed the flat gravel road and made his way purposefully onto Quince property. His expression did not alter, and his gaze did not for a moment leave the single light burning in a window at the top of the house.

Without even knocking, Lord Bradford threw himself against the doors, which gave way with a metallic snap of the feeble lock. Never wavering, he took the steps of the grand staircase four at a time until he stood at the top. He turned toward the light he had seen from the front of the house. In seconds he had reached his destination. Without pausing, he hurled the bedchamber door open and stepped into the faintly-lit room.

His abrupt appearance was met by a shrill cry and the sight of a startled female, whose dainty lawn nightgown had slid, in her hurry to sit up in bed, from one creamy shoulder, exposing more flesh than would have been revealed by even the most immodest demirep's ball gown. She blinked sleepily, clutching a tattered copy of Byron's *Childe Harold's Pilgrimage* to her breast.

It appeared that Genevieve Quince had fallen asleep while reading, thus explaining the still-burning candle whose light had shown Lord Bradford the way to her room. Her cinnamon curls hung in disarray over her shoulders and bosom, obscuring Miles's view of the perfect ivory mounds.

His nostrils flared. He took a deep breath. "Miss Quince!" he roared at the startlingly lovely apparition. He strode furiously forward. "What the devil is the meaning of this?"

"I beg your pardon, sir?" Genevieve gasped. *Childe Harold* slid to the floor unnoticed. She sat stiffly, quivering beneath the comforter she had hastily pulled up to her chin, as she stared at him, vivid blue eyes wide.

"I will not have it! I tell you it shall not be! Just who in God's name do you think you are? Disrupting first my peace of mind, and now the beauty and quiet of my country estate! And me with a fiancée arriving any day! I tell you, I will not have it!" His voice echoed through the chamber, and the poor girl shook beneath the covers, unblinking and terrified as she struggled to comprehend what crime this madman was accusing her of.

Unable to understand why the fiery wench who had defended herself so staunchly before would turn to a quivering mass of jelly now, Lord Bradford peered at her curiously.

Then, with sudden clarity of mind, the enormity of his impetuous act hit him full in the face, and he stood openmouthed with dismay, glancing around the bedroom uncertainly, thinking frantically that he would certainly be better off in purgatory than standing on the worn rug in this unprotected female's boudoir.

"I . . . I . . . ah . . ." he stammered.

As he stood there strangling in horror, something huge, hairy, and incredibly ferocious hurtled through the bedroom door and landed on his chest, pushing him to the floor. He would have cried out in alarm, had the breath not been knocked from his body. He gazed up into a set of gleaming white teeth the size of shoehorns, and a pink tongue that dripped on his face as the beast snarled viciously.

"Down, Jasper," Genevieve commanded, beginning to chuckle.

Miles noted distractedly that, although the chit was still confused, her fear was rapidly dissipating and was being replaced by delighted hilarity. Furiously he pushed the dog off his chest, giving no thought to the massive jaws so near his face, and rose to confront the woman. Jasper snarled and stepped forward menacingly, and Lord Bradford wisely paused.

"I do not find anything amusing, Miss Quince," he growled as he glared past the angry dog.

"Ah, but I do, sirrah. And as it is my house you have broken into, it is fortunate indeed that I am amused, would you not agree?" Genevieve mocked in near-perfect mimicry of their initial encounter. She felt quite safe with the mastiff now holding her tormentor at bay behind a wall of fangs.

A muffled gasp in the doorway behind him caused Lord Bradford to turn sharply.

"Jenny!" Miss Pramble cried anxiously. Her face was smothered in a layer of white goo, and her graying hair was tucked up under a mobcap. "Who is this man, and what is he doing in your bedchamber?"

"He is a complete cur! An unscrupled ruffian! A boorish cretin!" Genevieve huffed.

Lord Bradford looked directly at Miss Pramble, who, suddenly recognizing his lordship from having seen his unforgettably handsome face before while on a jaunt to London, paled considerably. She breathed deeply and drew herself up to her full height. "Well, sirrah! I would have expected better of a man of your station! Taking advantage of a poor, innocent girl like Miss Quince in such a disreputable manner! Suppose you tell me exactly what designs you had on her virtue, and then perhaps we can go down to the parlor to discuss wedding arrangements." The governess's voice was gravelly with disapproval.

"Marry *him?*" Genevieve cried with distaste. "Pigs might fly first! Why, the very thought fills me with even more terror than when he came barging into my chamber! Well, perhaps not terror, exactly," she said thoughtfully, staring up at the ceiling as she mused. "Perhaps more like disgust. Yes, that is it. Disgust." She gave a satisfied nod.

"Miss Quince," growled Lord Bradford in a malevolent voice, directing his attention back to the girl in the bed. "I came here tonight to tell you that I will not allow you to turn my country estate into a brawling playground for Cits and merchants. I intend to become affianced shortly, and I will not not have my bride-to-be see a mockery made of our class. Do you hear me?"

By now Genevieve was fuming. "You come barging into my bedchamber in the middle of the night to tell me that you will not allow me—not *allow* me?—to entertain whomsoever I please in *my* home because *your* fiancée will not approve? If that is not enough to make the cat laugh! You have exactly three minutes to be off my property, sir, or Jasper will lead you off by the seat of your pants."

"Miss Quince, I do not think you understand—"

"Oh, you are *wrong*, sir. I understand all too well. You thought that since I was a woman alone that you could come barging into my house with your ridiculous demands and that I would cave in immediately. Does it not strike you as ludicrous that you would find fault with my actions, when your own leave much to be desired?" she snarled. "You are so worried that your bride-to-be will not approve of *my* behavior, and yet here you stand, in an unwed lady's boudoir, calling me unreasonable for trying to earn my keep in the only way I have at my disposal. What would your dear fiancée say if she knew you had practically attacked an unchaperoned lady of Quality?"

"Just so, sir!" said Miss Pramble hotly. "Imagine invading Miss Quince's home in such a manner and then refusing to do right by her! Insisting that your disgraceful action was to protect the sensibilities of your *betrothed!* As if you could possibly wed anyone but Miss Quince now! It is too much to be borne! It is the outside of enough!"

"Silence, woman!" Lord Bradford shouted with rage, towering over the feisty but frail governess, making her quail and back up a few steps.

The dog let out a warning growl.

"Be still, Pramble," snapped Genevieve. "I would not have this madman for a husband if he were the last man on earth! Don't even put such an unthinkable idea into his head!"

The two combatants eyed each other mutinously for several moments, ignoring Miss Pramble's glares, and then Lord Bradford snorted rudely. "I should have known better than to try reason with a female. Especially as she is a Quince!" he snarled, and stalked furiously from the room.

For a moment Genevieve contained herself, but when she heard the front doors slam, she hurtled from the bed, raced down the stairs, and threw the doors wide, shouting a command to the mastiff, who responded with obvious delight.

"Jasper, sic 'im!"

Jasper streaked across the lawn, and it gave Genevieve intense pleasure to see her archenemy break into a run, Jasper's teeth mere inches from his backside as the dog rousted the intruder from the property.

When, mission accomplished, Jasper came trotting happily back across the lawn, Genevieve led him upstairs and reentered her bedchamber to find Miss Pramble sitting, shaken, on the edge of the bed.

"My dear, have you any idea whom we have just insulted?" asked Miss Pramble in an amazed voice.

Genevieve looked at the governess with blatant disbelief. "Whom *we* have insulted, Pramble? Are you gone mad? As I already told you, the man is a cur. A ruffian. Why, he accosted me once before in my own garden—grabbed me quite out of the blue and kissed me! On the mouth! 'Struth, I think he is probably an escaped Bedlamite." She stopped, looking thoughtful. "I suppose we really should alert the proper authorities so that they can nab him and take him back, do you not agree?"

"My dear girl! That 'Bedlamite' was none other

than Miles Bradford! One of, if not *the*, most powerful, richest men in all England!" Her eyes were
huge in her cream-whitened face.

"Quite," Genevieve said firmly, remembering
the stories she had heard while growing up. "Only
a Bradford could possibly be so crude. Besides,"
she said hotly, "the man got no more than he deserved!"

"I certainly hope you know what you're doing,
Jenny," said Miss Pramble gravely.

"Of course I do," replied Genevieve stoutly.

But secretly she wondered what power this man
had that every time he appeared she flew into an
uncontrollable rage and her body quivered in a
way she had never before experienced. She said
nothing to this effect to Miss Pramble, though,
merely insisting that they return to their beds and
get some much-needed rest. Then she was dismayed beyond words to find that her sleep was
repeatedly interrupted by the most disturbing
dreams of a tall, dark, devilishly attractive man
kissing her in the midst of a shower of rose petals.

6

Lord Bradford rolled over in his enormous feather bed, blinking groggily at the beam of sunlight that burst through the windows and hit him full in the face. His head ached abominably, and he was overwhelmed with a sense of foreboding, as if he had something unpalatable to do and had not yet become coherent enough to remember what it was.

He rubbed a hand across his gritty eyes, pushed his fingers through tangled black curls, and leaned up on one elbow. This small movement brought back the previous night's escapade with blinding clarity, and he groaned as he fell back onto his pillow.

Genevieve Quince.

No sooner had he slammed the doors of Bradford Hall in the face of that hairy beast called Jasper last night than Miles knew that an apology to Miss Quince was once again in order. Damn the woman! Surely asking for a little cooperation, a little peace and quiet in which to woo and win his new bride, was not so unreasonable? Not that that was even an issue anymore. This morning there was something even more distasteful to proffer than an apology.

Lord Bradford knew full well that, under the circumstances, there was only one thing he *could* do. After the dread task was completed, he would send a short missive to his mother, informing her of his approaching nuptials. She, at least, should be elated, he thought with disgust.

With renewed, albeit depressed, resolve, Lord Bradford climbed out of bed and rang for Benson, who arrived immediately, carrying his master's breakfast and a large pot of strong coffee on a tray. After the repast, Miles dressed in pale breeches of fawn leather and a fine linen shirt topped off nicely by a cravat tied with exquisite simplicity. He stared grimly at his reflection in the cheval glass, then made his way downstairs.

Aunt Hester was busily arranging a few early flowers in a crystal vase. She glanced up, looking as if his presence took her by surprise, frowned, and went back to her work.

Lord Bradford paused on the top step of Bradford Hall, gazing with distaste at the opposing estate. Then, squaring his shoulders, he accepted the inevitable and began striding purposefully across the drive. He crossed the perfectly manicured lawns of his own property and made his way closer and closer to the forbidding, dilapidated stronghold of the Quince family, keeping an eye out for the hungry mastiff.

Jasper did not make an appearance, and Miles successfully reached the doorstep. He raised the heavy knocker and rapped it sharply. Once. Twice. On the third knock, the heavy oak doors swung open.

The elderly woman answering the summons eyed him doubtfully but finally seemed to decide that he looked sane enough to allow inside. Besides, this was her young friend's future husband standing on the step.

"Miss Pramble, I presume," Miles said soberly, bowing rigidly from the waist.

"That is correct, Lord Bradford. I assume you are here to do the proper thing by Miss Quince."

At his terse nod, Miss Pramble unbent a little and smiled approvingly. "At least you will live up to the nobility of your name." she said, gesturing him into the hallway.

"You know who I am, madam?"

"Of course I do, my lord. Who in England would not recognize such an esteemed member of Society?" She curtsied respectfully.

"I cannot tell you how appalled I am at my behavior of last night, Miss Pramble. I can only assure you that I was not myself. I hope you can find it within your heart to forgive me. Especially as we will soon be seeing a great deal of each other, if, as I assume, you live with Miss Quince."

"Of course, sir. When one is overwrought, one is apt to do unthinkable things. No harm done, so long as the correct reparations are made," she said graciously.

"You are altogether too kind and understanding, madam. I only hope that Miss Quince will be so. I fear she thinks me quite a boor."

He looked so downcast at the thought of having to propose to Genevieve that Miss Pramble chuckled softly and patted his hand gently. "I cannot speak for Miss Quince, my lord, but as for myself, I find that you are all that is honorable and well bred. Come. Let us make bygones be bygones and start afresh, shall we? Now, then, if you will excuse me for a moment, I shall fetch Miss Quince so that you can get on with things." She smiled approvingly once more and led the way into a small, comfortably warm room off to the left of the vestibule.

Miles noted with discomfort the large, furry

lump resting by the grate, but short of thumping his tail weakly, Jasper did not stir. Both room and furniture were worn but had a lived-in, faintly appealing quality, Lord Bradford observed as he seated himself on a maroon horsehair sofa. Miss Quince had evidently been working very hard at making her home a livable residence once more. Still, that did not warrant her taking such a drastic step as allowing commoners to dwell in her ancestral home—much less to act as their maid herself, he thought.

He forced his mind back to the reason he had come. Once his wife, Miss Quince would accept his support gratefully, and she and Miss Pramble could retire to Bradford Hall, where he could leave them to enjoy a life of ease without being forced to behave in such a ridiculous fashion. Quince House would come down, and— His mental meanderings halted as a rustle of movement in the parlor doorway caught his attention. He stood quickly and turned toward the sound.

"Lord Bradford, I believe?" said a soft, melodic voice, which, for some reason, when combined with the warm, blazingly blue eyes that took in every detail of his appearanace, made him catch his breath.

Genevieve Quince looked at him silently. To her credit, she appeared calm and collected, every inch a gentlewoman. Miles gazed at her and for a moment completely forgot what he had come to say, so entranced was he by the delicate rosy glow of her cheeks and her lustrous strawberry curls, which were tied back with a slightly frayed cherry-colored satin ribbon. A sudden, unbidden memory of those curls streaming over her ivory bosom assaulted him, and he had to clear his throat. Although the gown she wore was obviously well-worn and not nearly in the height of fashion, the chit was entrancingly lovely in the morning sun that flowed in through the freshly washed windows. And the modest dress somehow did more to enhance the lush, ripe bosom beneath the bodice than it did to hide her charms.

Miles caught his wandering eyes abruptly, forcing them to meet hers. "Miss Quince, I have come to offer you my sincere apology. I realize that my behavior last night was absolutely unforgivable, but I hope that you will not dislike me so much that you will not give thought to what I am about to say."

For a moment, Miles was dumbfounded when he realized that, riveted as he had been by Genevieve Quince's loveliness this morning, he had actually been *eager* to offer for her. He cleared his throat again in confusion before continuing. Drat her blue eyes, he thought savagely, and turned away in order to regain control over his wandering thoughts.

"Yes, Lord Bradford?" said Genevieve, lips quivering. *God help me,* she thought madly. *He's really going to do it! He is going to ask me to marry him!* Immediately her heart began to race and she struggled for breath as her mind fought with the conflicting emotions assaulting her. She lowered her eyes demurely and turned toward the window as she tried to still her pounding heart. Should she say yes, marry him to save her honor? But what if that was not her true reason for accepting his suit? And what if— Her frantic thoughts were cut off in midstream as Lord Bradford spoke once more.

"It is obvious to me that a young woman of quality such as yourself would never consider lowering herself to such dire acts as your advertisement in the *Times* suggests unless she had no other alternative."

"That is very astute of you, my lord," Genevieve said. "But you see—"

"As such," he interrupted with a cursory wave of his hand, "because I would not be able to consider myself a gentleman unless I offered you an honorable way out of your current situation, and unless I offered recompense for my own behavior last night, I find that I must make you an offer you cannot refuse. 'S truth, I have no choice in the matter, but, nonetheless, my offer, that of a gentleman, is freely given. Truly, you would be mad to refuse the offer, since it is either accept what I propose, or engage in what we both know is a lewd and incorrigible act for one as well-bred as yourself, namely, selling the honor of your family name."

Miles cleared his throat, conscious once again that his attention was wandering to Miss Quince's glowing red-gold curls, making him wonder if they truly would smell of warm cinnamon if he were to bury his face in the thick tresses.

"I am prepared to make you my wife," he continued firmly, "even though said act is distasteful in the extreme to both of us. You will then be able to forget this mad venture and retire in the country with reputation intact, living in comfort and ease for the rest of your life. Once you have provided me with an heir, I shall, of course, leave you to your own interests. Now then, what is your answer?" He waited confidently, the thought of a negative response never entering his arrogant mind.

Genevieve turned to look at him, her eyes wide with shock. "You wish to marry me to save me from making a fool of myself?"

"Naturally. Is that not what I just stated?"

"And so that I may provide you with an heir?"

"Of course!" Lord Bradford snapped, annoyed at the inquisition. "And once we are wed, you will reside at Bradford Hall. Finally, Quince House will be demolished so that our view of the woods behind your disgracefully unkempt home is not obstructed." He spoke as if she would, naturally, agree wholeheartedly with his plan.

Genevieve stared at him without speaking.

"Come now, Miss Quince, what else could I possibly have intended? Did you believe that I had come because of my undying devotion to you?" Miles huffed uncomfortably, for one horrifying moment feeling disconcertingly close to expressing exactly those plebian emotions.

Fortunately for Lord Bradford, at just that moment Genevieve took the matter out of his hands. Without even attempting to understand all the convoluted reasons for the rage boiling up within her, she rounded on him furiously.

"What else indeed, my lord? Heaven forbid we consider whether we suit. But on further reflection, judging from your actions last night, I suppose I should be relieved that you have not come offering something quite different—what men of your standing and wealth do when a woman has nothing to offer but herself. "But I was wrong, was I not, in believing I had nothing to offer. I have something to offer you, my despicable Lord Bradford. Something your family has tried to wrest from my own for generations, and that you thought you could at last acquire in my time of need!"

She drew herself up straight, her eyes blazing. "No, sirrah! I will not sell either my family home or my body to you. I would prefer to starve! You have wasted your time and my own in coming here and making this disgusting offer. Now if you will be so kind as to leave at once, I will busy myself in preparation to receive my first guests!" She stopped, breathless from her verbal exertions, her ripe bosom heaving.

Miles stared, wide-eyed, at the beauty so viciously dressing him down, and he found to his amazement that there was only one thing in the world that he wanted to do. Acting on this impulse, he strode forward and seized Genevieve by the wrist, jerking her close to him. Jasper growled and jumped to attention.

"Down, Jasper!" commanded Lord Bradford in a tone that demanded obedience, and Genevieve was astonished to see the mastiff drop like a stone to the rug, eyes alert as he awaited further instructions.

Beyond the point of thought, Miles took possession of Genevieve's full, soft lips and pressed her ripe young body along the entire length of his own, kissing her masterfully and completely until she was limp in his arms and chastising him no longer.

Genevieve was awash in outrage yet overcome with newfound emotions that she could not begin to understand. Only when Lord Bradford's hands strayed to the bodice of her gown, arousing even more confusing sensations within her, did Genevieve murmur incoherently and struggle in his grasp. Abruptly Miles came out of his desire-fogged haze and back to reality. He pulled away from her abruptly, releasing his hold as if her flesh burned his hands.

Genevieve fell to the horsehair sofa that rested behind her knees, unable to stand on her trembling legs. Her mind had gone blank, and her body was still oddly warm from his nearness and his kiss. She stared up at his dark, angry face with wide, blank eyes.

"Now I will leave you, madam. While you shall no doubt disbelieve me, I have harbored no burning desire to obtain your precious Quince House. I merely wished to help a lady out of an undesirable situation, while at the same time do what was proper after my behavior of last night. However, as you would obviously prefer to prostitute your name rather than become my wife, I shall not stand in your way. The only thing I ask is that, when I have obtained a *suitable* wife, you stay away from her. I will not have you tainting her."

He smiled nastily in an attempt to hide his confusing disappointment. "However, should you find that your madcap ideas do not come to fruition and you wish to earn a more certain living, I shall be only too happy to oblige you in setting you up as my mistress. And I shall not apologize for my actions just now. You did nothing if not practically beg me to bed you," he sniped. He stalked out of the room.

Genvieve heard the front doors slam behind him. She was still sitting there in the parlor when Miss Pramble wandered in from the rose garden with a dozen or so lovely buds in a crystal vase.

"Look at this beautiful vase I found in one of the kitchen cupboards, my dear. And all these lovely roses! How nice that they are blooming so early. Just the thing to brighten the parlor, wouldn't you agree? How was his lordship? When is the wedding to be held? It would be nice if the roses were in full bloom—you could hold the ceremony in the garden," she said blissfully, placing the vase on the mantel. Then, looking at Genevieve's pale face, she gasped. She rushed over and took the girl's hands, chafing them to warm the chilled flesh. "My dear, what on earth is the matter?"

Genevieve looked up at her, unseeing, and, without uttering a syllable, rose and walked out of the room, up the stairs, and into her bedchamber, where she closed and bolted the door behind her. It was not sorrow that drove her to seek refuge, or fear. It was amazement that, for one brief moment, when Lord Bradford had made his second, shameful offer, she had seriously considered accepting.

During the days that followed Genevieve forcibly put Lord Bradford out of her mind as she and Miss Pramble turned the house into a reasonably acceptable vacationing place for wealthy commoners. Although they both dropped into their beds exhausted at the end of each day, by the time a week had passed they had scrubbed the white pillars outside the house, aired and cleaned all the bedroom suites inside, and raked the dead leaves off the extensive lawns. Even now the dried piles smoked in huge thimble-shaped lumps.

One morning while Miss Pramble was busily washing windows with lemon-vinegar water, Genevieve wandered around to the back of the house to inspect the outbuildings more closely. After rummaging around a bit, she decided that the small carriage house would be perfect for housing a few dozen chickens. The stables would be satisfactory for the visitors' horses as well as perhaps a cow or two for fresh milk and cream. Also, to her delight, she discovered several old uninhabited beehives. There had been an old bee tree half a mile or so from the house at one time. One day soon she would have to investigate, since it was spring and the bees would be swarming, some of them eager to leave the winter-crowded hive for a new home.

The next morning Genevieve and Miss Pramble hitched the gray mare up to a dilapidated wagon and set out for the neighboring village of Dunheath, which was—fortunately for the dainty

mare, who was unused to pulling such a vehicle—
only two miles away.

Since most of the shopkeepers and nearby farm-
ers had known Genevieve since she was a girl, by
the end of the day she had purchased on credit
two dozen chickens and a fine, strutting cock, several bales of hay and straw for the guests' horses
when they arrived, and, to Genevieve's utter delight, one large-boned, soft-eyed Jersey cow. The
farmer they bought her from promised she would
give enough milk for all the guests Quince House
could hold. In addition he had thrown in, free of
charge, one frisky black-and-white nanny goat,
which he swore produced milk that made the best
cheese in the country.

It was this straggling train, winding its way
down the road toward the two estates, that met
Lord Bradford's dubious gaze that evening. He
had been assessing with grudging admiration the
shining windows, neat gardens, and glistening
white pillars of the estate opposite Bradford Hall.
Damned fine job the two lone women had done
with the place, he had to admit. But suddenly his
attention had been snatched away from the mansion and fixed in astonishment on the sight before
him, this odd group that looked like nothing so
much as a caravan of Gypsies.

At first he was outraged, certain that now the
inimitable Miss Quince would turn the neighborhood into a barnyard. But then Lord Bradford's
mouth twitched in the faintest quirk of a smile,
both corners lifted slightly, and finally he collapsed in a chair, shaking with laughter as he
imagined Genevieve's delicately pointed chin lifting stubbornly as she tried to figure out how to
milk a cow! Surely that experience would hasten
her into seeing the folly of her ways, and soon
thereafter she would surrender Quince House to

his demolition crew. And then he would be free of the maddening wench forever!

Behind Quince House, Genevieve and Miss Pramble spread a thick layer of straw in the stall that was to serve as home for the cow, whom they christened Angelina. With light hearts they also put fresh, sweet-smelling hay into the mare's box, spread more straw along the shelves in the old carriage house so that the chickens could roost comfortably, and, after tethering Vashti, the goat, to a post in the yard, went into the kitchen to have a bite to eat before settling down for bed.

Lord Bradford need not have worried about how the ladies would manage to milk the cow, for two more determined women had never lived, and so it was not long before both of them could not only milk Angeline and Vashti, but had also learned to churn the sweet cream into the best butter and cheese for miles.

With their fresh eggs, milk, and butter, along with flour they purchased in the village, they were soon had preparing cakes and loaves of fresh, crusty brown bread to serve their guests at tea.

If any of those guests ever arrived.

Lord Bradford rolled over groggily and opened one silver eye. What the devil? A loud, raucous shrieking filled the air, rattling the glass in his windowpanes. At first he was dumbfounded and could not figure out what it could be. As he lay there, however, growing more and more irritated, the source of the insane clamoring became clear.

He rolled over and pulled an enormous feather pillow over his head in an unsuccessful attempt to muffle the horrid screeching. Finally, unable to block out the sound or to sleep, he climbed out of bed, lit a candle, and tried to read. The clock on his nightstand read 3:00 A.M. Evidently Genevieve Quince was being much more successful in her barnyard endeavor than he had given her credit for.

When the sun was high in the sky the rooster finally stopped crowing, having done his job in alerting everyone that a new day was coming. To Lord Bradford, the cessation of the noise came too late, for by this time the clamor in his head had reached a deafening crescendo, and he was forced to remain in bed for the rest of the day, cursing the hour that had brought Miss Genevieve Quince and her lovely eyes of cornflower-blue into the world.

7

Genevieve stretched. The early-morning sun streamed in through the windows she had been able to leave open during the warm night for the first time that spring. Now a fresh, clean-smelling breeze brushed aside the gauzy white curtains, and Genevieve jumped out of bed feeling refreshened and optimistic. To her delight, she and Miss Pramble had already been able to pay off many of their grocery and livestock bills by selling butter, cream, and eggs in the village, and she was looking forward to the new day.

Lord Bradford had also risen early, dressing in riding boots of pale champagne-colored calfskin and breeches of the finest wool. Both items were new, having been delivered from London only the previous afternoon, and although he was not a dandy—indeed, he thought those foppish creatures excessively foolish—Miles was well pleased as he straightened his cravat and scrutinized his reflection in the mirror.

His good mood was heightened when he found, to his satisfaction, a letter from Dobbins informing him that the first young candidate had been found on a pleasingly large and prosperous estate only a mile from his, bordering Bradford Hall on the west. His lordship promptly dispatched a missive inviting the young woman and her chaperone to come to Bradford Hall for the weekend. Her name was Lady Lucinda Wheatley, and from the solicitor's description, her face was as lovely as her fortune.

It was with this pleasant thought in mind that Miles collected his mount for his morning ride, cantered off across the lawn, and rode into the surrounding woods that bordered both his and Miss Quince's property. It was a spectacular spring morning, the warmest yet. Tiny purple-and-white violets peeped up through the crust of dead brown leaves on the forest floor, and here and there a startlingly bright wild rose burst forth yellow against the deep green of its foliage. After a brisk trot to warm Fury's muscles, Lord Bradford urged the stallion into a gallop, and horse and rider flew over the ground like the mythical winged Pegasus.

At last Miles reined the bay in, slowing to a sedate walk. As rider and steed neared a clearing at the edge of the forest, Miles became aware of an odd splashing sound, and he urged the horse forward into a cautious trot. His eyes widened when he saw where the noise came from. Good heavens! What would the damned woman be up to next?

After a hearty breakfast of fresh toasted bread and scrambled eggs, Genevieve had decided that the time was ripe to tackle de-clogging the lake, the one serious cleaning project left to take care of before any of her guests arrived. Bright and early she had donned her oldest, most threadbare gown and, without rousing Miss Pramble, went straight outside to start the job. Having eyed the vast expanse of lilies with a sinking heart, she had at last decided to clear away only enough so that the cygnets she intended to purchase would have enough room to swim and feed. And she had hiked up the skirts of her worn cambric gown, tucked them into her waistband, and waded in to proceed.

The effect was startling, as Lord Bradford could attest, and he found himself growing increasingly uncomfortable as he watched her from the shadow of the trees. Her white lawn pantaloons clung to her hips and thighs, showing off the young, slender limbs beneath. Miles caught his breath and swallowed; shifting in the saddle and tugging at his fashionably fitting wool breeches. While a perfect fit a short time ago, they were now becoming uncomfortably snug.

Her arms filled with blooming lilies, Genevieve looked like a naiad sprung from the lake on an early morning, frolicking at a time when she would not be seen by mortals. Lord Bradford watched as she waded out of the water, and for a split second he could see, through the dampened and now nearly transparent lawn of her underclothes, the dark triangle of curls at the cleft between her legs. He clenched his teeth and fought down the urge to ride down to the lake, sweep her up onto the horse, and carry her off into the woods.

It appeared that she had finished for the morning. After tugging her skirts down into place, Genevieve disappeared behind the house.

Lord Bradford had just decided he had best return Fury to the stables when he saw her coming back around the southern side of the mansion, tugging a large object behind her. What the devil? It was a *boat*. Now what on earth did she intend to do with that? Despite Fury's irritated shuffling and champing at the bit, Miles grinned and settled down for the rest of the show.

Genevieve launched the dingy, wondering if it

would float or merely sink to the bottom of the pond. To her happiness, it floated as well as an inflated pig's bladder. Cautiously she set one foot into the vessel, balancing herself on the bank just in case it decided to sink after all. When it did not fill with water, she swung her other leg in, and, after standing uncertainly for a few moments, finally sat down on the bench at the rear and began to row herself out into the middle of the pond.

The uncertainty of her movements made Lord Bradford conclude that she could not swim, or she would not have been so cautious. Grudgingly concerned for her welfare, he stayed where he was, intent on the scene before him.

The boat, which Genevieve had hastily patched with bunches of straw from the stables, served admirably for a time. Smiling, she began to think that there was nothing she could not do. Most of the lilies that she wished to remove were out in the middle of the lake, so she headed in that direction. It was an easy task to lean over the edge of the boat, grasp the lilies just below the leaves, and pull them up into the prow of the vessel. So intent on her work was she that she failed to notice that the straw, which had worked so well for a short time, was now sodden, and the water that was not soaked up was rapidly filling the bottom of the boat. Piece by piece the straw came loose, drifting silently to the pond floor.

At first she thought that the water beneath her was merely from the lilies, having run off the wet plants that she kept piling in the boat. However, as five more minutes passed and the depth had reached nearly an inch, she noticed with sudden alarm that the cause was no such thing. She began to row as fast as she could toward the edge of the lake. The sudden movement of the boat, however, had a detrimental effect on the straw, which pulled loose more quickly now, rapidly sinking out of sight.

As Genevieve had rowed quite some distance into the lake, she had not gone far toward land when the boat filled completely and sank from beneath her, leaving her thrashing about in the icy water. It had not seemed so cold while she waded, but now that it covered her waist and breasts, it took her breath away.

Fortunately Genevieve's forebears had not dug the lake very deep, insisting upon having one of their own only so as not to be outdone by the pond excavated by Miles's great-grandfather. Wanting more to antagonize the Bradfords than to have a true lake, they had dug it large in circumference but shallow enough that the water barely reached Genevieve's shoulders.

Lord Bradford, however, was not privy to this information, and, being certain Genevieve could not swim, knew he could not let her drown, no matter how irritating she might be. In an instant he had leaped from Fury's broad back, appeared from behind the trees that had concealed him, and dashed toward the water.

The situation might have been clearer had not Genevieve chosen this moment to catch her foot in a clump of lily roots at the bottom of the lake and found it necessary to duck beneath the surface in order to release her trapped limb. Her action merely strengthened Miles's certainty that she was in grave peril, and he quickened his strides, dove headlong into the water, and, fighting the clinging vines, swam toward her.

No sooner had Genevieve freed her foot and surfaced than she found herself grasped around the neck by an unknown assailant. As she struggled furiously, one of her hands made contact with an oar that had not, like the boat, sunk to the bottom. Hefting it awkwardly, Genevieve swung it into the air behind her, clubbing Miles firmly on the head.

He swore viciously, tightening the grip of his elbow, which was wrapped around her neck, ruing that drowning people had to panic and make a rescuer's task that much harder. During the struggle, his prized boots of pale calfskin became lodged deep in the thick black sludge at the bottom of the lake, and as he pulled the squirming, hysterical woman onto the bank, Miles discovered to his chagrin he had to leave them behind. Great clods of clayish, sticky mud clung to the stockinged toes so recently graced with such elegant new footwear.

"Unhand me, sir!" Genevieve cried angrily. When he did not immediately comply, she lowered her head and bit him firmly on the forearm.

And as if the loss of his boots were not bad enough, the ruin of his new breeches, now muddied beyond hope of repair was not sufficient, now Miss Quince had to chastise him loudly and furiously, attempting to do him bodily harm, after he had just done her the honor of saving her life! He could bear no more.

"Damnation, wench!" he cursed, lowering her from his arms and thrusting her away from him. "Is this how you thank someone for saving your life?"

"Saving my life? More like killed me, you did, squeezing my throat like that! And me just minding my own business, clearing the lake of lilies for some swans I wish to purchase!"

"You haven't even the decency to thank me politely for hauling you out of a watery grave! Instead you draw blood!"

"You thought I was drowning?" Genevieve laughed scornfully. "How like a man to think that just because a woman has a little mishap, she is in dire need of his manly services!" Her hair hung in stringy clumps and was dripping with bits of algae, twigs, and water lilies.

"Then there is the matter of my new riding boots, which are even now embedded in that filthy pond somewhere! And look at my new breeches! Ruined! And what about clubbing me over the head with that oar! You ungrateful wretch, I've a mind to turn you over my knee!"

"You just try it, sirrah, and you'll come away with worse than a clubbed head!"

Infuriated, Miles took a step toward her.

Genevieve, fearing the worst, reached around behind her, hoping she would find some weapon with which to defend herself. Unable to find anything else, she grasped a bundle of water lilies from the pile where she had been dumping them. "Come no closer, I warn you!" she cried, holding her lilies before her like a sword.

Suddenly caught by the absurdity of the situation, Miles laughed.

Genevieve, on the other hand, was filled with a burning rage that he should once again find her so amusing. Running forward, she caught him full against the side of the head with the muddy mass. Lord Bradford's smile disappeared, and in its place Genevieve saw a determination that definitely boded no good.

Wrenching the lilies from her hands, Miles gripped Genevieve by the wrist and twisted her arm, forcing her to turn around in order to avoid agony. Dropping onto the damp grass, Miles pulled Genevieve down with him, forcing her across his lap. With his free hand he jerked her drenched skirts up and began to render a resounding spanking. It was only after he had delivered several slaps that he realized what he had done.

Miss Quince was struggling fitfully across his thighs, and her bottom, clad only in her damp, translucent pantaloons, lay nearly bare beneath his hand. He could see it turning scarlet from his slaps. Miles caught his breath and unthinkingly made to massage the blushing flesh. The girl froze in his grip, and, to his horror, Lord Bradford realized that he was merely compounding his offense. Appalled at his behavior, he gasped, then pushed the woman away from him.

Genevieve sprawled forward onto her knees and scrambled to a standing position. They stared at each other, openmouthed and breathing heavily.

Finally Miles rose, turned sharply, and, without a word, headed back toward his horse. Swinging up onto Fury, he kicked the horse viciously in the flanks with his muddy, stockinged feet and galloped off through the trees.

Genevieve's hands flew to her burning face, and she ran for the house, not stopping until she had reached the safety of her room. How could she ever dare step foot outside the house again, for fear she would run into the man?

At last Genevieve tamped down her fiery shame, reminding herself that there was work to be done. She emerged from the sanctuary of her bedroom and saw that the post had finally been delivered. There were two letters awaiting her inspection. Dismissing the appalling incident with Lord Bradford in a trice, she snatched up the mail and took it into the parlor to read. After seating herself on the horsehair sofa, she carefully pulled apart the wax seals and opened the first of the letters.

When Miss Pramble came into the room a few minutes later, she started with surprise at the look of delight on Genevieve's face. "What is it, dear?"

"You'll never guess, Pramble!" cried Genevieve

happily. "Our first guests will be arriving in one week's time. Do you think we will have everything ready by then?"

She looked so hopeful that Miss Pramble hastened to assure her that they would.

Then Genevieve remembered that she had not yet completed her task in the lake, and her face fell.

"Is anything wrong, my dear?" asked the governess with a concerned frown.

"Oh, it is only that I still need to finish pulling lilies out of the lake, and I find that I am allergic to the pollen given off by the blooms," she lied uneasily.

"In that case, I forbid you to go near them again, Jenny," said Miss Pramble quickly. "It can be most distressing to fall prey to one's allergies. And I hear those who suffer are especially susceptible in the spring. Do not worry, child. I will be happy to complete the job."

Genevieve smiled gratefully. "Oh, thank you, Pramble. That will leave me free to check on that bee tree in the woods. I do hope it is still there; it would be so pleasant to have fresh honey."

"Yes," replied Miss Pramble uncertainly, "but, my dear, are you certain you know how to gather the honey without disturbing the bees?"

"Oh, don't worry, silly goose," laughed the girl, rising from the chair and walking to the doorway. "I'm sure it can't be all that difficult. I mean, what's to do? Just stay calm, reach in slowly, and gather the honey, right?" she said. She had no doubt whatsoever that she would be successful.

"Still, you mind yourself, Jenny. Be careful," called Miss Pramble doubtfully as Genevieve disappeared down the hall.

If Genevieve was to be honest, she did not have the first idea how to go about raiding a beehive.

However, her successes thus far with the estate had made her a trifle smug, and she honestly believed that the bees would be no trouble. So it was that she dressed in a gown of especially heavy cotton and searched around until she found a pair of old gloves and a hat with a heavy veil, the old-fashioned type that covered not only the front of her face but the back of her head as well, drooping down well past her collar.

Filled with self-importance, she wandered out to the small toolshed behind the house. The rickety door opened with a squeal, and Genevieve peered inside, glancing with distaste at the thick cloud of spiderwebs that clustered about the ceiling and eaves. Motes of dust stirred up by the door danced in the sunbeams that poured in through several large cracks in the roof.

In one corner she found a large metal bucket, which she scrubbed until it gleamed. Then, after digging around a bit longer, she was rewarded with the discovery of an ancient, rusted saw, which she promptly added to her bee-hunting supplies. With these tools at her side, Genevieve walked into the forest toward the place where she remembered the tree to be.

Before long she began to regret that she had dressed in such a heavy gown, for it was no longer cool, and she was feeling sticky and damp with perspiration. But being a woman of strong resolve, she did not pause in her search, and in a while she had reached a small stand of maples and oaks. The steady hum that came from an old, dead beech-tree trunk off to one side made her smile. Genevieve strode forward, armed with bucket, saw, and, as she was soon to find, an over-supply of confidence.

8

Lady Lucinda Wheatley arrived with pomp and circumstance the same afternoon.

Lord Bradford stood on the steps of Bradford Hall with Aunt Hester, who had roused herself enough to greet her nephew's prospective bride, even though she looked every bit as puzzled as she had by the rest of Miles's visit. Together they watched the crested carriage pull up the long drive, Miles with a smile painted on his face and relief in his heart that he was to be given a diversion to take his mind off Genevieve Quince, and Aunt Hester wishing that she could have done with visitors—including Lord Bradford—and be left once again in peace.

The carriage rolled to a stop, its wheels crunching as the brakes were applied, and the tiger jumped off his seat behind the main compartment. He flung the door wide with a flourish, Lady Lucinda stepped out, and Miles felt his breath catch at the young woman's beauty.

Her hair was pale-gold, gleaming like fresh grain in the sunlight, and her scent reminded him of rosebuds. She was all that was entrancing and delightful, and he smiled more sincerely as she looked up at him with huge twin pools of sky-blue.

"My Lord Bradford, how delightful to meet you." Her voice was musical and high-pitched, like a flute.

"The honor is mine, my dear. I am so pleased that you have come. Ah," he said congenially as a plump, matronly woman emerged from the carriage, looking as if she had just awakened from a long hibernation, "this must be your chaperone, Mrs. Simms. Charmed, madam. Please allow me to present my dear Aunt Hester, who will be in charge of your comfort during your stay here at Bradford Hall."

The lady nodded sleepily in Miles's aunt's direction.

Lord Bradford stifled a grin and took Lady Lucinda's arm to lead her into the house, accompanied by Mrs. Simms and Aunt Hester. "In one hour we shall dine. I will have Benson, my butler, show you to your rooms, as I am certain you will wish to freshen up before dinner."

Benson had appeared immediately, and the women, led by Aunt Hester, who said not a word, followed him up the great staircase. Lady Lucinda cast a last smile in Miles's direction as they disappeared.

Miles smiled to himself, a very satisfied smile. She would do. Yes indeed, she would do nicely.

At the appointed time Miles was dressed in an immaculate coat of pale-gray and breeches of charcoal, his cravat tied carefully in the Oriental and his hair combed so that not a strand was out of place. He stood at the bottom of the stairs waiting for the woman who was already, in his mind, his fiancée. When Lady Lucinda appeared, wearing a pale-blue gown of gauzy silk and a demure necklace of blue topazes around her slender, swanlike neck, he smiled brilliantly and extended his hand.

Mrs. Simms, much like Aunt Hester, did not offer so much as a single comment during the meal but ate as rapidly as Aunt Hester did slowly. Miles began to worry that the waistline of her black bombazine gown would split. For that matter, Lady Lucinda did not say anything, either, until the meal was over. When finally she spoke, Miles felt a shaft of ice shoot through him.

"I cannot tell you what a tiring journey we had," she said. This was not the sentence that worried him. It was, rather, when she chattered gaily, "But now I feel wholly rethted. You mutht call me Luthy, and I thall call you Mile'th."

Miles swallowed heavily, the happy dreams of nurseries and hours conversing with his delightful new wife dispersing like smoke in the wind. "Luthy?" he said hoarsely.

"No, thilly!" she trilled gaily. "Luthy."

"Lucy?" he said in a whisper, choking on a sip of wine.

"Yeth! Luthy, Mile'th. Now then, what entertainmenths have you planned for our thtay, Mile'th?" Lucinda batted her eyes at him in what would have, before she spoke, been a very effective manner.

Miles felt a terrible sinking sensation in the pit of his stomach as he explained that he had ordered three mounts to be brought round after their meal so that they could take a tour of his eth—he cleared his throat—estate.

When Lucinda opened her mouth to exclaim with joy, he hurriedly filled the gap.

"No, dear lady, do not thank me. Drinking in your beauty is all the thanks I need!"

Lucinda snapped her mouth shut like a turtle, obviously uncertain whether he was being rude or flattering. Evidently she chose the latter, for she beamed at him, remaining silent for the rest of the meal.

When Mrs. Simms had devoured the last course and graciously offered to finish off Aunt Hester's strawberry pie, the visitors went upstairs to their chambers to dress in riding clothes, and Hester wandered outside to do some weeding.

It took Miles a scant five minutes to change, and as he waited below he wondered which of his horses would be able to bear the weight of Lady Luthy's chaperone. Nearly thirty minutes later, at which time Miles was beginning to hope that maybe both ladies had packed their things and beat a hasty retreat from Bradford Hall, rustling sounds at the top of the stairs heralded their coming.

It was all Miles could do not to burst into disbelieving laughter as soon as he set eyes on Lady Lucinda. While Mrs. Simms was still dressed in black bombazine, albeit this time in a semblance of a riding habit, Lucinda was dressed more appropriately to adorn a fashion plate than a horse. Her habit was of impossibly impractical pale-yellow satin with a wide sash of spring-green and boots and kid gloves in a matching shade. While in truth she looked lovely in the outrageous costume, what left Miles openmouthed with wonder was her hat. If such it could be called. For upon Lady Lucinda's head rested the most incredible concoction he had ever seen. At least three feet wide and a foot high, the bonnet accompanying her habit was the gaudiest piece of headgear that Miles was sure had ever been invented.

"Do you like thith bonnet?" lisped Lady Lucinda, noticing his riveted gaze. "I dethigned it mythelf."

A multitude of flowers—roses, violets, daffodils,

asters, pansies, verbena, and daisies; orchids, sweet William, buttercups, and lilies of the valley; cowslips, jack-in-the-pulpit, begonias, geraniums, and phlox—surely all these and more were piled on top of one another in a concoction of shades, each more raucously brilliant than the next.

Miles nearly had to turn away from this fashion disaster, for it made his eyes ache just to look at it. But instead of uttering the exclamation of horror that rose to his lips, he clamped them firmly shut, smiled weakly, and nodded politely before leading the ladies out of the house to where their mounts were waiting at the foot of the steps.

After first lifting Lady Lucinda's petite form into the sidesaddle, Miles turned toward Mrs. Simms uncertainly. She beamed at his gentlemanly attentions and nodded toward Lucinda approvingly. Clenching his hands together, Miles gritted his teeth and placed his hands at the horse's belly to give Mrs. Simms a leg up. With a gay little laugh the chaperone, obviously feeling much more the thing after her enormous meal, simpered at him and lifted her oversized foot into his hands. Miles grunted as she put her weight down into his interlaced fingers, nearly dragging him to the ground. Stifling a groan, he heaved the woman into the saddle, ignoring the mare's sorrowful, rolling eyes as she sagged beneath her burden.

Feeling as if he had put his back out for the rest of eternity, Miles mounted Fury, smiled even more weakly at the women, and, as the group cantered off down the drive, madly racked his brain for some scheme that would make Lady Lucinda decide he would never do as a prospective husband.

Genevieve approached the tree stump, listening to the vibrating hum within. She cocked an ear toward the trunk, estimating where the buzzing was situated so she could decide where to saw. For why not bring the entire hive intact to Quince House and better her future honey harvests?

She placed the bucket on the ground at her feet, rested the teeth of the saw on the dead wood, and began to cut. The humming grew louder and louder, and Genevieve began to question the wisdom of her actions.

What Genevieve did not know, as she began to cut her way into the tree trunk, was that the insects that lived inside were not honeybees but rather a particularly vicious species of hornet. It did not take long for her to discover this, however, as a stream of screaming, indignant creatures came boiling up out of the dead gray stump.

For a moment she could do nothing but stare in amazement at the savage, ever-increasing cloud forming over her head. Outraged, the hornets spun round and round, searching for the presumptuous invader who had disturbed their afternoon.

It was very lucky that Genevieve had dressed so carefully before launching on her honey expedition, for in seconds she was covered from head to toe with a writhing mass of hornets. With a screech she flung her arms outward, flailing blindly as she raced away from the clearing.

At this moment, riding peacefully through the trees, the three sojourners from Bradford Hall were approaching the area where Genevieve had fallen into such grave misfortune.

"I thay, what ith that?" lisped Lady Lucinda, craning her neck, her preposterous hat tipping precariously as she peered into the trees at the odd-looking spectacle stumbling toward them.

What the riders were ignorant of, the horses figured out in record time, rearing frantically.

"Help! Help!" cried the hornet-covered human—if indeed human it was.

"Oh, God, no," groaned Miles as he reined Fury in abruptly, recognizing the all-too-familiar voice in an instant. "Miss Quince!" He turned and looked behind him to where, only a moment before, Mrs. Simms and Lady Lucinda had been. To his consternation he noted that both women had lost their seats and were now flat on their backs, dumped by the frightened mares, which had disappeared in the opposite direction.

Realizing from their shouts that help was nigh, Genevieve lumbered blindly in their direction, arms waving madly.

"Oh!" cried Lucinda, scrambling backward on her bottom as she tried to escape the monster that was coming ever closer. Her hat was dangerously askew, tilting over her eyes and obscuring her vision.

If Lady Lucinda had had the foresight to discard her floral masterpiece at this time, what happened next might have been averted. Instead she clutched at it, desperately pushing it back into place, more concerned with glamour than danger.

As Genevieve closed the remaining distance between her and rescue, the hornets, sensing a new player in the drama, took leave of her and zoomed toward the screeching, moaning form prostrate in the leaves. Fortunately, instead of swarming over Lady Lucinda as they had Genevieve, they were instantly attracted by the brilliant array of flowers, and they clustered thickly on the large, luminous blossoms.

Genevieve, now able to see, looked about to determine who had saved her. Her eyes widened as they took in Lady Lucinda, terrorized under her outrageous hat, and Lord Bradford, who was sitting in mute shock on his stallion. Nearby, a very fat middle-aged woman clambered to her feet and ran off into the woods, shrieking madly. Suddenly Lucinda, too, jumped to her feet and, with a horrified, unintelligible cry, began to run.

"Damn you, Miss Quince! Now look what you've done!" roared Lord Bradford as he kicked Fury into a gallop and raced after his prospective fiancée.

Genevieve swallowed nervously and, without another thought, turned and flew on winged feet back toward Quince House.

In a matter of seconds Miles closed the distance between himself and Lady Lucinda. He reached out one hand, which was, unfortunately, not gloved. Gripping the offending headpiece between his fingers, he wrenched it, pins and all, from Lucinda's head and flung it as far into the bushes as he could. For his troubles he received at least a dozen excruciating stings.

Lady Lucinda stopped running. She looked up at him through glittering, tear-filled eyes, looking even more lovely, as dishevelled as she was, than she had the moment they had met. However, tilting her chin back regally, she eyed Lord Bradford with an expression of intense hatred, letting him know in no uncertain terms that she held him completely responsible for the entire horrifying incident.

"I think, my lord, that we thall not thuit." Then she turned and walked swiftly in the direction of Bradford Hall.

Miles looked down at his rapidly swelling hand, then back toward the bonnet in the bushes. Then he began to laugh, hearty, relieved, gleeful laughter that did not stop until he reached Bradford Hall, where he was forced to maintain a disappointed, sober demeanor while Lisping Lady Lucinda and her chaperone departed.

Aunt Hester merely shrugged at their hasty retreat.

"Oh, Pramble!" moaned Genevieve tearfully as she stood at the window in the governess's bedchamber, peering out from behind the curtains in the direction of Bradford Hall. "You have no idea how embarrassing it was. Those horrid w-women and that awful L-Lord Bradford staring at me as if I were some sort of m-m-monster, and then the ladies being t-t-tossed off their horses because of me. And then those hornets! How was I to know they were not b-b-bees? Can't you just imagine that . . . that *beast's* rage when his fiancée flings her engagement ring in his face, and all because of m-m-me?" She paused, sniffling, her attention caught by a sudden movement at the opposite estate. "Oh, no! I knew it! Look, Pramble, there they go. Oh, dear. Lord Bradford looks so stern!"

Miss Pramble watched Genevieve with an amused frown as the girl paced back and forth in front of the window. "My dear, how can you possibly see Lord Bradford's expression from this distance? I am certain that you overrate his unhappiness. I mean, if this young woman responded to the incident in such an appalling manner as you say, then perhaps his lordship is only too happy to be rid of her."

Genevieve sniffed, brushing tears from her cheeks. "No, Pramble. He is absolutely livid. I am certain of it. I can tell by the way he is standing there watching the carriage pull down his drive."

If she had actually been party to Miles's thoughts at that moment, she would have been flabbergasted to know that he was thinking with all sincerity that if Miss Quince were there, he would grab her and kiss her from head to toe for getting rid of Lithping Luthy. He would really

have to write and tell Dobbins to be more careful
whom he sent next.

But as she did not know how pleased Lord
Bradford was, despite his enormously swollen
hand, Genevieve spent the remainder of the day
berating herself. She did know without a doubt
that she needed to apologize. But how? She could
not simply waltz over to a man's house and say, *so
sorry for chasing off your fiancée. I hope you will have
a happy life anyway.*

As she was attempting to sort out her trouble-
some thoughts by making a batch of fresh bread,
a possible solution occurred to Genevieve. The
sudden memory of how furious his lordship had
been to lose his new boots in the bottom of her
lake made her pause in her kneading. There, at
least, was something she could remedy. Leaving
the dough where it lay, Genevieve wiped her
hands on the flour-covered apron she wore and
rushed outside.

Miss Pramble was already down by the lake,
and, having hired some men from the village to retrieve the dinghy from its watery grave and repair
it, was busily pulling up water lilies and piling
them in the boat. When she saw Genevieve she
rowed back to shore.

"Hello, dear," she called gaily as she approached. Genevieve helped Miss Pramble unload
the lilies and then insisted that the governess take
a break for a spot of tea and a biscuit. As soon as
the woman disappeared into the house, Genevieve
climbed into the mended rowboat and slipped
across the water.

It was not difficult to find the spot where her
craft had capsized, for when it had sunk it had
pressed all the lilies beneath it to the bottom of the
lake, leaving a boat-shaped gap in the thick foliage. It was difficult, however, to locate the pair of

boots in the murky water. At last, after peering into the water and poking about with the oar for nearly half an hour, she gave up and rowed unhappily back to shore.

That night, as Genevieve strained unsuccessfully to sleep, an idea occurred to her. Surely, even if she had been able to find the missing boots, they would have been beyond repair. Why not have a new pair made for Lord Bradford? Very pleased with herself, she drifted off into slumber.

The following morning Genevieve raided the tea canister that contained their money and told Miss Pramble that she would be be back shortly. She saddled Storm and set off across the fields toward the nearby village. There she made her way confidently toward the cobbler's shop. After tethering Storm outside, she went into the store.

"Afternoon Miss Quince. May I help 'ee?" asked a small man with a very shiny bald pate who stepped out of the shadows and brushed his hands on his leather apron.

Genevieve smiled. "Good afternoon, Mr. Bateman. "Yes indeed. I would like to have a pair of riding boots made."

"Riding boots? Then 'ee've come to the right place. Sit down, miss." Genevieve sat on the low stool he indicated. "Now, what do 'ee have in mind?"

"Something in calfskin, I think," she said in a businesslike tone. "They are to be a gift."

"Of course. May I see your foot, please?"

"Certainly," said Genevieve with an uncertain smile, lifting one of her dainty riding boots with the tiny brass buttons for his inspection.

"Would 'ee be looking for something like this, then?" he asked, examining her boot.

"Well, I suppose," replied Genevieve, "but quite

a bit bigger. About the size of yours, I would think."

"Fine," said the shopkeeper. "Now then, can I interest 'ee in anything else?"

"No, thank you," said Genevieve. "When will the boots be finished?"

" 'Ee can come back tomorrow afternoon. For a fine lady like yourself, I will work all night to have them finished." He beamed at her, and Genevieve smiled in return as she stood, paid him in advance, and left the shop.

It was not until she was nearly home that Genevieve wondered whether the boots would fit Lord Bradford. Then she sighed contentedly. The cobbler had certainly seemed to know his business. Surely if he had needed more specifics, he would have asked. Probably all men had similar-sized feet.

9

For some reason she did not want to explore, Genevieve kept her business in the village a secret from Miss Pramble. Rising early the next morning she hastily wrapped up several loaves of the fresh bread and a large number of pastries she had baked the previous day, sneaked out to the stables, and saddled Storm, placing the large bundle before her on the saddle. In a short time she had sold the items at the baker's and earned enough money to cover the cost of the boots, so that Pramble wouldn't notice the missing funds. Thereafter, she rode directly to the cobbler's shop.

Mr. Bateman saw Genevieve before she even dismounted and he came rushing out of the store with her package, a broad smile stretching his lined face. "Good morning, miss. I done like I promised 'ee. Been up all night working on these riding boots. 'Ee going to love 'em. I put a little extra effort—something special 'ee might say—into 'em, as ee'll see when 'ee open the package."

The package was wrapped tightly and tied securely with thick twine.

"I'm sure I shall, Mr. Bateman. Thank you so much for your efforts. You may be sure that I will come back here next time I find myself in need of boots." She flashed him a brilliant smile as she took the box up onto her lap, and he beamed in return before disappearing back into the store.

Genevieve supposed that there was no point in opening the box beforehand, as the package was very well wrapped, and a man like Mr. Bateman must certainly have done a superb job if he had stayed up so late working on them. Turning Storm, she headed back the way she had come.

Losing a bit of her nerve, she had nearly decided to go home and take Lord Bradford his boots and apology later in the day. But then she sat up straight in the saddle, telling herself that she was only putting off the inevitable. Besides, if Lord Bradford had not gone riding yet, he would be able to wear his new boots. She smiled at this thought and headed toward Bradford Hall.

As Storm cantered up the gravel drive, Genevieve wished wistfully that she had had something prettier to wear. Then she paused, wondering why she was so concerned about such a thing. After all, this was not a social call, and she had no need to impress Lord Bradford. For some reason this did not make her feel much better about the worn condition of her pale-green kerseymere habit with its tattered black trim or the bedraggled ostrich feather adorning her cork hat.

Nevertheless, Genevieve straightened her shoulders and held her chin high as the liveried footman standing outside the door at Bradford Hall came forward to help her dismount. She tucked her package under her arm and walked sedately up the steps, ignoring the man's knowing grin. No doubt the servant thought a young woman visited an unmarried gentleman's house unchaperoned for only one good reason.

After giving the butler her name and allowing him to lead her into a bright, spacious drawing room, Genevieve seated herself in one of the comfortable rose-pink armchairs and waited nervously. She began to wish she had not come, for everyone she encountered sent her such suggestive smiles.

She glanced around, noting the exquisite Oriental carpets on the polished wood floor. In one corner of the room sat an enormous pianoforte. She wandered over to the lovely instrument, lifted the cover, and plunked one key before nervously returning to her chair.

A sound in the doorway startled her, and Genevieve looked up from examining one faded kid glove. Lord Bradford stood leaning on the jamb, a bemused smile on his face and a large white bandage wrapped around one hand.

"Miss Quince. What a . . . singular surprise. I heard you admiring my instrument. Do you play? So do I. In fact, until my . . . accident with the hornets, I had not missed a day of playing for five years." He grinned at her stupefied expression. "You have never heard of a gentleman enamored of the pianoforte? Perhaps you thought music was essential only for females of good breeding?"

Genevieve's face reflected that that had been exactly what she had been thinking.

"I have an unconventional mother to thank for my talents."

"I see," she replied uncomfortably, although she obviously did not.

Miles finally acknowledged the reason for her discomfort. "You do know, of course, that it is not the done thing for an unmarried woman to come unchaperoned to a gentleman's home. Perhaps you would like me to have Benson fetch my Aunt Hester so that you can be sure I will not accost you? Or perhaps . . ." He raised his eyebrows expressively, then smiled easily at the quick negative shake of her head. "Very well. So, what can I do

for you? Perhaps you have come to borrow honey,
since your foray proved fruitless?"

Genevieve stared at him in surprise.

"Yes, Miss Quince, I deduced what you were
doing, as I later found your bucket and saw. They
await you even now out by the stables. I'll have a
footman return them to Quince House this afternoon. Odd honey-gathering tools, I think, but
then, I am sure you know more about that than I
do." He grinned at her amiably.

"You . . . are not angry with me, my lord?"
Genevieve stammered finally, unable to tear her
gaze away from his handsome, calmly amused
face.

"Angry? Why would I be angry with you, Miss
Quince? Ah . . . I begin to understand. You mean
because Lady Lucinda Wheatley beat such a hasty
retreat—is that it?" He smiled, his teeth startlingly
white in his tanned face.

"Y-yes, my lord. And because you were unfortunate enough to lose your boots and ruin your
pants while attempting to . . . rescue me."

"Well, as you can see, I am surviving the loss of
my ladylove, and I have found both extra boots
and breeches. Although of the three, I must say
that parting with my boots caused me the most
pain." He laughed and seated himself opposite
her, propping one Hessianed foot on the opposite
knee.

"Actually, my lord, therein lies the reason for
my visit. I wished to apologize for your losses,
and I have brought you a gift in recompense. Well,
two, really. A loaf of my freshly baked bread, and
. . . and this. I hope it will in some part make up
for your losses. I'd have brought you a new set of
breeches, but I fear I do not know any men's tai-
lors." At the thought of such intimate apparel,
Genevieve flushed, handing him the tightly

wrapped package and the loaf she had set aside at the bakery.

"What is this? You come bearing not only apologies but gifts as well? I begin to wonder at this sudden change of heart, Miss Quince. Should I suspect a trap?" Lord Bradford chuckled at Genevieve's discomfiture. Truly, he thought, he had never seen a prettier creature than Miss Quince looked at this moment, seated in his parlor. "Allow me to serve you some tea, ma'am, before I unwrap this surprising offering. I declare you have arrived before I have even had my breakfast. We shall dine on tea and fresh bread."

"Oh, dear," said Genevieve, half-rising. "I am sorry, my lord. I cannot imagine what you must think of me, appearing so precipitously."

"Don't be ridiculous. A very pleasant surprise, having such a pretty creature show up on my doorstep first thing in the morning. Sit down, Miss Quince." He had jumped to his feet and now took her forearm to press her back into her chair.

At his touch Genevieve gasped, looking up into his silver eyes, amazed at the heat his fingers seemed to send through the thin stuff of her blouse. Momentarily, both man and woman froze, gazing into each other's eyes in bewilderment. Just then, however, a maid carried a pot of steaming tea into the room, and the spell was broken.

"Will you pour, Miss Quince?" said Miles gruffly, struggling to hide his ruffled composure.

"Of course," replied Genevieve, glad to have something to occupy her shaking fingers.

Meanwhile, Miles unwrapped the loaf of golden-brown bread, exclaiming softly at its sweet scent and airy texture as he cut several slices. "Delicious," he said approvingly as he took a large bite. "You are a virtual treasure trove of unexpected talents. It is fortunate, however, that we had honey already available, so that we were spared the necessity of braving the ... bee tree again. I do not think my other hand could have stood it."

Genevieve laughed merrily, definitely the prettiest sound Miles believed he had ever heard. Both had regained their composure as they sipped their tea and ate the bread thickly spread with butter and honey.

Finally Miles picked up the package he had set aside. He turned it back and forth in his manicured fingers, and Genevieve watched him, wondering why she had not noticed before how attractive his hands were.

"Well now, I wonder what this could be. Perhaps, if I am lucky, it will contain another loaf of your superb bread. No? Well, then, perhaps it contains a bronzed lily, reminiscent of our watery escapade. No? No, I think not. Then I suppose I am forced to admit my lack of prescience and resort to less ingenious measures."

Using the knife with which he had cut the bread, Miles slid the blade under the twine and slit it. It fell from the box, and Genevieve held her breath as he lifted the lid. From where she sat she could not see into the box, but she watched his face intently.

For several moments Lord Bradford was silent. Then a smile began tugging at the corners of his lips. "Miss Quince," he said tremulously, "I do not know what to say. Truly. I do not know what to say." He paused. "In fact, if I were to think on this gift for several days, I daresay that I should still not know what to say." He looked up, and the smile that had been begging release now broke out fully across his face as he replaced the lid on the box.

He seemed barely able to control the chuckles

bubbling up from inside. Finally he began laughing uncontrollably, nearly sliding off the chair and onto the floor.

Genevieve frowned, looking at him as if he had gone mad. "Are you quite all right, my lord?"

"Never better. Miss Quince, I commend you. I have never before met a woman possessed of both beauty *and* such a tart sense of humor!"

Genevieve jumped to her feet and grabbed the box just as it fell from Lord Bradford's lap. With a final perplexed glance in his direction, she pulled the lid from the lower half of the container. Pushing aside the tissue paper, she looked down into the box.

Lord Bradford managed to control his mirth, emitting only a snort now and then as he watched her. But as he noted her odd expression, his laughter ceased altogether, and he gazed at her uncertainly.

Nestled carefully in the bottom of the box, two riding boots of the palest pink calfskin lay side by side. Twin rows of tiny, intricately carved, mother-of-pearl buttons climbed their sides. They looked as if they have been made for a very large woman with extremely big feet. Mortified, Genevieve closed the box, unable to bring her gaze up to Lord Bradford's. Without saying a word she threw the box to the floor and flew from the room, down the hall, and out the door. In her haste she jumped onto Storm's back so quickly that the mare reared, terrified. Giving the horse a sharp kick, Genevieve urged the mare into a gallop and rode pell-mell toward Quince House.

Behind her, Lord Bradford stood in his doorway, watching her with a disturbed expression, not understanding why she would present him with such a joke and then not laugh at her own strange sense of humor. He turned as his aunt wandered into the hallway, wondering at the commotion.

"Here now, boy," she said gruffly, "what's amiss? Burglars? So much noise!"

"It's nothing, Aunt Hester. Don't fret."

His aunt nodded, satisfied, and wandered off absently.

Although perplexed by Miss Quince's behavior, Miles did not have time to worry overlong, for that very afternoon he received a letter from Dobbins informing him of the imminent arrival of one Miss Eunice Eubanks, the second of his prospective brides. The missive contained no more enlightening details than to inform Miles that "the lady's fortune and breeding more than make up for her slightly average appearance." When Lord Bradford read this sentence he narrowed his eyes suspiciously, but he barely had time to dress appropriately before he heard a vehicle rattling up the drive toward Bradford Hall. The woman was certainly prompt!

Taking a deep breath, Miles drew himself up tall and walked down the stairs toward the vestibule. Even before he had reached the bottom of the grand staircase he heard voices, heralding Miss Eubank's arrival, and that sound nearly sent him scurrying for the nearest hiding place. If Miss Eubanks looked anything like the way she sounded, Miles vowed he would put her right back into her carriage and send her packing.

Upon entering the vestibule, however, he did not get a chance to speak, because the lady in question was too busy assessing her surroundings. Aunt Hester stood nearby, watching the proceedings with a confused stare, as if she hadn't a notion in the world why all these people were invading her sanctuary.

Miss Eubanks's hair was an undesirable shade

of gray, Miles noted, pulled severely into a bun at
the back of her minuscule head. Perched atop her
beakish nose, silver wire-rimmed spectacles
glinted as she searched the room with a predatory
gleam in her squinted hazel eyes. As one hand
knowledgeably fingered the small enameled boxes
on the foyer table, testing them for weight, the
other was busily running over Sevres vases and
several delicate pieces of Dresden china.

Her tall, thin body had a scarecrowish look
about it, clad as it was in a wretched print of char-
treuse paisley. She nodded approvingly when she
noticed a few Fabergé eggs resting in a display
case and clutched greedily at the velvet drapes
covering the long hall windows, judging them for
thickness and quality. She frowned slightly as her
fingers twitched the heavy green-and-gold brocade.

"He'll have to do better than this if he expects to
mingle his blood with mine," she muttered con-
spiratorially to the smaller, gentle-looking woman
with her.

When Miss Eubanks had completed her visual
and tactile examinations, she finally turned in a
businesslike fashion and addressed Miles, obviously not recognizing him as Lord Bradford. Perhaps because Miss Eubanks was fifty if she was a
day and had obviously been expecting someone
considerably older than himself.

"Rude of him not to be here to meet me. Obviously doesn't know how to impress a lady. Not an
auspicious start. Stand aside, my good man, and
allow me to go to my room so that I may refresh
myself before meeting my bridegroom." Without
further ado, Miss Eubanks rushed up the staircase
as if he and Aunt Hester were not there.

Miles stared after her in amazement, wondering
which bedroom she would choose and praying it

would not be his. Then he noticed the short, plump woman standing beside him, eyeing him quizzically. She smiled, and he found himself liking her immediately.

"*You* are Lord Bradford, are you not?" she asked softly.

"Yes, ma'am." He inclined his head.

"I must apologize for Miss Eunice. Her eyesight isn't what it once was. I must confess that I was surprised when your solicitor wrote informing Miss Eunice's father that you wished to meet her. I can only assume that it was not for the purpose she has taken it to be."

"No, ma'am." Miles smiled at her. "That is, it was my purpose, until I discovered that Miss Eubanks was . . . shall we say . . . a bit more *mature* than I had realized. I cannot imagine how my solicitor made such an unfortunate mistake."

"I quite understand. Do not worry, I am certain Miss Eunice will find enough wrong with your household to decide that you and she will never suit. Will you excuse me? I really must go find her. Oh, by the way, I am Mrs. Olsen, Eunice's companion." She smiled at Aunt Hester and scurried off up the stairs.

Aunt Hester departed gratefully in the opposite direction.

Miles frowned as he wandered into the drawing room and closed the door behind him. This was one of his favorite rooms, and now he needed its seclusion desperately. Odd that one thought in his mind was how very different both Lady Lucinda and Miss Eubanks were from Miss Genevieve Quince.

To his delight he noticed that a careless maid had left the teapot and loaf of bread still sitting on the table. Ignoring the cold tea, Miles cut a thick slice of bread, spread it with honey, and devoured it as singlemindedly as if nothing else existed in the world. A contented smile passed over his handsome features, and an amused chuckle erupted from his broad chest as he glanced at the pink boots, which still lay where Genevieve had dropped them.

As Miles walked down the stairs for dinner, he hoped that Mrs. Olsen would prove correct in her assumption that Miss Eubanks would find him lacking and quit his house sooner rather than later. Just prior to descending, he had sent a most scathing missive to Dobbins concerning his choice of potential brides and was feeling much more the thing for having vented his spleen upon the solicitor. It did not occur to him that the solicitor was merely doing as instructed: choosing a female for his lordship according to birth, fortune, landholdings, and, last and least important, as stressed by Lord Bradford himself, beauty.

The ladies were waiting for him to lead them in to the supper table. Miss Eubanks was still annoyed that Lord Bradford had not appeared to entertain her, and her sniffs of disapproval were growing louder and more frequent. Apparently, Miles thought with relief, Mrs. Olsen had not given his identity away. Aunt Hester had pleaded a headache and excused herself from dinner, which would prove fortunate, since she undoubtedly would have exposed her nephew as the real Lord Bradford in a trice.

As Miles stepped back to help seat the companion, Mrs. Olsen smiled up at him, and he could have sworn she winked.

The small group was silent as the soup was served, a delicious concoction of quail eggs and cream with a touch of white wine. Mrs. Olsen waited until her mistress had taken a large spoonful into her mouth before speaking. "I say, dear boy, I must confess to a bit of curiosity. I am sure that my mistress wonders also but is too well bred to speak of it—but when might we expect Lord Bradford to make an appearance?" She raised her eyebrows pointedly at Miles, only a slight quirk of her lips.

Miles did not miss the interested gleam in Miss Eubanks's watery eyes as he paused briefly, appearing to give consideration to the question. "That I could not say, madam. It could be anywhere from four days to four weeks. You see, his lordship was not altogether thrilled with the idea of taking a new wife and agreed to do so only upon the urging of his solicitor, who felt it necessary to remind Lord Bradford that the last collection date on his enormous morass of debts was rapidly approaching, and that he had no money with which to pay them." He smiled congenially at Miss Eubanks, who had gone an unusual shade of gray.

"You don't say," replied Mrs. Olsen. "Well, that sort of thing is all too common these days, and it is not in the least unusual for a man to expect his new bride to bring something of value to their union. Nothing at all wrong with that as long as he loves the woman."

"Love?" Miles said in a surprised voice, he eyebrows raised in mock horror. "I do hope Miss Eubanks does not expect his lordship to stoop to such a plebian emotion as love! No, ladies, his lordship is far too superb a personage to ever experience such common feelings."

"Oh," said Mrs. Olsen. "Well, I suppose that is also not at all unusual in our day and age, and a woman would just have to be willing to accept it, with, of course, the understanding that her husband would remain faithful to her, love or no."

"Faithful? Surely you jest, madam," laughed Miles. "It is common practice for Lord Bradford to keep as many as three mistresses at once. Of course, of late his lordship has not had the financial means to do so, but once Miss Eubanks and he are married, well ..." His voice trailed off meaningfully, and he peeped at Miss Eubanks from beneath lowered lashes.

"Ah," Mrs. Olsen sighed mournfully. "Even so, one can not be too choosy these days, especially when one hopes to marry a titled gentleman like Lord Bradford. After all, at least one could look forward to her son's inheriting a title."

"I beg your pardon, ma'am," said Miles in a gruff, displeased voice. "Did no one tell you? Lord Bradford is my father, and I, as his eldest son, will inherit everything, from his title to the lady in question's fortune when he dies. No, dear lady, there is no question of that, for I assure you that I have no intention of deserting either my title or whatever moneys are due me."

Miss Eubanks, who had remained silent for this whole time but had been going paler and paler, now jumped to her feet, eyes blazing. "I see!" she cried in a forbidding tone. "I am only to be his banker, am I? Well, sirrah, I think not! You may tell his lordship that, having given proper consideration to the matter, I have decided that there shall be no match! Tell him to find his gambling and wenching money elsewhere, for he shall have not a penny of mine!"

Miles forced a hurt, confused expression to his thrilled face. "I say, madam," quoth he in a stern but worried tone. "Not at all the thing to back out like this, you know. I mean, what shall Father do for his debts? And what shall I do for my inheritance? You cannot mean this!"

"You'd better believe I do, sir! Come, Mrs.

Olsen, we shall pack our belongings and leave this Satan's dwelling at once!" Glaring at Miles one last time, she strode grandly from the room.

Mrs. Olsen rose, grinned at Lord Bradford, who nodded gratefully, and followed her mistress.

As the women climbed into the carriage that would take them home, Miles presented his ex-fiancée with a special gift he told her Lord Bradford had had made especially for her. This simple act nearly won the lady over again—until she remembered that her entire fortune was at stake and his lordship was a money-hungry rascal. With a gracious if strained smile Miss Eubanks accepted the pink riding boots from the man's handsome son, wondering how his lordship had known her exact size.

10

Genevieve found a bucket and decided to search for a few early strawberries so that she could make a pie for her soon-to-be-arriving guests. Just one more day before they would be here, she told herself, wondering why the idea did not send the same thrill of excitement running through her as it had when she had first concocted the scheme. After telling Miss Pramble that she would return in a few hours, she whistled for Jasper and the two of them set off across the fields toward the spot in the woods where Genevieve knew a thick patch of berry bushes thrived. The air was fresh, and the sun was barely peaking over the eastern horizon.

The plants were not on Quince property. Actually, she would be trespassing on Bradford land. But she would be extremely careful to avoid Lord Bradford himself. The man was a hazard, forever upsetting her sensibilities and making her a laughingstock.

Jasper bounded happily from tree to tree, marking a shrub here and a tree there, constantly looking back to ensure that his mistress was still following. In no time at all they had covered the half mile to the strawberry patch. While Jasper flung himself contentedly into the shade of a large lilac bush, Genevieve set down her pail and began plucking the plump, juicy berries.

Eventually the bucket was filled to overflowing. Genevieve inhaled the scents of ripe fruit and rich, damp earth and glanced around for Jasper. He was no longer in his bed of ferns beneath the shrub, and she looked around the clearing, calling out and whistling for him.

Cursing softly, Genevieve shouldered her heavy bucket of strawberries and began to search for the mastiff. Finally she heard a far-off yip, and she changed direction to follow the sound. In a while she became aware that she had gotten quite close to Bradford Hall. She paused in the dim shadows at the edge of the woods as she peered anxiously around the lawns of the great house.

Damnation! she thought furiously. There was Jasper, looking in her direction, wagging his tail mischievously, and approaching the back door of the mansion. He paused, and soon Genevieve saw why. A man wearing a white apron and cap emerged, holding hands with a serving girl. They giggled in unison and vanished behind one of the outbuildings, never giving the dog a second glance. They had left the door ajar, and Genevieve watched, chewing her lip anxiously, as Jasper nudged his way into Bradford Hall, his wagging tail visible for a fraction of a second before he disappeared inside.

Clutching her bucket of strawberries, and keeping close to the grape arbors and rose trellises that decorated the yard, Genevieve crept closer to the house. When she neared the back door, she stopped, in a quandary about what to do. This was decided for her as a resounding crash echoed from within Bradford Hall.

Genevieve sped toward the open door and followed the noises down a long corridor, clinging to the hope that she would be able to stop any further damage from being done.

Jasper however, had other ideas. A quick glance into the kitchen showed Genevieve the tail end of the mastiff protruding from beneath a large table. As she cautiously inched into the room, the dog turned his massive head to peer at her with a toothy, mischievous grin, a ham clutched in his immense jaws. Nearby on the floor was a large silver platter, gravy drippings spattered every which way around it.

"Jasper," she hissed furiously. "Come out of there immediately!"

The dog wagged his tail and took another bite of his prize.

Genevieve knew that she had to retrieve her dog and vacate the premises at once if they were to escape undetected. The chef might reappear at any moment. Thinking quickly, she dropped to her hands and knees and crept forward.

"Here, boy," she coaxed. "Good boy, Jasper. Mama's not angry, boy. Come on now."

Just as she prepared to lunge and capture the dog by his leather collar, Jasper dove out from beneath the table and raced for a door. Genevieve gave her all, throwing herself forward but missing as his tail slid through her gravy-slick hand. "Oh, damn," she muttered, and "Ouch!" she cried as she scrambled to her feet, knocking her head against the table.

She grabbed her bucket and reached the door, only to see Jasper's back half disappear through a second larger and more ostentatious door, which obviously led from the servants' domain into the main hall. Afraid to call out to him for fear of being discovered, Genevieve hurried through the door and saw the dog scamper happily up the great staircase, still clutching the huge hambone in his slathering jaws.

At least, early as it was, none of the servants seemed to be up and about except the cook, who had undoubtedly been preparing the succulent ham for his lord's breakfast. Genevieve took a deep breath and began creeping quietly up the stairs, cursing the day Miss Pramble had brought the dog to Quince House. She reached the top and looked frantically about the dimly lit hallway for her missing canine. Her steps muffled by rich, thick Oriental rugs, Genevieve proceeded quietly from room to room. Bradford Hall was possessed of many more bedchambers than Quince House, and she wondered how she would ever find the dog in this maze.

Fortune smiled upon her at last, however, as she reached the end of the hallway and discovered a door slightly ajar. A few telltale gravy drips marred the perfection of the carpeting just outside. Genevieve took a deep breath and, praying silently that the room would be unoccupied, pushed the heavy door wide. No inhabitant was visible, but the bedclothes had clearly been slept in, and atop them Jasper grinned at her, the moistly pungent hambone resting majestically on his forepaws, tail thumping energetically on the pillows as he eyed his mistress.

Genevieve groaned inwardly, praying to every god she could think of and promising all kinds of sacrifice if they would just get her out of her predicament unscathed. She quietly set the bucket on the dressing table and stepped toward the bed.

"Benson? I would wear the buff pantaloons and chestnut coat today, if you please," called a deep, warm, all-too-familiar voice from behind a closed door, apparently a dressing chamber off the main bedroom.

Genevieve froze. It couldn't be. It couldn't be!

The rattling of the knob on the other side of the closed door spurred her into action. Searching about frantically, she at last dove for the bed, wriggling underneath it. Above her, Jasper yipped happily, overjoyed that his mistress was playing with him.

The door opened, and from her position under the bed Genevieve watched Lord Bradford's bare feet pad across the rug and stop short.

"Jasper?" said an amazed voice. "What the devil are you doing on my bed? Get off at once, you scurvy mutt!"

Lord Bradford apparently flung a slipper at the mastiff, for Jasper let out a yelp, and one leather romeo landed with a plop in front of Genevieve's nose. The dog jumped down from his resting place and trotted over to Miles, dropping the hambone on his lordly feet.

"Well, thank you, sir," he said wryly, "although I cringe to think where your offering came from. I'd wager that Chef Antoine is even now having one of his fits."

If Genevieve had not been so frightened she would have laughed, but as it was she lay still and clenched her eyes shut. Perhaps if she could not see him, he would not see her. At this moment, though, a bit of dust tickled Genevieve's nose. She held her breath to stifle her sneeze, desperate but not daring to move. Then a terrible thought occurred to her. The bucket of strawberries sat right on top of Lord Bradford's bureau! She opened her eyes slightly and peeped over at the desk, which she could just barely see. Yes, there sat the pail, and there stood Lord Bradford, looking down at it, a perplexed expression on his devilish face.

Suddenly he smiled, picked up a berry, popped

it into his mouth, and disappeared from her view. He walked around the bed and lay down on it.

There was silence for quite some time, and Genevieve began to wonder if perhaps he had dozed off. Jasper, still looking very pleased with himself settled down to doze by the door. If only she dared sneak out. But what if Lord Bradford was not sleeping? Genevieve remained still beneath the bed for what seemed forever, praying he would rise and leave the room.

At last the bed creaked, but as Genevieve peered out anxiously her nemesis's nose appeared upside down, only an inch from her own.

"Truly, Miss Quince, if you wish to share my bed, I would prefer to have you on top of it rather than under it. I think I told you once that you need only to ask and I would be pleased to welcome you with open arms."

Genevieve swallowed convulsively, flushing a violent pink, and Miles climbed off the bed, leaving her to extricate herself from her humiliating predicament. He smiled with open appreciation at the shapely bottom that inched its way out from under the bed. Quivering with rage, Genevieve stood and turned on him, eyes flashing a brilliant blue. "You! You ... you ... you ... *horrid* man! You knew I was under there all the time! How could you?" Enraged, she flung out a hand and struck him across the face.

Miles stood very still, his jaw clenched. Finally he reached out, grasped her by the waist, and abruptly pulled her toward him.

Genevieve stared into his rage-darkened eyes, terrified, as she slammed against his hard, male body.

When he spoke, his voice was nearly a whisper, every word filled with anger held precariously in check. "Damn you, Genevieve Quince. You need to learn some manners very badly, and I believe that I am just the one to teach them to you. Your dog steals my breakfast, you come sneaking into my bedchamber, and, last but not least, you strike me—for the second time—hard enough to shake my brain loose from my skull. But I say this to you, wench, you push me too far, for I am not made of steel." His fingers clenched her small, pointed chin tightly as he turned her face up to his and brought his mouth down to her lips.

Genevieve was still for a moment, in sensual shock. Then she realized that the man was kissing her just to make a mockery of her again, to taunt her about her presence in his room. Wrenching her face away, she lifted her hand yet again, only this time, before it met with flesh, it was caught deftly and held firmly in Lord Bradford's iron grip.

His lordship smiled, his teeth very white in his tanned face. It was a dangerous smile.

11

"Very well. If that is the way you want to play." He laughed softly.

Before Genevieve knew what was happening, Miles had bent swiftly and grasped her behind the knees, hoisting her into his arms as if she were as light as a feather. She cried out and wrapped her arms around his neck, afraid of falling.

"That is more like it, my dear. You learn quickly." Turning swiftly, he dumped her unceremoniously onto the mattress.

Genevieve bounced twice, her long curls tumbling from her loose bun and falling about her shoulders.

Lord Bradford's expression darkened as he stared at the cinnamon-colored locks. He turned suddenly and strode to the door. Genevieve thought perhaps he had come to his senses and was about to leave, but a small clicking sound told her he had simply locked the door, effectively imprisoning her.

"We wouldn't want dear Aunt Hester to walk in on us and have an apoplectic fit, now would we?" He turned, smiled at her, and dropped the skeleton key into the pocket of his full length silk dressing gown.

"My lord, please," she whispered, shimmying her bottom toward the edge of the bed.

He caught her before she jumped off, pulling her back next to him.

He wore no shirt beneath the dressing gown, Genevieve noticed suddenly as her gaze was drawn to the curling black hair that covered the muscular expanse of his broad chest peeking from between the edges of his robe. She gasped as he gripped her head firmly, tilting it to plant moist, passionate kisses along the slender column of her neck. To her horror she found herself unable to resist him, felt herself instead responding, arching her neck to facilitate his outrageous act.

So assaulted by unfamiliar sensations was she that Genevieve did not notice when his dressing gown slipped from his shoulders. One moment she was clinging to the silk, and the next to bare muscle, biceps bulging into her palms as she clung to him as if he were a lifeline and she a drowning woman.

Miles drew a shaky breath, holding on to a mere shred of sanity. He buried his face in her thick curls, inhaling their sweet scent. "My God," he murmured huskily. "You smell exactly as I dreamed you would, of roses and cinnamon."

Then his mouth reclaimed hers, and Genevieve, stunned, gave herself over to his caresses. She kissed him as if she would die if he broke contact, clinging to his lips desperately, hungrily, with a passion she had not dreamed she possessed.

Miles shivered as her fingertips brushed his nipples. When he could stand no more he grabbed her hand and pulled it away, smiling down at her. "You will shatter my self-control, little one," he whispered brokenly.

"Oh, Miles," Genevieve whimpered helplessly.

She was on fire, and he the only source that could quench her burning thirst.

"Yes, Jenny. Soon," he answered, fiercely thrusting his sanity away. His hands found the buttons that ran up the back of her threadbare dress, releasing them with finesse and parting the fabric so that he could stroke the satiny flesh beneath. Her skin was hot to the touch, and she lifted herself slightly to give him greater ease. His tongue forged a trail over her exposed shoulders, lingering in the deep, sweet hollow at her collarbone.

Genevieve closed her eyes, drowning in startlingly unfamiliar but blissful sensations. She moaned softly as he tugged the dress down a little farther, baring the top of her white lawn chemise and the ivory skin above it. Her nipples were clearly visible through the thin fabric, and Genevieve's back arched as Miles lowered his head to take one into the warm wetness of his mouth. He suckled her through the cloth, running his tongue over the rough cotton and making her cry out with startled pleasure.

He slowly raised his head, his nostrils flaring slightly as his eyes took in her creamy skin, her nearly naked breasts, and the nipples glowing rosy pink through her chemise.

"You are so beautiful," he whispered, looking down at her intently. Genevieve felt as if his gaze was burning her bare flesh, so clearly was desire written in his eyes. "Let me love you, Jenny." Without waiting for her response, he again took possession of her mouth, nibbling on her lower lip as if it were the greatest delicacy. His tongue flicked into her mouth, caressing that intimate cavern, and Genevieve squirmed at the odd sensation. Miles caught his breath and pulled one of her small hands to the curls on his chest.

At first her touch was shy, tentative, as she began to explore his superb, masculine body. Her fingers ran lightly over his flesh, downward over his taut, muscled belly, pausing uncertainly when they reached the tied belt of his dressing gown.

Miles arched his hips toward her hand, urging her to rid herself of her fear. But as her fingers began to slip nervously toward the rock-solid mound beneath his robe, he gasped, sanity surging back upon him in a disapproving tide.

Groaning, he pushed her hand aside, holding her away from his burning body so that he might reclaim the last shreds of his self-control.

Genevieve looked at him, feeling a wave of disappointment she did not understand wash over her. "My lord?" she said uncertainly, wondering what he wanted her to do.

Miles sighed heavily, regretfully, and took the quivering girl back into his arms. He smiled tenderly down at her wide, upturned blue eyes. "You are such a sweet innocent, my darling Jenny. Let us keep it that way—for now." He held her for a long time, until the tumult of the morning caught up with her, and she fell into an exhausted, confused slumber.

Lord Bradford dressed slowly, watching her sweet face. She was smiling in her sleep, and he wondered if she were dreaming of him. At the thought he grinned ruefully, faintly annoyed at having caught himself in such an immature, romantic fancy. Then, after planting a final kiss on her sleep-parted lips, he left the room.

When Genevieve awakened, she was horrified to see her surroundings. She tugged her disheveled clothing up, hoping beyond hope that Miles would not return while she was dressing.

He did not, and cautiously she hefted her pail of berries and slipped out of the bedroom, keeping a sharp eye out and an ear peeled, and managing to creep out of Bradford Hall without being seen.

Miss Pramble eyed her curiously as Genevieve entered Quince House, wondering why the girl appeared so flushed and where she had been for so long, especially since Jasper had returned quite some time earlier. Then she dismissed the question from her mind, as Genevieve hurriedly reminded her that their guests would arriving on the morrow. Remembering that she had a cake in the oven, Miss Pramble hastened to the kitchen to remove it so it would not burn.

Genevieve sank down into a chair, her head cradled in her hands. From a corner of the room, Jasper peered at her, head cocked. Genevieve glared at him and sighed heavily, promising herself never to allow such a shameful thing to happen again. At last she walked slowly upstairs toward her room.

For his part, Miles could not have been happier, and he took care of his estate affairs as quickly as he could that afternoon, hoping that Jenny would still be asleep when he returned to his bedchamber. He longed to waken her with a kiss, sweep her into his arms, and tell her that he loved her and could not live without her antagonizing, irritating, delightful presence.

To say that he was disappointed to find her gone would have been a severe understatement.

Drawn by an unseen force to the hall window, Genevieve gazed out toward Bradford Hall. She caught her lower lip between her teeth when she saw Lord Bradford's mount carrying him ever closer toward the inevitable confrontation. Anger welled up within her as she thought of how many times she had suffered indignity and humiliation at the man's hands, and she made a beeline for her room. She plopped down on the bed, picking up a powder box from the vanity to throw at him should he dare appear at her bedchamber door once more.

Miles maintained a cheerful smile as he saw Miss Pramble come out of Quince House and walk swiftly toward him. Soon she was standing beside Fury's broad shoulder. "Lord Bradford," she said with a nervous smile, torn between courtesy and disgruntlement toward this man who had compromised her young friend and never found a way to make things right. At the lowing of a cow from behind the house she hastily said, "What can I do for you? I do hope our animals are not being an inconvenience. I know the rooster has an uncomfortable knack for crowing rather prematurely, and—"

"Not at all, dear lady," he lied with his famous heart-stopping smile, dismounting with easy grace. "Actually, I have come to see Miss Quince. Would you be so kind as to beg me a conference with her?"

"To be sure," said Miss Pramble, smiling in return as things began to look better.

She turned and went inside, and Miles watched her, silently praying that the silly wench he had fallen in love with would not produce any further problems today.

With steps more spry than those she had taken in years, Miss Pramble skipped up the grand staircase, beaming indulgently as she popped her head into Genevieve's room. Her smile vanished as an object suddenly hurtled through the air toward her. She ducked, and it smashed against the wall beside the door, emitting a thick white cloud as pottery shards tumbled to the floor.

"Oh, I'm sorry, Pramble!" exclaimed Genevieve.

"I was certain it was going to be that . . . that . . . *creature* from next door."

"Even so, my dear, is such violence necessary? Why, pray tell, would you wish to bean his lordship?" The governess shook her head and looked at Genevieve with grave disapproval. "Now, Jenny, Lord Bradford wishes to speak with you, and if I'm any judge, he's going to ask you something very important. Stop acting imbecilic and come down at once." She spoke in a voice as stern as she could muster.

Genevieve slid back farther onto the mattress, face stormy. "I have no desire to speak to Lord Bradford. Tell him . . . tell him that I am ill."

"I will do no such thing. You are not ill. If you wish him to be told that you are, then you had best come tell him yourself."

Although part of Genevieve longed to rush downstairs and into Miles's arms, she could not face the shame of telling him that she accepted his request to become his mistress, as, after her wanton behavior this morning, this was undoubtedly the important thing he had to say to her.

She looked up at Miss Pramble. "I shall not." She paused, took a deep breath, and then continued. "You may tell Lord Bradford that if he so much as dares step foot on Quince property again, I will sue him for trespass."

Miss Pramble stared at her, mouth agape.

"Go, Pramble. This is the only message I will give his lordship. Now or ever."

"Where is Miss Quince?" Miles asked softly as soon as the governess stepped outside.

"She will not come down."

"What did she give as reason?" When Miss Pramble remained silent, he looked at her intently. "What did she say?"

"She . . . she asked me to tell you that if you so

much as dared set foot on Quince property again, she would sue you for trespass." Her eyes brimmed with tears.

Lord Bradford, a man of such importance and power that no one had ever dared cross him before, did not know how to handle this defeat. He could not stand the heart-wrenching ache that welled up inside his chest, and he shoved it behind a screen of anger.

"You may tell Miss Quince that I shall not trouble her again," he replied with icy nonchalance. "Tell her also that while I would sooner walk through the gates of hell than set foot on her property, I will walk when and where I please if fate so directs. And tell her that if she tries to sue me, I will ruin both her and this disgraceful inn-keeping endeavor of hers. Good day, madam." He jumped onto Fury's back, his face a mask of controlled rage, and galloped down the drive, back toward Bradford Hall.

12

"Jumpin' Jee-hoseefat, Ma! Lookit that fishin' hole!"

"Shore 'nuff, Laddy. And just lookit them roses. I can't wait to get my shears in gear. Hey, see the little maid waitin' to take our stuff to our rooms? Don't she look a mite small to carry our luggage?"

"Prob'ly stronger than she 'pears, Ma. I hear tell these country gals, even the noble ones, is strong as men, not deli-cat like the girls back home in Philadelphie."

"I 'spect you're right, Laddy. Leastways she'd better be, for the heap o' money we're payin' to stay in this place."

"Yeah, Ma. And if I know you, you'll get your money's worth! 'Sides, she's purty 'nuff. I know I can find somethin' she'd be good at, even if she ain't per-tic'larly strong!" The unseen boy, Laddy, guffawed heartily. Their words and laughter carried clearly from the end of the driveway.

Genevieve had stood proudly on the landing of Quince House, smiling at the carriage that rattled up the drive. As she heard these words, however, her smile faltered. It had struck her as odd that the very first visitors she would entertain were to be Americans rather than the English middle class, as she had expected, but that they should be *this* crude . . .

Genevieve was too grateful that the advertisement had finally been answered to truly care, though, even if Americans *were* rumored to be far more plebian than their English counterparts. Besides, beggars couldn't be choosers. And the second letter inquiring about lodgings, which she had received on the same day as the Americans', had come to nothing. She took a deep breath and stepped off the landing toward the vehicle.

In the last day or so the rose gardens had burst fully into bloom and looked glorious against the velvety emerald lawns. Genevieve tried not to think of all the hours of toil it had taken her to make them look decent, or of Mrs. Featherweight's shears. For the enormous sum they had paid to stay, the woman had the right to cut every single rose on the estate if she wanted to.

The carriage rolled to a stop, and, before the coachman or tiger could leap to the ground to help the occupants disembark, the portly form of Mrs. Featherweight and the skeletally thin figure of her son, Laddy, barreled out of the vehicle like racehorses from the starting gate.

Keeping her smile pinned carefully in place, Genevieve stepped forward with a gesture of welcome. She had dressed carefully in a gown that was worn but lovely, hoping to impress but not intimidate her guests. Her eyes widened in shock, however, as she took in the Featherweights' apparel.

Dressed in a heavy maroon velvet gown with black maribou feathers trailing from the sleeves, hem, and bodice, Mrs. Featherweight looked like a refugee from the London stage. Her pudgy cheeks were heavily rouged, and nestled in deep, dimpled cleavage exposed by a very low neckline glittered the biggest pigeon's-blood ruby Genevieve had ever seen. Every one of the woman's thick, stubby fingers was covered with masses of ostentatious diamonds, and from each wrist hung several gem-encrusted bracelets. Her earlobes were stretched like a Buddha's under their burden of two more hefty rubies.

That the woman was encased in velvet on a day that could not be much under eighty degrees astounded Genevieve almost more than that Mrs. Featherweight was wearing enough jewelry for ten women and enough face paint for an entire troupe of actors. Then she glanced at the woman's son, and her already wide eyes flew open even wider.

Laddy Featherweight could easily give any flashy London dandy cause to turn and stare. Dressed in breeches of lemon-yellow silk so tight they left nothing to the imagination, a coat of apple-green satin, and a shirt veritably frothing with lace ruffles and frills, the boy was obviously convinced that he cut quite a dashing figure.

He turned toward Genevieve, picked up the quizzing glass nearly buried in the lace encrusting his chest, and eyed her appreciatively through the lens. Placing one hand on his hip so that the object of his lust could not fail to notice his fashionably painted crimson nails, Laddy Featherweight favored Genevieve with a broad leer.

Genevieve was hard-pressed, despite her horror, not to burst out laughing. "Welcome to Quince House," she stammered, biting back the chuckle that rose in her throat. "I am Miss Quince. Won't you come inside?"

"Well, of course we will. Didn't pay you a small fortune so that we could camp on yer doorstep, did we, gal?" Mrs. Featherweight raised her nose snootily and shoved past Genevieve nearly colliding with Miss Pramble, who had been preparing the guests' dinner and had emerged upon hearing voices.

Miss Pramble's eyes widened as she took in the two figures, and she gave Genevieve a questioning glance.

"Ah, Miss Pramble," Genevieve said hastily, worried about what the governess, who had disapproved of the venture from the start, might say. "This is Mrs. Featherweight, and her son, Laddy. They are Americans, don't you know," she added in subtle explanation.

"*Mr.* Featherweight," the boy said hastily, sniffing at Genevieve's lack of respect.

"Mr. Featherweight," repeated Genevieve apologetically, smiling at him.

He sniffed again but looked somewhat mollified.

"How do you do?" said Miss Pramble stiffly, boiling inside that this upstart provincial's son should speak so to a well-born English lady like Jenny.

Genevieve leaped into the breach. "Miss Pramble has been laboring all day in preparation for your arrival. I'm sure she has prepared a delectable feast for dinner." She smiled again, although her face was fast beginning to ache with the strain. "Now I am sure you are both exhausted and would like me to show you to your rooms," she said hastily, taking her female guest by the arm and hurrying past Miss Pramble.

Genevieve headed for the stairs, eager to get her paying guests out of the way of Miss Pramble's ire. Laddy followed slowly, ogling everything in sight through his quizzing glass.

"This is your room, Mrs. Featherweight. I had it completely redone just last week," she lied smoothly as she opened one of the doors lining the hallway of the second floor, hoping that the woman would believe the worn furnishings were prized antiques.

She did. Mrs. Featherweight allowed a slow smile to pass over her heavily powdered face and plopped down onto the feather bed, bouncing up and down as she ran her chubby fingers ecstatically over the rose brocade coverlet. For a brief moment Genevieve saw her mask slip, and the country girl beneath the gaudy facade beamed at being allowed advantages usually reserved to a privileged few. Just as Genevieve's heart warmed toward this fellow victim of deprivation, the woman caught herself and slid back into her snooty demeanor. "Yer letter said a king slept here once. This the room? I specifically requested the king's room, an' you better not be gyppin' me, missy."

"Yes, indeed," Genevieve improvised. "King Sven of Denmark. A very rich, very powerful king. He and his wife slept here over a hundred years ago. Rest assured, though, madam, that we here at Quince House are every bit as honored to have you and your son as our guests as we were to have King Sven." She smiled demurely at the fat woman, crossing her fingers behind her back that Mrs. Featherweight's knowledge of history was no better than her taste in clothes.

"Ah, King Sven," replied Mrs. Featherweight grandly. "Of course."

Genevieve was hard-pressed not to giggle, but a snort behind her made her turn toward the door, whipping her crossed fingers apart.

"Hurry up, gal. I'd like to find my room before I pass out from exhaustion." Laddy, standing not a foot from her, yawned with delicate affectation, once again displaying his crimson nails. He turned and minced out into the hall, taking very small

steps in the high-heeled, ruby-red pumps at the
ends of his silk-stockinged legs.

"Yes. Well then, Mrs. Featherweight. If you need
anything, just give a tug to the bellpull beside the
door. Dinner shall be served at seven. I look forward to seeing you then, and I trust your stay
with us will be as pleasant for you as it is for us."
With a final subservient smile Genevieve curtsied
deeply, catching Mrs. Featherweight's approving,
pleased expression out of the corner of her eye as
she left the room.

Laddy Featherweight had disappeared down
the hall, and Genevieve wondered where he could
have gotten to. She scurried off after him. As she
rounded the bend in the hallway, a hand reached
out from a dark corner and jerked her into the
shadows.

"King Sven? Come now, my pretty. We both
know that they ain't' no King Sven and never was.
You cain't fool Laddy, gal, 'cause I finished the
fourth grade. Now let us understand one another.
You rub my back, and I'll rub yours. An' I'm sure
we'll rub along real good together. Unnerstan'?"
He leered down at her, caressing her back lustfully
through the thin stuff of her gown.

Fortunately for Genevieve, at this moment Miss
Pramble wandered up the stairs. Laddy released
Genevieve abruptly.

"Do hurry, Jenny dear," said Miss Pramble innocently, pretending not to have noticed the boy's
furtive motion. "I need your help in the kitchen.
Come now, you go downstairs, and I will accompany Mr. Featherweight to his room."

"Oh, don't bother yerself," Laddy said hastily.
"I'll send her right down to you as soon as *she* has
shown me where to sleep."

"Don't be ridiculous, Mr. Featherweight." Miss
Pramble smiled tightly. "'Twould be remiss of me

not to show you the courtesy of accompanying you to your room. Come along now." She moved off down the hall, leaving Laddy to follow, cursing softly. Once he had been ensconced in his chamber and Miss Pramble had gotten Genevieve alone in the kitchen, the governess turned on the girl furiously.

"I suppose you still think this is a good idea, miss? Now, I'll admit I went along with you, but only because you were so insistent, and because I wanted to be here to make certain no harm befell you. You very nearly had me convinced that you could handle this venture. Now I'm sure that you don't know what you are doing, Jenny. You almost got yourself raped in the hallway! And by *that!*" she hissed. "An American, of all things! That pair is pure trash," she huffed. "Trash, Jenny. Those gaudy jewels! Those outlandish clothes! Did you see his fingernails? And their manners! I think we should just forget this entire idea, and you should come home with me at once." She paused, breathing heavily from the delivery of her tirade.

Genevieve drew herself up, looking Miss Pramble directly in the eye. "I thank you for your concern, Miss Pramble," she said stiffly. "However, I will not so easily be discouraged from retaining my newfound independence. It is quite out of the question for me to throw myself on your mercy, and I have no intention of returning to Cousin Marybelle's and taking my place as her household harlot. I just cannot quit so easily. If you choose to leave, however, I will understand." Her eyes glistened with unshed tears, but she held firm.

Miss Pramble, too, looked teary. "I cannot say that I like this. But I will not desert you now, Jenny. If you insist on continuing this mad venture, I will stay as long as you need me. And at

least those two will only be here for the weekend."
She sniffed daintily, then drew herself up straight.
"Now, however, we have a dinner to lay out. And
we have luggage to carry upstairs. I'm sure our
young fop would not wish to risk cracking his nail
polish by carrying his own baggage up to his
room."

"Oh, Pramble!" Genevieve laughed. "You are
priceless."

Had Miles known that Dobbins had not received his scathing letter before sending out the
next lady, he would not have thrown himself quite
so heartily into the preparations for the third con-
testant in the battle of the brides. But so certain
was he that this time Dobbins would not dare
send him anything except the very *crème de la
crème* of English society, he even went so far, due
to his fury at Genevieve, as to have an entire suite
redecorated in anticipation for the new lady's arrival.

Now he entered the suite and examined the
rooms. The walls had been re-papered in a fabric
of palest blue, embroidered with tiny forget-me-
nots. The carpets had been replaced with rich,
thick wool the same shade as the blossoms on the
walls.

Miles tried not to think of the lovely pair of eyes
that had inspired this room, or of the person who
should, by rights, be occupying it. But his traitor-
ous heart would not allow him to forget that he
had personally selected each delicate piece of
Chippendale for one person in particular. The furniture was white with accents of gold, and the
huge bed, covered with a white satin comforter,
sported a canopy of blue silk that hung in filmy
splendor from the ceiling, making the bed look
like a cloud in the summer sky. Even Aunt Hester,

normally remote, had voiced her admiration at the effect.

Miles smiled slightly. The room was perfect. And this time, *she* would be perfect. He would not allow it to be otherwise. With a final, determined, angry glance at the enormous bed, Miles left and closed the door behind him.

A muffled cough indicated that Benson had been awaiting his master's exit for some time.

"Yes, Benson? What is it?"

"The young lady, my lord. She has arrived. Your aunt is already below." He raised his eyebrows expressively at his master.

"Delightful, my good man." Miles rubbed his hands together in anticipation and smiled brilliantly. "What is her name?"

"Lady Hortense Figg, my lord."

"Hortense Figg?" Miles arched his eyebrows, certain he had misheard.

"Yes, my lord."

"Good God!" he said in a mock-horrified voice. "Well, no matter. I am sure that she will be lovely enough to warrant a suitably charming nickname."

"Oh, I don't know, sir . . ."

"What don't you know, Benson?"

"Well, my lord . . . she does look rather as if she *should* be named Hortense Figg."

Miles glanced at him, eyebrows raised.

"My lord?" asked Benson, feigning ignorance.

"Is she not everything you would expect the future Lady Bradford to be?"

"Well, my lord—"

"I have no doubt that she is as lovely as a summer's day, is she not?"

"Well, my lord—"

"And has a figure that would have inspired Michelangelo?"

"Well, my lord, as you have told me before, it is not my place to say."

"Your reticence to engage in gossip about your new mistress is most admirable, Benson, but I give you my permission. Now tell me, is she not a vision of loveliness, of all that is perfect?"

"I repeat, my lord, it is not my place to speak of your, er, bride-to-be."

Lord Bradford emitted an impatient snort. "For heaven's sake, what is it, man? Spit it out. Is she not possessed of immense proportions of beauty, wealth, and breeding?"

Benson brightened momentarily, happy to be able to agree with his master at last. "Oh, yes, my lord. Immense proportions." Then his frown returned. "But that is just it . . ."

"*What* is 'just it'?"

"Well, my lord. That is . . . you see . . . it is just that . . ."

"Come, come, Benson. Obviously you are so impressed with the young woman's qualifications that you are speechless. Do not let us stand here dawdling all day. Let us go down and greet my bride-to-be!" He tossed the valet an irritated glance and strode off down the hall.

"But, my lord!" called Benson in an agonized tone.

"What is it, man? Hurry up, for God's sake." He turned and glared once more at the valet before continuing down the corridor.

"As you wish, my lord," Benson sighed mournfully to Miles's departing back. He followed Lord Bradford with resignation.

Miles smiled happily as he heard the lilting, feminine voice that wafted up the grand staircase. He moved down the stairs lightly, beaming with anticipation.

"I have been telling Martha here, my maid, that

this must be the loveliest house I have ever seen, my lady," an unknown voice commented politely.

Miles supposed she must be addressing Aunt Hester. He slowed his pace that he might listen in, unnoticed. His aunt made no answer. No doubt she was in awe at the lady's beauty, he decided, smiling.

"I hear tell that Lord Bradford is the handsomest, most charming, richest man in England."

His smile grew wider.

"My nephew is, of course, a gentleman."

Aunt Hester's words were decidedly chilly, and Miles's eyes narrowed with annoyance. Did she fear she would be displaced when he married the unseen goddess?

"Martha," she said to the aforementioned maid, "how do I look?"

Miles could imagine his beautiful fiancée leaning close to the looking glass that hung in the hallway, peering at her flawless face with worried eyes.

"As well as you ever have, my lady."

Miles frowned slightly, wondering why the maid's flattery was not slightly more effulgent. No matter. She was probably just jealous. Apparently the lady was not concerned, for there was no answering rebuke.

"I do hope we will have dinner soon, Martha. I declare I am simply famished. Will we be eating soon, Lady Hester?"

"I could not say, madam."

"What do you think we shall dine upon? Roast suckling pig? Capon? Lobster patties? I would really enjoy some lobster patties right now, Martha. Do you know if his lordship likes lobster patties, Lady Hester?"

"At this moment, I would not be willing to hazard even a guess at my nephew's tastes, madam."

Miles frowned darkly, even more perplexed at Aunt Hester's daunting behavior. He continued to eavesdrop.

"No? I suppose it is probably just as well that we ate recently at the posting house. Although traveling always makes me hungry, and the mutton pie the innkeeper served us was dreadfully small, was it not, Martha?"

"As you say, my lady," Martha answered quietly.

"Martha, why don't you just run down to the kitchens and see if you cannot find a little something to tide me over until we dine. Anything at all. I'm sure Lady Hester won't mind."

Miles could imagine Aunt Hester's sniff of rebuke.

"Yes, my lady."

However, before the unseen Martha could depart on her mission of mercy, Miles called out a greeting from his position just outside the hallway. "Never fear, Lady Hortense, we shall eat within the hour. Welcome to Bradford Hall," he said as he rounded the corner into the room. "I trust Aunt Hester has made you comfortable." He glanced about to find the exquisite Lady Hortense but realized she was seated in a large wing chair whose back was to him.

He rounded it, bent in a low, graceful bow. "Allow me to introduce myself. I am Miles Bradford." He raised his eyes, prepared to drink in her loveliness, but the breath caught in his throat, and the smile of welcome froze on his lips.

Lady Hortense thundered to her feet. All three hundred pounds of her.

For a split second Miles thought she would not be able to stop the momentum of her ample bulk and would tumble forward and crush him in her exuberance.

"La, sir. You do make a lady feel welcome."

Two hamlike fists reached out and gripped his hand painfully, pulling him into her squishy embrace. It felt as if he had been engulfed by the world's largest marshmallow, Miles thought frantically, his face buried between Lady Hortense's massive, boulder-sized breasts, his mind racing as he sought the proper words to extricate himself from this mess. He struggled for breath.

"Ooh, my lord," crooned the lady, "you are so passionate, and us not even wed yet! I do hope you will have the patience to wait until we are legally man and wife." She giggled.

Miles managed to pull away and stood gasping for air. When at last he could speak, he found that he had nothing to say. His mind went completely blank as he stared at her florid face. He could not even discern the color of Lady Hortense's eyes, which glittered at him like tiny pinpoints of light from within the fat padding her broad, glistening cheeks.

His fascinated gaze wandered downward, noting that her head, thinly covered with carrot-colored hair dressed in ringlets, appeared to be connected immediately to her shoulders without benefit of a neck. Her skin was pale-white, except, he amended silently, where it was dotted with great reddish-brown freckles.

Lady Hortense was dressed in what appeared to be a curtain, complete with heavy gold braid fringe that passed over one thick hip and around the hem of the gown. Of crushed mulberry velvet, it was definitely the most remarkable garment Miles had ever seen. But then, Lady Hortense was the most remarkable woman he had ever seen.

Just beside his bride-to-be's great bulk stood a

tiny, stick-thin woman whom Miles assumed to be the invaluable Martha, without whose help Lady Hortense would undoubtedly starve. For a moment he fought an insane desire to giggle at the unlikely prospect.

At last Miles grappled his ruffled composure into place, replacing his frozen grimace with a smile of welcome. "How do you do, ladies?" he managed hoarsely.

"Well enough, thank you, my lord," simpered Lady Hortense. "But absolutely famished. Perhaps you could have someone show us to our rooms so that we might change for dinner? I do so hope you have planned a special repast for our arrival!" Her eyes widened in anticipation, and he thought perhaps they were green.

"Yes. Yes, of course." Miles turned uncertainly, eager to have this whale off his hands. "Ah, Benson!" he cried with relief. "Do take her ladyship to her room."

"The blue room, my lord?" asked Benson respectfully, with only a faint quirk to his lips giving away his amusement.

"No, I think not, Benson," said Miles sharply. "The . . . er . . . the violet room I think."

The valet bowed and indicated with a sweep of his arm the direction in which they were to proceed. As the ladies followed the estimable Benson, Miles could not help noticing the gargantuan wicker basket Martha clutched. At the same moment that he noticed it, he felt a sneeze well up from deep within him, and he sneezed so hard that he thought for a moment that he had burst his immaculate cravat.

"Ah, Martha?" he called, sniffling into his handkerchief.

"Yes, Lord Bradford?" The woman looked back.

"Could I fetch someone to help you with whatever you are carrying?"

"Oh, no, thank you, my lord," she said gratefully with a shake of her graying head. " 'Tis just her ladyship's Persians. She'd never rest if anyone but myself carried them." She turned and hefted her burden up the stairs after her mistress.

Miles's face fell even further. Cats. Of course. He had been allergic to cats since childhood, and after he'd suffered a particularly violent case of hives, the creatures had been forbidden within miles of the Hall. He shook his head, cursing Dobbins yet again before smothering another explosive sneeze.

Aunt Hester harrumphed before sweeping majestically away.

13

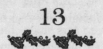

After retrieving her latest prize, a perfectly shaped, golden-brown strawberry pie decorated with tiny, delicate pastry leaves, Genevieve closed the heavy open door, wiping her sweating brow with the edge of her gingham apron.

When Miss Pramble had admired the creation, the two ladies sat back with cups of tea, surveying the splendid meal they were to serve their guests in less than an hour. Their silence was a comfortable one, broken only by an occasional snort from the mastiff sleeping beside the table, paws twitching as he chased rabbits in his dreams.

"I must admit, Jenny, that things have worked out better than I expected," said Miss Pramble with an admiring nod. "You are a superb cook. If all else fails, you can always aspire to that position," she teased.

"It will not fail, Pramble, and you mustn't say such things. It's bad luck." Genevieve laughed, a contented smile on her face.

"I don't think you need luck, my dear. From all I have seen, there is next to nothing that you could not handle with flying colors. I must say, I am impressed."

"Just between the two of us, so am I!"

They laughed companionably, then rose to begin the last preparations for the evening meal. Each course was laid out in order upon the cupboards to facilitate serving, and when all the crystal, which they had discovered with delight while searching the cellars for a few of the remaining bottles of wine, was in place on the table, sparkling in the candlelight, they sighed and looked at one another.

"I guess we had best change. You must sit with them, Pramble, as hostess, while I serve."

"Oh, my dear! Surely you are better suited to such a task. Why, the grandest dinner I ever attended was when an Irish cousin of mine married a country squire. I am not sure I would know how to go on."

"Don't be silly. You'll do fine. Besides, this is my venture, after all, and I promised to serve." Refusing to take no for an answer, Genevieve bustled Miss Pramble off up the stairs to change for dinner, while she returned to the kitchen for some last-minute touch-ups.

She entered the room only to gasp with horror. The pie was gone! Frantically Genevieve searched the counters for the misplaced dessert, only to discover that everything else—from the capon to the crab puffs—was also missing. Huddled beneath the table, Jasper was happily licking crumbs from his forepaws.

"Jasper! My pie! My crab puffs! My stuffed capon! How could you?"

At her horrified cries, the dog hung his head and managed to look suitably sorrowful, although his tail thumped against the floor, and his liquid black eyes gleamed hopefully.

"You mangy cur! What am I to serve now? That meal took me all day!"

Jasper rolled over, cocked his head at her, and lifted his ears.

"Why, I've a mind to serve *you*, you ungrateful beast!" Then, to Jasper's great surprise, his mistress burst into tears, dropped into a chair, and buried her face in her apron. The dog heaved to his feet and ambled over to her. He propped his massive paws on her knees and licked her face with his huge tongue, wiping away the salty tears. When she shoved him away, he whined pitifully.

"Go away, Jasper! Either you should find another dinner to serve my guests, or you should find another home. For we will have no home after tonight. All is ruined!"

Jasper looked at her, huge black eyes blinking dolefully. Then he dropped back to the floor, whirled about, and was out the kitchen door in a flash.

Genevieve felt too desolate to care where he had gone.

Miles dressed for dinner with a sinking heart. His sneezing had grown progressively worse, and his nose was as red as a ripe tomato. He sneezed again, and Benson handed him a fine lawn handkerchief, looking at his lordship sorrowfully.

"Bless you, my lord."

"Thank you, Benson," Miles said, sniffing. "But if you truly wished me blessed, you'd get those blasted felines out of my house, and their mistress with them! Why the devil didn't you tell me what Lady Hortense was like?"

"As you have told me in the past, it was not my place, my lord."

"Well, it is now. If I manage to extricate myself from this predicament, I grant you all rights to speak to me as you see fit."

"Thank you, sir." Benson opened Lord Bradford's chamber doors, standing to one side as his master strode from the room, stifling another sneeze. The valet sighed and shook his grizzled head.

Miles descended the staircase as grandly as his dripping nose would allow, relieved to discover that he had beaten his visitors downstairs. He headed for the sitting room just beyond the dining chamber and poured himself a double brandy from a crystal decanter on a side table. He swallowed it in one gulp as Aunt Hester entered the room, her shock at this latest invasion made apparent by her doing the unthinkable—dressing for dinner. She looked every inch the grand lady in her evening dress of rose crepe, matching pink slippers, and shawl of Brussels lace. The long rope of pearls Miles himself had sent her last Christmas was draped around her neck.

As the brandy burned a path to his empty stomach, Miles heaved a deep breath, feeling much more the thing. He managed to wrench his disgruntled features into a grimace of a smile as he heard Lady Hortense approaching. She sounded like a rhinoceros on stampede.

As if the necessity of dining with Hortense Figg was not distasteful enough, when Miles saw what the woman carried in her arms, he very nearly returned to his room pleading a headache. It would not have been fabricated, either, he reasoned, shrugging his broad shoulders to relieve the tense throbbing that increased with each step nearer Lady Hortense came.

Aunt Hester's thin mouth had formed an enormous 0; she was speechless with horror.

"My dear Lord Bradford, Lady Hester," Lady Hortense cried gaily, lifting her burden toward them. "Just see who has come to share our supper! This is Eustace"—she lifted an enormous calico

Persian and waved its limp arm—"and this is Herb!"

Miles shuddered, sneezing heartily into his handkerchief. "I see."

"They are so happy to meet you. Aren't you, my preciouses? Come now, my lord. Tell them you are happy to meet them, too, or you'll hurt their feelings."

She swooped down on him, brandishing the furry lumps in his face, and Miles jumped back, barely escaping a swiping paw.

"Of course. Delighted." Lord Bradford backed away, only to find to his dismay that Hortense followed as if she were glued to him.

"Bad boy, Herb. Naughty, naughty boy to swipe at your new daddy!" she simpered, winking at Miles.

"Yes, er, about that, Lady Hortense. I fear that there has been some mis—"

"We cannot tell you how happy we are, my lord. But just now we are simply famished. Let us go in before we simply die from hunger!"

As if in agreement her mountainous stomach emitted a rumble of thunder, and Miles could have sworn he felt the floor vibrate beneath his feet. Lady Hortense sailed grandly out of the salon. Miles proffered his arm to Aunt Hester, who took it and stepped forward, bristling.

Lady Hortense stopped in the dining-room doorway. "Ooh! This is just grand, my lord. How beautiful your home is. I shall be so thrilled to be a part of it. I cannot tell you how honored I was to receive your proposal."

"My dear lady!" Miles fairly exploded. Then he tempered his voice. "My lady, there was never an actual . . . an actual proposal. This was intended to be more of a trial visit, a holiday, if you will. But if my solicitor made some mistake, made my invitation sound like an offer, we really must—"

"Oh, dear!" cried Hortense, noticing for the first time that the place settings were miles apart at the enormous table of gleaming mahogany. "This will never do. How are we to get acquainted if we must shout in order to speak?" She bustled forward, setting the porcine cats down on the table as she made to rearrange the china and chairs. The felines began nosing the side dishes of butter and cream, and Miles stifled a disgusted comment and sneezed again even more violently.

The fringe on Lady Hortense's latest gown jiggled almost as magnificently as her great jowls as she dragged a second chair down the length of the dining hall, then looked at her host expectantly, waiting for him to seat her.

Miles sighed resignedly, pulling out the chair. Lady Hortense beamed and sat down, the delicate Chippendale chair groaning beneath her bulk, and Miles summoned up a burst of strength to heave chair and woman to the table. He bleakly did the same for his aunt, then took his own seat at the now crowded head of the table.

"Now then, what are we to dine upon, my lord? I do hope your chef has cooked a superb meal. I always say that there is nothing a good meal cannot solve or cure, don't you agree?" Without waiting for him to reply she beckoned to a footman who stood nearby, bearing a great tureen of turtle soup. He scooped the rich mixture into her bowl, and she plunged her spoon into the liquid as if she had not seen a meal in weeks. Then, as the man made to carry the tureen away, she caught his arm and instructed him to leave it beside her bowl.

The cats, having remained on the table, scampered forward and began lapping Lady Hortense's soup. Miles had never seen such a revolting display, but their mistress chuckled merrily and patted their heads. "Aren't they sweet? I can never decide which of my babies I love the most. The rest will be down shortly."

Miles's attention was suddenly riveted upon his obese guest. "I beg your pardon?" he rasped. Another volatile sneeze echoed around the great hall.

"The rest of my children. Turtle soup is one of their favorites, you know."

The sight was too much for Lord Bradford, and he turned away so that he would not lose his brandy, which was by now roiling in his stomach. "I see. And how many . . . 'children' do you have, my lady?"

"Ten in all."

"Ten?" he said hoarsely.

"Yes, but Bathsheba is having kittens just now. It nigh broke my heart to leave her during her confinement, but I couldn't disappoint my beloved, could I?" She blushed femininely, batting what Miles could see if the stubby lashes buried in their folds of fat.

He looked at her with a stunned expression and then buried his face once more in his handkerchief, sniffling.

"At any rate, the other seven should be down at any time. They always eat with me."

Miles closed his eyes and leaned back in his chair, unable to eat a bite and feeling more ill by the second.

Aunt Hester, unable to take any more, rose to her feet, and, in blatant disregard for her position as chaperone, removed herself from the dining room, leaving them alone. Miles watched her retreat, wishing he could do the same. He turned to Lady Hortense.

"Where is your maid? Surely she should be with us, acting as your chaperone. I shall send for her."

Lord Bradford made to rise but was halted by
Lady Hortense's iron grip on his wrist. "My chaperone? Not at all, my lord. Since we are to be married, I told Martha to stay out of our way so that
we could ... become better acquainted."

"Really, Lady Hortense, I feel that we must
come to an understanding. There is much that has
been mistaken here." His attention was caught by
a faint, rumbling sound, and in the next moment a
veritable army of cats flew through the dining
room door. Several promptly jumped upon the table and began attacking the joints of beef and slabs
of veal. One very brave black specimen began to
devour Miles's soup.

Miles pushed his chair back so violently that it
nearly tipped over. He surged to his feet, sneezing
ferociously. He glared at Lady Hortense through
swollen, red eyes. Ye gods, it was the outside of
enough! "My lady! I must insist that your cats
leave the room at once!" he roared angrily.

The lady in question looked up at him in innocent surprise, her slit-like eyes widening. "What?
Why, I couldn't possibly do that to the poor children! They would be so hurt!"

"I assure you, my lady," Miles said in a muffled
voice, handkerchief over his nose, "that if you do
not remove these vile creatures from my dinner table at once, that is exactly what they shall be!"

"Well! I have never been so insulted in all
my—"

Their argument was interrupted as a huge, furry
creature thundered into the room, barking furiously. It threw itself at the table, intent on its prey.
Cats flew in every direction; clouds of feline hair
swirled around the two humans' heads.

Amid another horrendous bout of sneezing,
Miles could only stare in wonderment at the cabal

ensuing in his usually orderly household. "What the—"

The great soup tureen which had been placed beside Lady Hortense's bowl began to rock madly, soup surging up the sides like a tidal wave. Lord Bradford and Lady Hortense watched, spellbound, as with a great crash it rolled to one side, spewing its contents over the lace tablecloth, the cats, and Lady Hortense. She sat there, mouth hanging open, as she struggled to comprehend what had happened.

Miles began first to chuckle, then to laugh madly, sneezing vividly in punctuation. "J-J-Jasper!" he hooted.

Snarling, the mastiff grabbed Herb by his tail. The cat spun around in a terrified frenzy, catching Jasper on the nose with its claws. The dog let out a pained yelp and lunged again. His great weight proved too much for the table, and the next moment the entire thing pitched to one side, spilling bowls and roasts, crystal and china, in a veritable waterfall of food and flatware.

Lady Hortense let out a grunt and pushed her chair back so forcefully that its delicate legs gave way beneath her. She hit the floor hard, soup dripping from her hair and a single lobster patty stuck to the side of her head, her face as red as a beet. "Oof!" she cried as Jasper landed on her great belly.

All the noise had alerted the servants that something was amiss, and in moments the room was filled with maids and manservants as well as the mass of squabbling animals. At first they were appalled to see proper Lord Bradford lying prostrate on the floor, laughing and sneezing with equal gusto. But as cats flew about screeching and the dog barked madly in hot pursuit, something of the hysteria seized them all, and soon the entire room erupted in crazed glee.

The footman picked up a leg of lamb and clubbed his lifelong enemy, the groom, up the side of the head; the cook, Antoine, seized an enormous dish of creamed peas and onions and poured it merrily over Benson, who responded by flinging an entire platter of lobster patties at his assailant. In moments everyone was flinging food and drink at everyone else.

Lady Hortense began to sob, her fat cheeks screwed up and brilliantly red. When no one came to her rescue, she heaved her great bulk up and stumbled through the crowd toward the doorway. Just before she escaped, a turkey pie hit her squarely in the back of her red sausage curls. She looked around furiously.

Lord Bradford was innocently examining his fingernails.

Huffing furiously, Hortense Figg stomped away.

"Well, that's that," Miles said softly to himself, smiling as he quietly left the room, not wanting to disrupt his servants' mad party.

When he reached the hall he called for Jasper, who obediently raced to his side. Lord Bradford contemplated the mischievous beast, then patted his head and said, "Good dog." Then he took the mastiff by the collar and led him outside, thrusting aside the memory of Jenny's threat to sue him.

14

Genevieve was still sitting at the kitchen table with her face buried in her apron when Jasper returned, Lord Bradford in tow.

Miles stopped dead in his tracks, concern flooding through him. It was an unfamiliar emotion, and it confused him momentarily. "Jenny?" he asked hesitantly, uncertain whether she would welcome his intrusion at such an obviously personal moment. When the girl raised her tear-filled eyes to his like two huge blue saucers, he felt his heart constrict and wondered how he ever could have been angry with her.

"Oh, Miles," she sobbed, "you were right. Of course you were right. I'll admit it now. I know full well that you are here to gloat over your triumph. You just had to witness my ruination, didn't you?"

"I beg your pardon?" he said, more confused than ever at this nonsensical outburst. "I came because I wished to return your dog. He has just frightened away yet another candidate for the position of mistress of Bradford Hall and has set my entire household on its ear. My servants are clubbing one another with joints of meat, and, if I am not mistaken, Lady Hortense Figg is even now racing away from me in a carriage."

Genevieve looked up at him suspiciously. "What are you talking about? Jasper has been with me. Too much with me, I might add, as he has just devoured the entire meal I was set to feed my first guests!"

Jasper slunk back behind Lord Bradford's tall figure, peeping out around the man's legs.

"I assure you, madam, that no one could have imagined what took place in my dining room not fifteen minutes ago. But that is neither here nor there. What do you mean, he devoured your meal?"

"The whole thing! I left the room for a moment, and when I returned, there he lay, under this very table, licking the last crumbs from his miserable chops. What are you still doing here, Jasper?" she groaned at the dog. "I told you that you must either replace my dinner or find a new home!"

"I see." A most peculiar glimmer of understanding surfaced for Miles as he gazed down thoughtfully at the naughty mastiff.

"How could you see? You have no idea how important this meal was to me! I worked so hard preparing Quince House for these guests, and if I fail with them, no one else will ever come. I shall be forced to go back to Cousin Marybelle's in shame. I shall be forced to succumb to her loathesome scheme, to play harlot to her husband's political cronies! I shall never again be able to look at myself in a mirror, for the shame of it!"

She had begun to cry again, and Miles, horrified at the heretofore unknown severity of her plight, fought the urge to pull her into his arms and comfort her as his mind raced to come up with a solution to her dilemma. The happy prospect of demolishing Quince House once its owner sold it to him because of her failure evaporated into nothingness in the face of Jenny's tears.

Finally he smiled confidently. "Stop crying, Jenny. Go dress for dinner, and I will see to your meal."

"But—"

"Don't argue. Just go."

Genevieve looked up at his handsome face, not daring to let herself wonder what he had in mind or why he would help her, only hoping that he could. With a last swipe at her teary face, she fled the kitchen.

Miles smiled again and walked back to Bradford Hall. In moments he had marshaled his staff into action. Fortunately Antoine, upon glimpsing Lady Hortense, had prepared mountains of food for her weekend stay.

Once his plan was under way, Lord Bradford went up to his room and put on his finest dinner jacket of black superfine with a black satin cravat. Then he returned to lead an entire retinue of food-bearing servants across the lawns toward Quince House.

Miss Pramble glanced out the window of the parlor where she and the two Americans sat waiting for their call to dinner. Her eyes widened. "Would you excuse me for a moment?" she said genially to the guests.

Mrs. Featherweight grunted, miffed at being kept from her meal for so long. Laddy said nothing at all, merely examining his crimson nails blankly.

Miss Pramble rushed upstairs and found Genevieve in her bedchamber, staring hopelessly at the pitifully worn gowns hanging in the wardrobe. Perplexed as to how and why such an elegant caravan was approaching Quince House at that very moment, Miss Pramble nonetheless wasted no time on gathering information but simply turned and ran as fast as her scrawny legs would take her down the corridor and into her own room. She rummaged around in her drawers and finally drew out a golden key. Then she hurried from her room, stopped in front of another door, unlocked it, and entered the chamber.

There she paused and looked around. Yes, everything was just as Genevieve's father had ordered it left. Even her ladyship's combs were still on the bureau. Without stopping to examine anything, Miss Pramble walked determinedly to the large wardrobe and threw open the doors. She sighed, relieved. Everything was still there, too. They were not new or in the height of fashion, but a girl with Genevieve's beauty could make one of these eighteen-year-old gowns even more lovely than they still were. She selected a gown of gentian-blue silk, the same shade as Genevieve's eyes, and found a pair of matching slippers.

When she made her way back to Genevieve's room, the girl was still staring hopelessly at her old gowns. "Jenny? I have come to help you dress. His lordship approaches even as we speak."

Genevieve whirled around, startled. "Dress? I have nothing to wear, Pramble. Oh, well, here, I guess this rose muslin will have to do." She reached out for the chosen gown.

Miss Pramble put her hand on Genevieve's arm. "No, my dear. You will wear this." She gestured toward the bed, where she had laid the lovely blue gown.

Genevieve's eyes widened. "Mama's?" she whispered reverently.

"Yes. I hope you do not mind, but I took the liberty of selecting it for you myself."

"Oh, Pramble! It's lovely," Genevieve said, fingering the silk with trembling fingers. "I had forgotten about Mother's things. Her room has been locked since I was a child. Where did you get the key?"

"I have kept it hidden since the time your father brought his first . . . lady friend . . . to the house. I didn't trust them to leave her things alone. As for your father, he was, God rest his soul, always too drunk to wonder where the key to your mother's room had gotten to. Come now. Let's get you dressed."

When Miss Pramble had buttoned the gown and combed Genevieve's strawberry tresses, she allowed the girl to look in the cheval glass. Genevieve turned slowly, glanced uncertainly at Miss Pramble, and then looked at herself. Her breath caught.

Once, when she was a small girl, when there was still money in the Quince coffers, Genevieve had seen an exquisite portrait hanging in her father's library. It had long since been sold to pay for her father's excesses, but it had been of a woman dressed in blue, like Genevieve was now. Genevieve had thought at the time that the woman was the most beautiful person in the whole world. Now, as she stared spellbound at her image in the mirror, Genevieve realized that the woman had been her mother, and this had been the dress she had worn.

Tears filled her eyes, and she smiled damply at Miss Pramble before throwing her arms around the governess's thin shoulders. Then the women walked downstairs and entered the parlor where their guests awaited them.

The first thing Genevieve noticed was the loud, raucous laughter emanating from the gaudily dressed Mrs. Featherweight. The second was the tall, immaculate, superb figure of a man who was entertaining her. The man turned, capturing Genevieve's eyes with his own.

Miles froze. He felt his breath stop in his chest as he stared, transfixed, at the vision in the doorway. Jenny had always been lovely, but tonight she was radiant! He bowed deeply. His experienced gaze had taken in that the gown was long out of date, but it suited Jenny far better than a more modern dress would have. The watered silk made her eyes lustrous, and the low-cut bodice exposed the rounded, faintly peach-colored tops of her firm young breasts. He cleared his throat and spoke in an effort to relieve his straying thoughts and rapidly tightening breeches.

"Miss Quince. What a pleasure to see you again. I was just having the most enjoyable discussion of American society with Mrs. Featherweight here. And her son, Mr. Featherweight, is a veritable treasure trove of amusing anecdotes. How fortunate you are to have such charming guests, and how fortunate I am to be among them!" He was rewarded with a girlish giggle from Mrs. Featherweight and a preening, pleased smile from Laddy.

"Why, Lord Bradford, I am delighted that you could join us tonight," Genevieve improvised with a relieved sigh.

Miles felt a glow of satisfaction deep within his chest at removing the pathetic, hopeless look from Jenny's blue eyes. He forced himself to turn back toward the visitors, proffering his arm to the colonial woman, who took it with a simpering smile. "Quite so, Miss Quince. Now then, dear lady," he said, delivering one of his world-famous, heart-stopping smiles to Mrs. Featherweight, who basked like a schoolgirl in its glory, "shall we go in to dinner?"

For a moment Jenny's face took on its haunted

look again, but Miles winked at her and led his giggling companion into the small dining room.

Genevieve held her breath as she entered the room behind the two laughing companions. Then she expelled it slowly through pursed lips, whistling silently. At the far end of the room, in the cavernous fireplace, flames crackled brilliantly, making the gleaming crystal glitter like a thousand stars. Footmen in deep-blue livery with gold braid stood behind each of the chairs surrounding the table.

When they were seated Genevieve stole a glance at Mrs. Featherweight. She was beaming happily up at her escort, eyebrows batting flirtatiously as she listened to his witty remarks.

The meal was a sumptuous feast, everything perfect, but Genevieve found her eyes straying more and more often toward the tall, dark figure opposite her. Now and then she saw that Lord Bradford's attention was on her, too, and she wondered if his heart could possibly be beating as fast as hers.

Following the elegant meal Miles suggested to Laddy that they take their port in the library and join the ladies in the salon afterward.

The boy led the way importantly, his chest thrust out like a banty rooster, and Genevieve smiled into Miles's silver eyes gratefully. Then she and Miss Pramble led Mrs. Featherweight to the sitting room for coffee while the servants cleared up.

"Ladies," said Miles when he and Laddy rejoined them. Smiling deeply into Mrs. Featherweight's eyes, he murmured, "I would be honored if you would dance with me. Miss Pramble, do you suppose you could play the pianoforte? Then Miss Quince shall play while I dance with you."

Genevieve stared at him.

"Of course. What a charming idea, my lord," replied Miss Pramble.

Once again Miles offered Mrs. Featherweight his arm, and, following suit, Laddy offered his to Genevieve. He seemed to have picked up a few manners in the brief time he had spent with Lord Bradford.

Miles danced three sets with Mrs. Featherweight, by the end of which the woman was breathing heavily and happy to sit down. He turned toward Genevieve, but she blushed prettily and pretended she had not seen, nudging Miss Pramble out of her place at the pianoforte. The governess stood and was wrapped in Lord Bradford's capable arms, her long dove-gray gown swirling about her legs. She laughed gaily.

At last Miss Pramble pulled Lord Bradford to a stop. "Not another step," she gasped. "I couldn't dance another step. Come, Jenny, let me take your place, and you dance with his lordship."

Genevieve looked up nervously, but Laddy insisted their hostess dance with him again. For the next two songs she endured his heavily scented embrace and his inane comments. Then Miles stepped forward. He tapped Laddy gently on the shoulder, and although the boy's eyes narrowed sulkily, he stepped back with a polite-enough bow.

Although held intimately in his arms, Genevieve found that she could not look up into Lord Bradford's eyes.

Finally he whispered softly, "Jenny?"

"My lord?" She forced her gaze up to meet his.

"Don't you like to dance?"

"Yes, my lord."

"Then why do you not look at your partner? Why do you not converse with me? I know you have things to say, for I saw you chatting with Mr.

Featherweight only moments ago." He raised his eyebrows at her inquisitively.

Genevieve blushed. "I am sorry, my lord. It is just that I do not know how to lightly discuss the weather when I stand here feeling so very beholden to you for your efforts tonight on my behalf. You have saved my life." His fingers tightened slightly against her back, and she felt her cheeks warm.

Lord Bradford stared down into her eyes. "I think not. I suspect you would survive almost anything on your own—from wild lilies to mad hornets. But let us discuss it no further now. Now, as you said, is the time for less weighty chatter." He smiled at her. "You look extremely beautiful tonight, Jenny. I wonder how I could possibly have mistaken you for a servant that first day in your garden."

Genevieve blushed again at the memory of that day.

Miles's smile widened, and he whispered boldly, "You look even more lovely than you did in my bedchamber."

That sparked Genevieve into conversation. "You should not speak to me so, my lord," she told him in an angry whisper.

"If I do not speak of it now, then when will I have the opportunity to do so? You have already threatened to sue me for trespass if I stepped onto your property again. I suppose after tonight I should expect a call from the local constable. Or perhaps you intend to feed me to that vicious beast, Jasper?"

Genevieve winced. "My lord, I must beg that you do not bring up the subject again."

"Of my being sued? But I should think it quite natural that I be concerned." His eyes widened with false innocence.

"You know that's not what I meant," she snapped. Then she sighed contritely. "I am sorry. Please forgive my foul temper. I have had an awful day, and I suppose it galls me a little to have the man I threatened to sue save me from certain failure. Especially when I know full well that he would have better enjoyed seeing my endeavor come to grief." She looked up at him. The expression in his eyes caught her off guard, and a flicker of unexpected warmth spread through her. And suddenly, despite herself, she remembered quite vividly what had, indeed, happened between them in Miles's bedchamber.

Lord Bradford opened his mouth to speak. "Jenny, I—"

"Please, my lord," she beseeched, gazing up at him with frightened eyes. "Let us never mention the matter again. I appreciate your help greatly, and when I can repay you, I will. Until then, please cede to my wishes."

Miles looked at her closely. Then he smiled gently. "Very well, Jenny. The subject is closed for now. But I warn you, only for now."

The strains of the waltz Miss Pramble was playing ended, and the partners drew apart. The remainder of the evening they all played whist, and although the time passed companionably enough, it seemed that an unspoken current of tension flowed between Miles and Genevieve.

At last Miles stood to leave. He bowed to Mrs. Featherweight, taking her pudgy hand in a last chivalrous gesture. "My dear lady, it has been an honor to make your acquaintance. I do hope you have enjoyed your stay enough that you will come back again, and perhaps tell your friends about Miss Quince's hospitality." He kissed the air a quarter of an inch above her hand and gazed flirtatiously into her eyes.

She blushed violently. "Oh, yes, yes, my Lord Bradford! To be sure!" she gushed. She curtsied, and elbowed her son in the stomach, prompting him to bow.

As they still had no butler, Genevieve walked Miles to the front doors. As they stopped at the outside steps, she suddenly felt terribly shy and looked at the ground, speaking hesitantly. "Thank you, my lord. What you did tonight was very, very kind. I do not know how I can possibly thank you enough, but if you ever think of a way I can repay your thoughtfulness, please tell me, and I will do so at once."

Miles said nothing, and Genevieve looked up at him.

The dangerous smile he gave her set off an alarm bell somewhere inside her.

"Ah, Miss Quince, as it happens, I already have."

Genevieve instinctively backed away a step. "Well, then, perhaps you can tell me what it is," she said hurriedly, inching toward the doors.

He grasped her lightly by the elbow. "Not so fast, Miss Quince."

"But just now I am extremely tired. Could you not tell me next time we meet? Now if you will excuse me—"

"Jenny," he said softly. "You can repay me with a kiss."

Genevieve's heart leaped into her throat. "I see," she said, her mind racing as she tried to think of a way to escape.

"No," he said quietly, his eyes never leaving hers, "I don't think you do, my dear, dear Jenny. But I am very willing to explain it to you. There are so many things I want to explain to you, to teach you." He pulled her by her elbow gently but

insistently toward him, and Genevieve powerless
to resist.

Like a rabbit trapped by the glittering eyes of a
cobra, she felt him fit her to the long, hard length
of him, felt the heat of his body radiate through
her own. The hand that was not holding her arm
cupped her chin and tipped her face up so that
she was forced to look at him. His silver eyes glittered in the moonlight as he gazed at her. Then his
mouth was coming closer, closer, and his lips
touched hers in a feather-light caress.

Genevieve was drawn to him like a magnet;
there was nothing she could do to avoid the over-
whelming onslaught of desire that raged through
her veins. She leaned toward him, pressing closer,
ignoring the clamor from her brain telling her that
she was behaving like a wanton. She felt Miles
smiling against her mouth as he whispered her
name, kissing her even more deeply.

His tongue outlined her full lips, and Genevieve's mouth opened to permit him entrance.
Their tongues mated in that indescribably sensual
gesture, sending shock waves through Genevieve's
innocent body. Somewhere in the back of her mind
she noticed that his hands were now spanning her
waist, then sliding up her midsection and closer to
her breasts, which were throbbing most oddly.

Then, without warning, Miles pulled away,
breathing heavily, and pressed her head against
his chest. She reveled in the warmth of his embrace, wondering at the hardness below his hips,
glorying in the maleness of him, wishing that the
wondrous feelings would never end.

"Jenny," Miles whispered hoarsely, "come with
me. Come with me to Bradford Hall now. Miss
Pramble will take care of your guests. I want you,
Jenny. Let me love you."

Fierce heat shot through her, and every fiber of

her body cried for some unknown satisfaction she was certain that only this man could give her.

Then, to her utter shock and dismay, just as she was about to capitulate and agree to anything, Miles released her abruptly, gently but firmly pushing her away from him, and shook his head as if to clear it. She grabbed the doorknob behind her lest her wobbly knees give way.

"I will come for you tomorrow," he promised solemnly, gazing at her in a way that made her flesh burn as if he had touched her, making her long for his touch in a way she did not understand but instinctively ached to experience. Then he turned and disappeared swiftly into the night.

Genevieve stood in the doorway, drawing deep breaths until she felt recovered enough to go inside. She found that her guests and Miss Pramble had all gone to bed, and she followed suit, even though she was certain she would never be able to sleep.

15

As soon as the guests at Quince House had departed the following morning, Lord Bradford called on Genevieve Quince, prepared to ask her, for the second time, a very important question. He dressed carefully for the event, and he cut a fine figure as he walked across the newly scythed lawn of his estate. It was, by the rules of Society, much to early to call, but Miles was unable to quell his desire to see Jenny after eight long hours without her. He tugged with uncharacteristic self-consciousness at the lapels of his charcoal coat, straightening his brilliantly white cravat nervously as he gazed at the opposing house. The nearer it came, the more nervous he got. He smiled to think that Lord Miles Bradford, powerful in both Society and politics, should be shaking in his boots at the mere thought of asking a young woman to be his wife.

For hours the night before he had paced the rug in his library, practicing exactly what he would say to Jenny. Still, nervous butterflies fluttered in his stomach, and as he walked he repeated his lines again and again to be certain he did not forget them.

At last the inevitable could be put off no longer,

for the steps of Quince House loomed large before him. Miles stood for a moment gazing up at the shining windows, then shook his head, clearing away the fog of unreasonable fear, and climbed to the double doors.

He rapped the knocker loudly. Genevieve watched him from an upstairs window. Though she thrilled to his tailored handsomeness, her heart was heavy, for she knew that she wanted to accept his offer more than anything in the world, but that becoming his mistress would mean her ruin as nothing she had done before had.

She, too, had been awake for most of the night, staring blindly at the canopy above her bed, crying miserable, hot tears. There was not a doubt in her mind that Lord Bradford would appear on her doorstep the next day with his dishonorable demand. She had not, however, expected him quite so soon.

If only things were different! If only Father had not died penniless and she had not been reduced to her current straits. Then perhaps Miles would be arriving to renew his proposal of marriage instead of asking her to live in sin until he tired of her. What would there be then, except to go on to the next man? And the next? No. It could not be. Although she was grateful to him for saving her newly begun business the night before, she was not grateful enough to abandon herself completely.

At last she had risen from her bed, refusing to cry another tear for what could never become reality, and she had dressed in the same faded blue gown she had worn when she had first met Lord Bradford in the garden. It was more than a dress, she thought; it was a statement of the differences between them. Differences she could not forget and was sure he would not.

Genevieve knew that Miss Pramble was still

abed, having stayed up so late the previous night, so when she heard the knocking on the front doors she walked slowly down the stairs, staring at them as if Death himself awaited entrance. She was tempted to turn and run back up the stairs, leaving his lordship outside, but to do so would be cowardly, and Genevieve was determined to be brave.

Miles rapped once more, thinking that if someone did not answer soon he would return to Bradford Hall and come back at a later hour. As he thought this, though, the doors swung open, and he found himself face-to-face with the object of his intentions.

Genevieve said nothing, only looked at him sadly.

Miles gazed at her, stunned by the power of his feelings for her as desire, love, and admiration poured over him in a landslide of emotion. Then he noticed the gown she was wearing. Why was she dressed once more like the servant girl? He frowned but followed as she turned and walked silently down the hall and into the small parlor.

She did not speak until she stood before the fireplace, staring into the flames. "My lord, I know why you have come." Her cheeks flamed, but she raised defiant eyes to his.

Miles, meanwhile, was so intent on remembering his lines that he heard not a word she said. God! She was so beautiful. He turned away from her and stared out the window, the better to concentrate on his delivery. "My dear Miss Quince, long and long have I pondered what is in my heart," he began grandly.

"My lord, I do not wish to hear—"

"And I have decided that there is only one avenue to take."

"I assure you, I have no intention of taking that avenue."

"I am sure, when you have heard me out, you will agree that we must travel that road together."

"I beg you, my lord, do not—"

"It is a path fraught with dangers, but it is also a path filled with intense, indescribable pleasures for those who are brave enough to tread it."

"It is not a question of bravery!" Genevieve snapped. "It is a question of honor!"

Miles looked at her blankly. "Quite so," he agreed, then returned his gaze to the window. "Now then, where was I? Ah, yes. It is obvious to me that you desire me as I do you, although I am certain you are far too innocent to realize that yet."

Genevieve gasped furiously, but Miles continued inexorably.

"It will be my utmost joy to teach you what is meant by both desire and pleasure."

Genevieve was growing angrier by the moment. "And I assure you that you will never—"

"Likewise, it will please me immensely to be able to care for you in the years to come."

"Well, at least you would have had the grace to keep me for a few years," Genevieve muttered to the air, for that was all that was listening to her. Impatiently she glared at his back, tapping her foot. Heavens, the man was obtuse! He was so caught up in what he wanted that he blindly assumed she would desire the same thing.

"I fully intend to arrange a special account for you at my bank in London, as well as at a branch in Dunheath. You will have everything you require and want. Rest assured that I am a most generous man. So then, my dearest Jenny. May I have your answer? Say that you will make me the happiest of men. Say yes, Jenny, and let me free you from this bondage, this crazy scheme you call independence." Having reached the end of his monologue, Miles turned and regarded her hopefully.

Unable to control her temper any longer, Genevieve exploded. Picking up a small vase from a side table, she hurled it defiantly at his head. Fortunately for Miles, it was not very heavy, and it simply bounced off his forehead and fell to the rug with a dull thud.

He stared at her, stunned, and raised one finely manicured hand to the quickly rising lump on his brow. He looked down at the vase, then back at Genevieve, with a complete lack of comprehension. Had he said something wrong, offended her in some way? What woman could possibly be offended by an offer of marriage?

"You deliberately struck me," he breathed. "I stand here, baring my soul to you, and instead of returning my sentiment or simply me telling me that you did not return it, you slam that vile object into my skull!"

"Yes, I did, and I'm glad of it. You haven't heard a word I said, you've been so busy ranting on about how well you were going to take care of me. Well, I have news for you, my Lord Bradford. I do not want to be taken care of. I do not want desire and pleasure. I do not want you to spare me from the necessity of keeping my home open for paying guests. I do not want your filthy lucre. But the thing I want least of all is *you!*"

Her breasts heaved; her cheeks glowed with fury. She had never looked more beautiful, and Miles had never felt more desolate. "I see," he said softly. "I am sorry that I have wasted both your time and mine in this fruitless effort. Forgive me for offending you, Miss Quince. I shall not trouble you again. I will show myself out." He bowed, turned and walked with dignified steps from the room.

Genevieve waited until she heard the double doors close softly, and then she collapsed onto the sofa, her heart crying out for her to follow him and say that she would do anything he wanted as long as he would love her. But he had not said he loved her, and she knew her answer could have been no different. Still, she could not prevent herself from bursting into tears.

Although Lord Bradford had insisted that Dobbins keep his bride-seeking venture quiet, word did manage to seep out, and even before the first candidate had arrived rumors were whispered on London lips. Indeed, it had been the chief topic of conversation in the carriage that rolled ever closer to Bradford Hall. Now, however, its occupants were silent, wrapped in thought.

After several miles the finely dressed woman within turned to one of her companions, a dowdy, shrewish female in a maidservant's garb. "We're almost there. How do I look?" she demanded haughtily.

"Ee look foine," said the maid sourly.

"My lady," growled the other, glaring at her servant angrily. "And stop being disrespectful. It's not seemly."

"Moi laydy," replied her maid saucily.

Her mistress, dressed in a traveling gown of deep-crimson brocade trimmed with black mink and a tricorn hat with a black net veil, was a beauty, with raven-black hair twined intricately over blackbird-wing brows. Her eyes were emerald-green and slightly tilted, giving her a panther-like expression. The tip of her pointed tongue slid out from behind perfect, pristine white teeth and moistened her ruby-red lips. Then she reached up and pinched her cheeks to bring out a rosy color, wishing she had dared use face paints. But his lordship was said to be a stickler for convention and would probably not smile on his future wife using cosmetics.

"I'm so tired of this carriage," she said blandly to the man seated opposite her, who was gazing out the window at the rolling countryside. "And this area is so dreary. I'll be glad when I'm Lady Bradford and can insist on living in London year round."

Her companion said nothing, only smiled wryly.

Lady Bradford! the woman exulted silently. Her mouth curved upward in a frigid smile. From her reticule she pulled a small gold-plated mirror, peering into it intently. Satisfied, she patted her hair and replaced the mirror in the handbag. She had heard of the three other women's failures, as had nearly all of London, but was undaunted. *She* would not fail. Of that she was certain. Sabrina, Lady Westwood, was too smart to fail.

"Smile, Crenshaw," she demanded, glaring balefully at the maid. "You look like you've been sucking a lemon. And for God's sake keep your mouth shut once we get to Bradford Hall. Your voice is enough to sour milk." The vehicle slowed near a copse of trees, rolling to a stop. "Get out, Sebastian."

The man eyed her with annoyance. "Watch yourself, my dear," he said tonelessly. "You wouldn't want to offend me. After all, you can't do this alone," he pointed out, reminding her of the plan they had mutually devised.

The woman ignored him. She had no intention of retaining her lover once she was Lady Bradford, even if Lord Bradford was soon conveniently dead. "I warn you, both of you. Make one mistake, and I'll see you in Newgate. Soon I will be in

a position to do just that. The wife of Lord Bradford will have ample power to dispose of two
criminals." She pushed the man out, jerking the
carriage door closed behind him.

He watched them drive away, his lips tightening. "I think not, my lady," he murmured. "'Twill
not be me who swings at Newgate. Although the
judges are loathe to hang women, they've done so
for far less than your crimes." And he turned and
disappeared among the trees.

The carriage turned up the drive of the finer of
the two homes that faced each other across the
road. The lady in red smiled again, peering out the
window eagerly as the vehicle rolled to a stop. She
patted the reticule she carried on one arm, ensur-
ing that the tiny derringer was still there. If worse
came to worst, she would not hesitate to use it, as
she had already proven.

Miles sat back dejectedly as Benson dabbed alco-
hol on the small wound on his forehead. "She will
not have me, Benson," he repeated for the fifth time.

The valet merely clucked his disapproval at the
maiden's ignorance.

"She will not have me!"

"No, my lord," he said mournfully.

Lord Bradford flinched at the sting. He was silent for several moments. "Benson?"

"Yes, my lord?"

"Do you find me unreasonable?"

"Unreasonable, my lord?" Benson inquired.

"You know, hard to get along with. A difficult
master. Do you find that I do not listen to you?"
He looked up inquisitively.

"Of course not, my lord," the valet murmured in
a reassuring voice. Faithful to the end, Benson
conveniently forgot the many times he had complained to Cook about that very thing. A bell

sounded in the hallway. "If you will excuse me, sir?"

Miles nodded, wrapped in gloom.

A few moments later Benson reentered the room. "My lord, there is someone to see you. She says you have been expecting her. A Lady Westwood."

"Lady Westwood? I don't believe I've ever met the woman, although the name is dashed familiar. What is she like? Another of Dobbins's witches in a debutante's clothing?"

"I do not know who she is, my lord. She is, however, if you will pardon my presumption, very beautiful. I put her in the gold salon."

Mildly glad for the diversion, Miles smiled faintly and walked out of the bedchamber. Westwood, Westwood, he thought. The name rang a bell. But where had he heard it?

He could hear her voice before reaching the salon. It was low-pitched and musical, sensual, like cool velvet, or like the smoothest cognac sliding down one's throat. Miles stopped in the corridor to listen to the unusual timbre. Then he rounded the corner and entered the room, where he promptly froze in his tracks.

"My lord," the voice said, but Miles was too spellbound to notice anything but the woman to whom it belonged.

She was quite tall, striking and willowy, with piles of blue-black hair that he knew would feel like satin if he ran his hand through it. She smiled, exposing teeth that were even and small, almost feline. Somehow she had managed to endow her two simple words with such intense sexuality that Miles immediately imagined sweeping her up in his arms and taking her to his bed.

"Lady Westwood?" he asked unnecessarily. Reining in his libido, he bowed gracefully. The

woman approached him. Immediately the desire
to make love to the elegant creature vanished, and
Miles was astounded to find, instead, the image of
a deadly viper come to mind as she slithered forward.

"Oh, dear," she murmured, mouthing the words
broadly with her superb red lips. "I fear that you
were not expecting me. I do hope that is not so, for
your solicitor, Mr. Dobbins, led me to believe that
you wished more than anything to make my acquaintance." She paused, looking mildly embar-
rassed.

On cue, since he was a gentleman in every sense
of the word, Miles leaped into the breach. "Ah,
that would explain it. How remiss of me. I'm
afraid I have not read my mail for the last few
days and must therefore have missed his corre-
spondence informing me of your arrival," he lied
smoothly, thinking that at last Dobbins had hit on
exactly what he had been looking for. She seemed
a trifle cold, for all her luxuriant beauty, but was a
far sight more eligible than the previous three candidates the solicitor had selected. "At any rate, I
am happy to meet you, Lady Westwood, and I
hope you will enjoy your stay at Bradford Hall."

As if satisfied with his response, Lady
Westwood extended her small white hand. "Please
call me Sabrina."

Miles took her fingers in his, surprised that the
image of the viper still remained. "Of course, and
you must call me Miles." Her hand was cold—he
could feel the chill even beneath her kidskin
glove—but that did not mean the woman was a
reptile. God, look at her! She was as appealing as
Eve must have looked to Adam after he took a
bite of the apple.

"Well, now that we are properly introduced, I
imagine that you would like to be shown to your

room to freshen up before dinner. It will be served in a little over an hour," he said gallantly. "Benson!" The valet silently appeared. "Please show Lady Westwood and her companion to the"—he paused, an angry flash to his eye—"blue room. She will be staying with us for a while."

"The blue room, my lord?" Benson questioned with wide eyes.

"Is that not what I just said?"

"Yes, my lord."

Maid and mistress made to follow Benson out of the room, but Lady Westwood paused in the doorway. "I am so glad to make your acquaintance, my lord," she said softly, running her eyes over his lithe, muscular body in open appreciation. "I hope we can be very good friends." Then she was gone.

Miles shook his head, wondering at the feeling that the woman had practically invited him with her eyes to come to her room. Impossible. Dobbins knew he was in the market for a wife, not a paramour. Doubtless this woman had all the proper credentials even though her title, Lady Westwood rather than merely Lady Sabrina, indicated her status as a widow instead of an innocent maid. And she was certainly beautiful enough for the part.

16

Genevieve weeded ferociously, tugging up bits of grass in the rose beds as if her life depended upon her removing every last blade. Within her head raged the fiercest war she had experienced in all her eighteen years, and within her heart a solid, wooden ache seemed to smother every breath she took. She longed to go to Miles, to tell him she was his to do with as he pleased, and devil take the future. So caught up in her thoughts was she that she did not hear the man step up behind her, his black boots crunching on the gravel of the narrow pathway.

"Miss Quince, I presume?"

"Yes?" Genevieve whirled around to face her inquisitor and just as rapidly felt her face warm for staring at him so intently. He was extremely attractive, but there was something about him that lent the image of a highwayman. His hair was very dark, almost as black as Lord Bradford's, his eyes the most startling, piercing shade of blue she had ever seen. Above his well-formed, full-lipped mouth rested a tiny, perfect mustache. His calfskin breeches were as dark as pitch, and his shirt, while obviously made of a fine silk, was also black. He stood with his hands resting on his narrow hips, smiling down at Genevieve where she knelt on the ground. She belatedly stood, and for a brief instant she wondered where Miss Pramble and Jasper were, wishing they were nearby, as she suffered an odd tremor of fear. Then she shook her head to rid it of its ridiculous, suspicious thoughts and smiled at the gentleman, for certainly that was what he was.

"Mr. Sebastian Crowley, at your service," he said with a polite bow. He smiled, extending his hand. Genevieve took it hesitantly, and the man raised it to his lips and kissed it, all the while gazing deeply into her eyes.

Genevieve flushed and pulled her hand away. "Is there something you need, Mr. Crowley?" she asked stiffly.

The man's eyebrows shot up, and he looked at her as if deeply hurt. "Why, Miss Quince! Surely you have been expecting me. I wrote to you over a month ago informing you of my desire to stay here at your charming inn."

"I am afraid I did not receive your letter, Mr. Crowley," said Genevieve with a frown, brushing her dirty hands against the skirt of the blue muslin gown.

"Oh, dear," he said unhappily, craning his neck to peer down the road. "I have already dismissed the public coach. It must surely be miles from here by now. However, I shall try to catch it."

He turned as if to leave. Genevieve put out a hand to stop him, although at the same time she wished to let him go. His arm felt wiry, strong. "I won't hear of it, Mr. Crowley. You are here now, and there is no reason you should not stay."

He breathed a sigh of relief and smiled at her. "Oh, thank you, dear lady. I am so pleased that you are not going to force me to continue my journey. I have been making a tour of the country, you see, and I would give anything for a soft bed and a good meal."

"Then you have come to the right place, sir. If you will go up to the house, Miss Pramble, the other lady who lives here, will see to your needs."

"Thank you again, Miss Quince. I shall be no trouble, I assure you." He bowed gracefully and took his leave.

Genevieve watched him go, wondering at the faint warning signal her brain was sending her. Then she dismissed the thought and turned back to her roses, happy to have a paying guest once again. Hopefully it would take her mind off her sadness.

True to his word, Sebastian Crowley was no trouble. He was very quiet, keeping to his room most of the time, and when he wasn't there he was either off walking around the countryside or riding Storm for hours. His manners were impeccable; even Miss Pramble could find nothing wrong with his gentlemanly demeanor.

Both ladies soon grew to enjoy his quick wit and dry humor, laughing with their guest over superlative meals. However, try as they might, the women could find out nothing about his situation in life, and he showed no sign of quitting Quince House or of paying his tab, saying only that he would prefer to pay all at once when he left rather in allotments.

For Lord Bradford's part, he found that Lady Westwood filled an aching gap in his life, always seeming to say exactly what he needed to hear. They spent hours together, riding around the countryside on his thoroughbreds or laughing over cards, cheese, and wine while Aunt Hester embroidered near the fire in the evenings. Lady

Westwood's maid kept to herself. Miles doubted if he had seen her twice during their entire stay.

It was soon obvious to Miles that all he needed do was knock on Lady Westwood's door at night in order to be welcomed with open arms, but he could not bring himself to give her more than a simple touch when lifting her into her saddle or offering his arm to lead her in to dinner. Even with her delightful companionship, Miles could not seem to rid himself of the emptiness that gripped him each time he glanced in the direction of Quince House.

This morning they were to ride through the forests and into Dunheath for a mug of cider at the local posting house. Miles tugged his boots onto his feet. "Do you think Lady Westwood is ready?" he asked Benson disinterestedly.

The valet stood to one side, holding his master's riding jacket. He held it out, and his lordship shrugged his broad shoulders into the fine wool coat. "I would presume so, my lord," he said in a careful monotone.

"What do you think of her, Benson?"

"She is . . . very beautiful, my lord."

"Yes."

"My lord?" said Benson hesitantly.

"What is it, Benson?"

"Perhaps I will offend, but there is something I feel I must say."

"Of course, Benson. You have been too good a friend to me to hold back now. What's on your mind?"

"I cannot help but notice that you have not been yourself of late. Do you not think that a visit to Miss Quince's would do you good? Perhaps she has changed her mind about your proposal. Such a warm, sweet woman, Miss Quince."

Miles shot him a look. "I do not think that I mistook Miss Quince's mind on our last meeting, Benson. Nor do I think she would welcome me. More likely throw something heavier this time and finish me off." He smiled wryly. "Although if I were killed, I would at least be spared the necessity of siring an heir."

"I hear from belowstairs that the ladies at Quince House have a guest. A male guest, who has been there for nearly as long as Lady Westwood has been here."

Miles frowned.

"You know, my lord," Benson ventured, "it might be a nice diversion for Lady Westwood to visit Quince House, or perhaps you could invite its occupants to go riding with you some afternoon. Miss Quince could find no fault in your wishing to give your fiancée some entertainment, and she would probably welcome the opportunity to entertain her own guest."

"Lady Westwood is not my fiancée," Lord Bradford growled.

"Oh. I was under the impression, since her ladyship has been here for so long, that she was to become Lady Bradford, my lord." Benson looked at his master innocently.

Miles ground his teeth. "Are you trying to sway me into a proposal, Benson?"

The valet looked shocked, the corners of his mouth turning down in dismay. "No, my lord! Certainly not! I was simply thinking that, whether or not Lady Westwood is or is not your fiancée yet, it might do you good, if you'll pardon my bluntness, my lord, to compare the two ladies in question before making your final decision."

He looked so sincere, that Miles could not help but feel touched at the man's concern. He laughed softly. "You don't like Lady Westwood, do you, Benson?"

"I cannot say that I like or dislike her, my lord. In truth, I cannot put my finger on how I feel about Lady Westwood. She is very lovely, but at the same time I do not hear the warmth in your voice when you speak of her that I used to detect when you talked of Miss Quince. Marriage is for a long time, my lord. And if you are not absolutely certain that you want to marry Lady Westwood, you might yet want to pursue Miss Quince in the future. In which case, you might be very curious about her gentleman guest. Don't you think inquiring after her is worth risking another blow?"

Miles chuckled ruefully, rubbing his brow in remembrance. "Perhaps. And just what would you suggest, my good man?"

"Well, at the risk of sounding impertinent, my lord," Benson said respectfully. "I was thinking that a ride would be just the thing. The four of you, or five, if Miss Pramble is of a mind to go. That way you could see the two ladies together, and your mind would be ever more certain."

Lord Bradford nodded at his valet's sagacity and promised to consider the matter.

Lady Westwood was awaiting Miles below, pacing back and forth in front of the grand staircase as she bit her lip and fumed over Lord Bradford's failure to come to the point. He seemed to enjoy her company. She knew he thought her beautiful. And she was ready and willing if he should happen to come to her room during the night. Why, the man would have to be blind to have missed all the hints she had thrown out, she thought with chagrin, the leather riding crop she held in one gloved hand tapping sharply against her thigh.

It was a good thing she had taken precautions for just such an event as Lord Bradford's failure to propose, she thought with satisfaction. She would give him until tomorrow, and then measures would be taken. At last she heard him coming down the stairs, and she painted on a sweet expression as she lifted her lovely face to gaze adoring up at him.

Lady Westwood looked stunning, Miles noted, and the fact irritated him for some reason. She was dressed in a pale-fawn corduroy riding habit, beneath which she wore a lemon-yellow blouse of airy muslin. On her head perched a delicate bonnet with a small veil trailing down her back. The entire costume was set off by black velvet braid which accented her raven tresses beautifully. Her waist-length hair had been skillfully arranged atop her head, with a few curls left artfully loose around her heart-shaped face and down her back.

Again Miles found himself racking his brain to understand why he was not smitten with her and what it was he could not recall about her most familiar name. Had he perhaps known her deceased husband?

"Well, my lady, you look exquisite, as always," he said.

"Shall we be off? I have chosen a particularly spirited mount for you this morning—Imp, the daughter of my favorite stallion, Fury." He smiled at her and proffered his arm. Lady Westwood took it with a charming smile, and they headed for the stables, where their horses waited, saddled and champing at their bits.

Miles led the way, and they rode off through the fields toward the forest. The meadows had exploded into bloom: daffodils the same shade as Lady Westwood's blouse, tulips as red as her lips, irises as blue as—well, thought Miles, as blue as Jenny's eyes.

The splendor of the day palled, and he turned to his companion just in time to catch a fleeting expression that looked for all the world as if she had been glaring at him. Of course, he must have been mistaken. She was merely squinting against the sun.

"I thought perhaps I would invite my neighbors from across the road to accompany us on our ride tomorrow, to provide you with some fresh entertainment," he said, missing the pleased look she sent him because at that moment Fury sidestepped a rabbit hole and Miles had to turn forward.

Behind him Lady Westwood smiled. "I assure you, my lord, that you are all the entertainment I require," she replied sweetly, batting her thick, sooty lashes at him when he smiled back at her appreciatively.

"Very sweet but not altogether true, I suspect. I know that women need the company of other women sometimes. You have, after all, had no such companionship but my rather taciturn aunt and your maid."

"But my lord, I swear to you that you are all the company I want. How could a woman not be satisfied when she has a man as handsome and as charming as you for her companion?" As he turned his attention back to his somewhat skittish mount, Lady Westwood's expression grew more sour, her green eyes stabbing him in the back. Being pleasant to the man was becoming more and more difficult. And she did not relish comparison with the fresh young chit Sebastian had told her about during one of their secret, illicit meetings in the woods behind Bradford Hall. Nonetheless, perhaps it was fortunate that his lordship planned, albeit unconsciously, to aid her in her trap.

"But, I insist, my lady. I know it will do your heart good. We shall ride tomorrow with my neighbors." He turned back to her again and was mystified when he saw what seemed to be blackest hatred glowing in Lady Westwood's eyes. Miles shook his head. Such imaginings! For truly she beamed at him in gratitude, as if he were the finest of men to think of her need for companionship.

"You did what?" Genevieve cried furiously. She was seated at her bureau, pinning up her hair.

Miss Pramble stepped back from the fury in her friend's eyes. "I accepted, by proxy, Lord Bradford's invitation for you and Mr. Crowley to go horseback riding with him and his guest, Lady Westwood. I thought it a good idea to offer our guest such a diversion. After all, the Featherweights were thrilled to hobnob with nobility. It's an excellent lure for Quince House. I already informed Mr. Crowley, and he was as delighted as I believed he would be. What on earth could be the matter with that, Jenny?" she asked concernedly, peering at the girl's face.

"Nothing, Pramble. Nothing at all. I simply have a headache. Perhaps I should stay home, and you and Mr. Crowley should go. I'd hate to be contagious and give everyone the plague or something."

Miss Pramble did not believe her complaint for a second, knowing full well that if Jenny had been contagious, as angry as she looked now, she would have thrown her arms around his lordship and kissed him full on the lips, just to be sure that the poor man took sick! "I won't hear of it, Jenny. You're not at all ill. You have been invited, and you shall go. If not for your own sake, then for that of Quince House. Honestly. I don't know what the problem is between you and Lord Bradford, but I must insist that you take yourself in hand!"

"But what would I wear on this outing with Lord Bradford's fancy fiancée?" Genevieve protested feebly.

Miss Pramble shook her head. Unless she was firm, Genevieve would pine away in Quince House forever, growing old and childless. "It doesn't really matter what you wear, Jenny, since you are lovely enough to outshine any other woman even if you sported sackcloth and ashes."

Her stern but gentle voice reminded Genevieve that her governess often knew best. And there was wisdom to her proposal. "Oh, all right," Genevieve sighed wearily. "But would you please bring me a headache powder? Now I truly am in pain." She turned away and finished dressing her hair before going about her morning chores.

"It is almost time for you and Mr. Crowley to walk over to Bradford Hall," said Miss Pramble, gaily a few hours later.

"Oh, Pramble! Must I?" Genevieve groaned.

The governess laughed. "Yes, you must. After all, you wouldn't want to hurt my feelings by refusing to wear my gift, would you? I have been working on it for quite some time."

"Gift? What gift?" Genevieve demanded, curious.

"Come to your chamber and see," said Miss Pramble smugly.

They hurried upstairs, and there, spread across Genevieve's bed was a brand-new riding habit of rich periwinkle-blue. A new pair of boots and gloves also waited for her to try them on. "Oh, Pramble!" the girl cried. "They're beautiful! Thank you!" The governess beamed as Genevieve hurriedly undressed, then slipped the garment over her head. When she was dressed she turned to the cheval glass nervously. The habit was a perfect fit, as were the new black riding boots.

"There is one other thing," Miss Pramble said softly, producing a hatbox from its hiding place under the bed.

Genevieve's eyes glittered with unshed tears at Miss Pramble's huge generosity as she drew the new bonnet from its bed of gauze. It, too, was periwinkle-blue, and sported a jaunty white ostrich feather against its wide brim. A broad ribbon of ice-blue satin, tied in a showy bow against her cheek, complemented her red curls. From the back a wide veil of pale-blue Brussels lace draped elegantly down her shoulders and back. She spun around gaily. "Oh, Pramble! It's the most beautiful habit I've ever seen. How can I possibly thank you?"

A soft, tender smile curved the governess's lips as she handed Genevieve her matching kid gloves. "Just be happy, my dear."

17

Genevieve could not help the warm glow of satisfaction she felt when she met Mr. Crowley at the stables and saw his eyes light up with appreciation at her appearance.

"Miss Quince!" Mr. Crowley said reverently. "You look stunning!"

"Thank you, sir," she replied, a blush staining her cheeks. "Shall we go?" She reached for Storm's reins, as he had been kind enough to saddle the mare, and they headed down the drive.

"We have a fine day for a ride," Mr. Crowley observed, stopping to pluck some bright-blue forget-me-nots as they approached Bradford Hall, where Lord Bradford and Lady Westwood stood outside awaiting them.

Miles's eyes narrowed angrily as he watched the unknown man tuck the spray of blossoms behind Jenny's bonnet ribbon in a manner he deemed far too familiar.

Lady Westwood hid her fury behind a placid smile, wondering, as she fumed, what had become of the little country mouse Sebastian had told her about. This chit was dressed to the nines, and Sebastian looked positively smitten! She glanced down at her own habit of pale-rose wool and patted her immaculate pink bonnet and veil to assure herself that she outclassed the wench.

Cursing silently as she assessed the overly young beauty, Sabrina hated Miles Bradford even more than she had before. She did not miss the angry gleam in his eye as he watched Sebastian touch the girl's hair, and she was glad that she had finally decided on a plan of action. "My lord," she murmured softly, taking Miles possessively by the arm and leading him down the steps, "shall we go down to meet your guests?" She was gratified by the tightening of his arm against hers and the brilliant smile he flashed down at her.

"Certainly, my dear," he replied amiably.

Damn you, Jenny, Miles fumed silently as he made the introductions. *You're behaving like a trollop.* Quite deliberately he became much more attentive to Lady Westwood than he cared to be, touching her at every opportunity when he sensed Jenny was watching him as he and Lady Westwood led the way to the other three mounts.

There was Fury, of course, as well as Imp for Lady Westwood—and an ancient, broken-down hack for Mr. Crowley. Miles noted with pleasure the dismay on the other man's face as he considered his mount.

Then Mr. Crowley considered Miles. "How kind of you to choose such a gentle steed for me, Lord Bradford. A practiced horseman I must confess I am not." He ignored the surprised glance from Genevieve, who was well aware that he took Storm, an extremely challenging mount, out riding every chance he got.

As the two couples cantered toward the woods at the edge of Bradford Hall, Genevieve found herself worrying about Storm and whether her cousins had yet returned to London and discovered the mare was missing. The mare *and* the money she had borrowed in their name. But the day was too splendid—and Genevieve too determined to show Miles Bradford that she did not care a fig for him—for her to dwell on the matter overly long.

Lady Westwood and Mr. Crowley chatted amiably, their horses slightly ahead of the other two. Lady Westwood smiled frequently at Miles and he rewarded her with his slow, lazy, flattering grin.

Slut, Genevieve thought savagely of Lady Westwood, all the while beaming fondly at Mr. Crowley.

Commoner, Miles fumed of dandy-handsome Crowley. The man had noticed that his mount was less than equal to the others, but, instead of becoming angry, he had acted as if Miles had done him the greatest favor in the world. Probably couldn't tell good horseflesh from dog meat, Miles thought.

Fake, Lady Westwood raged to herself. Obviously, pretty Miss Quince was out to capture Lord Bradford. The way she avoided his eyes—a certain ploy to get his interest. She wished *she* had thought of it. Perhaps she had been too available. A man like Miles Bradford was likely to need a challenge.

Bastard, snarled Mr. Crowley inwardly of Lord Bradford. Beneath the leather saddle the horse's backbone, bony and uncomfortable, pressed insistently into his crotch. Unable to take revenge, he simply smiled gratefully at Miles, patting the nag as if to show his great appreciation.

In the shuffle of horses and smiles and charming chitchat, Lady Westwood and Mr. Crowley ended up several lengths ahead of their companions after a while, but both were assured of their partner's affections by the effusive smiles bestowed upon them each time they happened to glance back.

They could not hear the angry words passing between Miles and Genevieve.

"What the devil do you think you're doing?" Miles snapped, glaring at the girl riding at his side.

Genevieve's eyes whipped up to meet his, blazing blue fire. "I fail to see where whatever I do is any business of yours, my lord," she said icily before returning her gaze to the fore once again. Their companions drew farther away.

"I suppose you think it of no concern to me that you are acting like a trollop in front of my fiancée."

"Your fiancée? Ah, another one, my lord? You do seem to have the most difficult time hanging on to them, don't you. I suppose it is due to your terrible temper. Or perhaps your lack of tact." Genevieve smiled at him nastily.

"Hold your tongue, Miss Quince. You may go too far. Of course, there is nothing at hand for you to throw at me, and with your paramour nearby, I suspect you would not risk a tasteless display of violence that might put him off."

Genevieve glared at him. "Is that a challenge, my lord?" In a flash she produced the braided leather riding crop concealed by her skirts.

Like lightning Lord Bradford's hand caught her wrist, twisting it deftly to secure the offending instrument. "Damn you, Jenny!" he ground out, leaning to jerk her from her saddle, bend her over his knee, and give her the spanking she deserved. Instead, however, he found himself cradling her in his arms, holding her slender body tightly against him.

Genevieve struggled for a moment but, then went still. "You simply cannot leave me alone, can you, my lord?" she said softly, her huge eyes filling with tears as bright as diamonds. "Here you are, with yet another fiancée in tow, and yet still you try to claim a mistress. You are despicable, sir, and I cannot imagine why I was so insane as to come on this ride with you. I suppose I am just weak. I cannot deny that I am in love with you, but it is too cruel of you to treat me like your whore."

"Mistress?" Miles gasped. "Is that what you thought I wanted, Jenny? Dear God, no, my sweet, fiery, tempestuous beauty! I wanted you to *marry* me. Oh, Jenny, did I hear you say you loved me?" Without even waiting for her response, he groaned, crushing her lips against his own.

Genevieve trembled under the intensity of his kiss, feeling as if he were taking possession of her very soul. A soft cry of delight escaped her, and she thought she would die of pleasure.

His kiss finally softened, and he leaned away and gazed deeply into her eyes.

"Jenny," he repeated in a shaky whisper. "Marry me, Jenny. Let me make you my wife, not my mistress. I would never sully you in such a manner, my little darling. Can you forgive me for my rash comments in the past?"

Genevieve gave a joyful laugh and threw her arms around his shoulders. "Oh, yes, Miles!" she cried, pulling his face back to hers with a tearful smile. "But only if you can forgive me for hitting you in the head!"

Lord Bradford did not reply. Instead he kissed her desperately once more. Finally rationality returned, and with a final kiss he reluctantly replaced Genevieve on Storm's back. "I do not want you compromised this time, Jenny," he explained. "I want to marry you with pomp and ceremony, not because Society deems it proper."

He urged their mounts forward, and no sooner had they rounded a clump of trees than they saw

Lady Westwood and Mr. Crowley merely thirty feet ahead. With a final, mutually affectionate glance, the lovers joined their companions.

Lady Westwood had pulled her mount to a slow walk the moment she became aware that Miles and Miss Quince were no longer with them, and now a quick glance told her that all she suspected was true. Miss Quince was practically glowing, and Lord Bradford looked as if he would far rather be in the bushes tending to his lovely little country miss than riding sedately along with herself and Mr. Crowley. Immediate action was necessary, for by the look on Lord Bradford's face, he might soon begin shouting his love for his little bumpkin chit aloud.

With a savage kick Lady Westwood brought the razor tips of her tiny silver spurs sharply against Imp's sides. The mare screamed in pain, rearing up on her back legs before bolting forward, almost knocking her rider to the ground. Lady Westwood clung frantically to the saddle horn. "Help! Help! She's bolted!" she cried in a mock-terrified voice.

Mr. Crowley looked pleasantly over at Miles, smiling slightly. "I cannot hope to catch her, my lord. You must save her."

Miles kicked Fury into a run, streaking after the runaway mare.

Lady Westwood leaned over the pommel, urging Imp to gallop faster, faster. They flew past bushes and trees, over stone fences, beneath low-hanging branches, and through rushing streams. Not far behind she could hear the thundering hooves of Lord Bradford's mount. She yanked her hat from her head, tossing it carelessly onto the ground. Then she rounded a hill, drew Imp to an abrupt standstill, and leaped from the mare's heaving, white-flecked back.

"Go!" she snapped, smacking the horse on the

withers with her open hand before carefully rip-
ping the bodice of her gown from neckline to
waist, exposing her full white breasts and falling
gracefully into a crumpled, dainty heap on the
fresh spring grass. She barely had time to arrange
her skirts so that she showed a fair amount of
shapely ankle before his lordship was upon her.

He barely missed trampling her. If not for Fury's
quick, instinctive swerve, Lady Westwood truly
would have had a fatal accident. However, the
horse reared to a stop as Miles yanked on the
reins. He jumped off and hit the ground at a run.
"Lady Westwood! Sabrina! Are you all right?" he
asked worriedly, kneeling beside her and cradling
her head on his knees. He leaned closer, examining her face for signs of life.

Lady Westwood moaned softly and opened her
green cat's eyes. Her lips parted slightly, and her
hands snaked up behind his neck, tugging his
head down until his mouth covered hers. Just
then, as fate—or, more specifically, a carefully arranged plan—would have it, Genevieve and Mr.
Crowley galloped into view.

Miles jumped back as if bitten by a viper, his
eyes bright with sudden comprehension as he noticed her torn bodice and realized what she had
done. He growled with rage, leaping to his feet
and dragging her with him.

Lady Westwood gave a skillful whimper, covering her breasts with her hands. "No, my lord!" she
cried in a trembling voice. "Please, no more! I
came to your home at your request to find a husband, not a rapist! Please, my lord, let me be!"
From her flushed cheeks to her heaving bosom
and her raven curls tumbled in disarray around
her face, she was the picture of an exquisite victim
of unbridled male lust.

Miles's eyes widened in horror, and he turned to

where Genevieve sat, stricken, on Storm's back, her blue eyes clenched shut with pain. "Jenny, let me explain." he gasped, abruptly releasing Lady Westwood's arm.

"I refuse to listen to any more of your *explanations*, my lord," Genevieve spat brokenly, casting him one last devastated look before turning her mount and kicking Storm into a gallop.

Nearby Mr. Crowley looked on. "I trust you intend to do the right thing by Lady Westwood, my lord?" he asked stiffly. Miles looked at him blindly, and Crowley continued. "For if you do not, I shall be forced to spread the tale of your violent nature all over England. I will return Lady Westwood to Bradford Hall, since I am certain that she has had enough of your company for one afternoon, and from there I will continue on to London, where I will watch the *Times* for your wedding announcement, just to make certain you take the proper action." He climbed down from the hack, carefully lifted Lady Westwood into his arms, and placed her on the horse's back. Without a backward glance, he led her away.

A shaft of pain so intense that he did not know if he could bear it shot through Miles's heart, and he sank down to the ground with a groan, head in his hands.

18

Genevieve rode hard, barely noticing the mare's steaming flanks. Blinded with tears, she relied upon Storm to find her way back to the stables at Quince House. Once there, she slid numbly from the saddle, removed her riding tack, and rubbed the hot mare down with a towel.

"I'm sorry, Storm," she whispered sorrowfully as she daubed the white flecks from the mare's mouth and neck. Then she began sobbing as if her aching heart had burst, and she sank down into the hay beside the mare, crying herself into exhaustion. At last she fell into a deep, dreamless sleep.

Some time later she awakened with a start, and her ears strained for the sound that had drawn her from the depths of slumber. Storm stamped impatiently, hungry for her ration of oats. Genevieve got up slowly, brushing stray bits of hay and straw from her skirt. There was that rumbling again. What on earth? She walked to the stable door and gazed out onto the Dunheath road. And what she saw made her heart freeze in mid-beat.

A gleaming black carriage was sweeping noisily toward the house. Although she could not yet distinguish the crest on the side of the vehicle,

Genevieve knew without a doubt to whom it belonged. In another few seconds her fears were confirmed as the carriage, wheels crunching on the gravel drive, rolled to a stop. The tiger jumped down from behind and opened the door with a flourish.

A man and woman climbed out and stood just below the steps. The woman was glaring up at the refurbished house with open hatred. The man gazed around blankly. Then, as if her evil heart could feel Genevieve's presence, the woman turned and stared as Genevieve emerged from the stable and approached the house.

Lady Merriweather waited to speak until Genevieve was at her side. "Your father's solicitor told us where you were, Genevieve. Shall we go inside for a cold drink and a bite to eat while we decide what to do?" Cousin Marybelle turned and walked up the steps on Augustus Merriweather's expensively clad arm, not giving Genevieve a backward glance.

Genevieve followed, mute and dumb.

"The house is looking well," said Cousin Augustus heartily, smiling at Genevieve.

Genevieve felt wary of his praise; politicians were fulsome with compliments only when they wanted something.

"I was just telling dear Marybelle as we drove up that I fully expected to find you lonely and hungry, waiting to be rescued and eager to return with us to London."

At this Genevieve's hackles rose. "I assure you, Cousin Augustus, that I am in no way in need of your help, and even if I were dying of starvation, wild horses could not drag me back to London to act as your whore."

Cousin Marybelle gasped at her crude wording. "Truly, Genevieve, I must say that living in the country has not done your manners any good." she snapped, her cheeks flushed with anger. Her plum-colored gown with its gaudy copper braiding rustled as she settled her bulk onto the horsehair sofa in the salon, exposing an underskirt of turquoise silk.

"And I see that a trip to the Continent has not helped your sense of fashion any, Cousin Marybelle," replied Genevieve. "Now then, let us stop pretending that we can stand the sight of each other. Tell me what you want, and then get out of my home."

Her cousins' eyebrows rose in unison.

"Now, now, gel," said Augustus gruffly. "Is that any way to speak to your only living family?"

"I have no family." Genevieve stared, unrelenting, into his faded blue eyes until he looked away.

Cousin Marybelle rose heavily to her feet and turned her furious gaze on her young relative. "I had hoped to reconcile our differences in a hospitable manner, Genevieve. However, I see that you are determined to make this as difficult as possible. Therefore, I must demand that you repay all moneys you borrowed in our name, as well as my mare, Storm, immediately. If you cannot repay us, while it will break my heart to be forced into such action, I'm afraid I shall have to call in the local constable and have you arrested for thievery." She beamed triumphantly.

Genevieve smiled. "If you will wait just a moment, Cousin Marybelle, I will get your money so that you may be on your way. Storm is in the stable. She is in fine condition, I assure you." She turned abruptly and walked out of the room.

The tea canister, which held the extra butter and egg money, as well as the fee paid by the Featherweights, sat in its place on the cupboard shelf. Genevieve was so relieved that she had the funds with which to pay her cousins that she twirled around twice as she entered the kitchen. But as she reached up to grasp the canister, a feeling of foreboding came over her. Her fingers wrapped around the tin and pulled it from the shelf, but she heard no ringing, metallic sound of coins against metal. It was empty!

Her mind raced. Only that morning it had been nearly full of coins! Miss Pramble? Ridiculous! Why would she steal from her own partnership? Genevieve sank down into a chair, clutching the empty container in one hand and the edge of the table with the other. She turned at the sound of footsteps.

"Hello, Jenny dear," said Miss Pramble as she entered the room, a bucket of strawberries over her arm. She lowered the bucket to the table and sat down with a satisfied grunt. "My, but it's hot out there today. Did you have a nice ride? Where did Mr. Crowley go? All of his things are gone. He did remember to pay you, didn't he? Such a charming man he was. I felt sure that he was going to come to the point with you. I hope you are not too disappointed, my dear. Ah, well, perhaps he has only gone to London to buy you an engagement ring, eh?" She laughed happily.

Genevieve blanched, just as certain that Mr. Crowley had absconded with their funds as she was that the sun would rise on the morrow.

Miss Pramble's smile faltered as Genevieve slowly raised her stricken eyes. "Jenny? What is it? What has happened?"

"The money. It's all gone. Every last cent. Mr. Crowley, I assume." She shoved the empty tin toward the older woman.

Miss Pramble looked at the tea canister blankly and fell silent for a few moments. "Well," she said finally with a forced smile, "what we did once we

can do again. And next time we will not be so le-
nient with charming gentlemen. They will pay on
the day they arrive, or they will not stay." She
sighed. "No use crying over spilt milk, Jenny."

The girl sighed miserably. "That is not all,
Pramble. Even as we speak, Cousins Augustus
and Marybelle wait in the salon for their money.
You know I bought all our supplies on credit before leaving London."

"Dear God," the governess said as the serious-
ness of the situation hit her.

"Exactly. Well, I had better go give them the bad
news." Genevieve dragged herself to her feet.

Miss Pramble watched the girl walk dejectedly
from the room, wishing there was some way to
help. If only *she* had a bit more money!

Genevieve's cousins glanced up expectantly as
she entered the salon. She noted that Augustus
had made free with the brandy they kept in a crystal decanter for their male guests.

"Well?" said Marybelle. "Where's my money?"

"I haven't got it. I'm afraid our last guest, one
Mr. Crowley, has made off with every penny we
had. If you will be patient, I promise I will have
your money within the month."

Augustus busily tossed back the last of the
brandy, and a delighted smile graced Marybelle's
homely face. "I see. And what can you offer us as
collateral while we wait?" she asked, an unpleasant gleam in her eyes as they wandered freely
over Genevieve's young, lush body.

"Collateral?"

"You cannot expect us to leave with nothing."

"But I have nothing, cousin. Surely you can find
it in your heart to grant me one month." Genevieve's blue eyes pleaded eloquently.

Marybelle laughed mirthlessly. "I assure you,

Genevieve, you have something that will do nicely as collateral."

"I don't understand," she said hesitantly.

"You will return with us to London. I am sure if you are willing to work in our house, as we agreed before dear Augustus and I left on our trip, for a month, we would be more than happy to grant you the time. For that matter," she said with a generous nod, "we would be willing to forget the money altogether."

"You cannot be suggesting—"

"Ah, can I not?" Marybelle smiled, showing her yellowed teeth.

"I won't do it. You will have to throw me into debtors' prison first!"

"Very well," said her cousin. "You *and* your dear Miss Pramble will rot in prison."

"What has Miss Pramble to do with this?" Genevieve demanded. "She has done nothing!"

"Hasn't she? Why, I was under the impression that she, too, was living here. At least so your father's ex-solicitor opined. A partner in crime, shall we say? At the very least she has aided and abetted a criminal."

Genevieve's mind spun.

"Now, dear, don't look so glum. After all, I have only your happiness in mind, even if you do not believe me," Marybelle said.

"No! I will get your money. I can have it by tonight!" It would be horrible and degrading, but she would borrow it from Lord Bradford, Genevieve thought with a sick lurch. Given the nasty evidence of his lustful nature she had recently had the misfortune to glean, he, too, might demand the ultimate favor in return, but *once* with him could not be as humiliating as a month of playing harem-girl for the Merriweathers. Besides, perhaps the sultry Lady Westwood would keep him too occupied to stray.

Cousin Marybelle grunted, her chubby face twisted into a sneer. "Spare us, Genevieve. You and I both know that I will not rest until you are back under my roof in London. Even if you came up with three times the amount, I could still have you arrested for horse thievery."

Genevieve sank into a chair, refusing to cry although tears pricked her eyes. "I see."

"Good. Now then, run along and pack your things. Augustus and I shall have your dear Miss Pramble make us some tea, just to make certain that you and she don't take it into your minds to run off before our business is settled." Satisfied that the matter was taken care of in her favor, Marybelle lumbered out of the room, calling Miss Pramble.

Now that the brandy was gone, Augustus turned his attention to his lush young cousin. "Ah, my dear," he said cheerfully, his eyes lingering on her full breasts, "it will be so pleasant to have you home again."

Genevieve ran from the room with a stifled sob.

Cousin Marybelle managed to keep Miss Pramble away from Genevieve until they were ready to leave. Now the traveling party stood by the carriage on the drive, ready to embark. Storm whinnied and tugged at the rope that held her tied behind the vehicle.

"Jenny, are you sure you must go?" asked Miss Pramble, her eyes clouded with concern.

Genevieve would not look at her. Cousin Marybelle had told her in no uncertain terms that if she so much as shed a tear at their departure, Miss Pramble would be arrested without further adieu. "Yes, Pramble, I must."

The governess watched the carriage roll down the driveway and turn onto the road. Then she turned decisively and walked toward Bradford Hall.

19

S omething was wrong. Something was terribly
  wrong. Amelia Bradford said as much to her
companion and long-standing admirer Lord
Stanfield as they sat down to enjoy an after-dinner
drink.

She had, of course, heard about the scandalous
bride lottery her son had engaged in. While not
approving of his methods, she had been too eager
to see him wed to interfere. Now, however, was
another story altogether, for dark whispers and
her mother's intuition told her that Miles's plan
had gone awry.

"What could it be, Amy?" Lord Stanfield asked
with concern. He had loved Lady Bradford since
his best friend, the late Lord Bradford, had
snatched her up from a crowd of debutantes and
married her when the girl was barely seventeen.
He himself had never married, remaining devoted
to Miles's mother for the fifty years he had known
her.

"I do not know, Reggie," Lady Bradford said
worriedly, wringing her hands. Her ivory cheeks
looked paler than usual, and Lord Stanfield
clasped her fingers in his own, chafing them to

warm the chilly flesh. "I only know that Miles is in some kind of trouble, and I must go to him."

She looked up at Lord Stanfield with eyes the color of spring rainclouds, and he managed somehow to smother the urge to ask her to marry him again, as he did so often. For now she needed firm resolve, not romance. And perhaps if he could prove his usefulness, she would accept his suit later on. "How may I help you, Amy?" he asked.

She smiled at him through unshed tears, squeezing his hands. "You are such a good friend, Reggie."

Lord Stanfield's heart constricted. He hated it when she said that. "I want to be much more, Amy," he said stiffly. "But I will not press you now. If you need my help, I am, as always, at your service."

Lady Bradford looked at him. Then she shook her head. "No, Reggie. Not this time. I will handle this alone. I have already instructed my maid to pack a bag, and I intend to go to Bradford Hall this evening."

Lord Stanfield turned stubborn. "I will not allow it, Amy. You cannot go racing about the countryside by yourself, especially if you think there is some danger involved. I am coming with you." He held up his hand. "No! Do not say anything. Either I accompany you, or I do not allow you to go. Do you doubt that your servants would stop you if I so warned them? They love you as much as I do, and I know that they will help contain you, if need be."

He looked so imperious that Lady Bradford lowered her eyes demurely and nodded her acquiescence. "All right, Reggie. But we must leave as soon as possible. And, Reggie?" she said, looking up at him. "Thank you."

Lord Stanfield stood and proffered his arm to

help her to her feet. They walked from the room together, and Lord Stanfield watched her ascend the grand staircase to her chambers. A crook of his finger brought the butler to his side. "I do not want her going out of this house until I return, Hawkins. It is a matter of her safety. Do you understand?"

The butler nodded, willing to go over his mistress's head only because he trusted this gentleman who loved her so much.

"Good man," Lord Stanfield said, and he turned and hurried out to his carriage. "Go!" he snapped to the coachman. "We must get home and back within half an hour. I don't want Lady Bradford leaving for the country without me, and if I know Amy, she will try to do exactly that. Stubborn woman." The coachman snapped the reins.

True to his word, Hawkins managed to keep Lady Bradford standing in the hall, bag packed, until Lord Stanfield returned with his carriage. Reggie could hear sharp words being exchanged as he dismounted from the vehicle. He took a deep breath, preparing for the storm to hit him full in the face when he opened the door.

"Reginald!" cried Lady Bradford furiously. "How could you? How dare you instruct my servants to disobey me? As for you, Hawkins, you may find yourself another position, for you are not welcome in my home after this!" She stamped her gold-tipped cane on the floor fiercely before stalking past Lord Stanfield and allowing the tiger to help her into the carriage.

Lord Stanfield shook his head grimly.

"Bring her back married, my lord. She needs you," Hawkins said in a moment of uncharacteristic bluntness.

"I need her, too, Hawkins. I shall do my best."

They shook hands, and Lord Stanfield stepped off the landing and into the carriage.

Lady Bradford refused to look at him, gazing stonily out the window into the darkness as they rolled down the street and out toward the countryside. In her traveling gown of mulberry corduroy, she looked like a betrayed queen on her way to her execution, Lord Stanfield mused with a quiet chuckle.

Fortunately for him, Lady Bradford was not ordinarily of such a sour disposition, and it was not long before the sun began to shine behind her stormy eyes. After all, they were on an adventure. A serious one, surely, but an adventure nonetheless.

After traveling for two hours she turned to her companion. "I wish I had thought to bring something to eat," she said with a rueful grin. "I was so worried about Miles during dinner that I scarcely ate a bite."

Lord Stanfield nodded with a smile and stood, leaning over in the low-roofed carriage. "Yes, I noticed. Never fear. Have I ever failed to take good care of you, Amy? How can you doubt me now?" He lifted the leather seat, exposing an inner compartment from which he drew a large rattan basket.

Lady Bradford's eyes widened, and when he opened the package, she beamed like a schoolgirl.

"What would you like, my lady? We have cold chicken, sliced beef, fresh strawberries, apple puffs, cheese, and a bottle of fine Burgundy wine."

Lady Bradford clapped her hands together delightedly, and Reginald was happy to see the worried, peaked look leave her face, if only for a little while. He served her royally, pleased that the strong wine was bringing color to her cheeks. At last they both leaned back, sated.

"I'm stuffed, Reggie," Lady Bradford announced, the heady wine relieving her of Society's standards for polite conversation.

Lord Stanfield laughed. "So am I. Fine dinner, fine company, and fine wine. Lovely combination. By the way, Amy, have I told you lately that I love you?" He could have kicked himself the instant the words escaped his mouth. He was relieved when the lady merely laughed.

"Many times, Reggie. If not in words, then in actions."

Heartened by her statement, Lord Stanfield pressed on. "If I help you discover whatever it is that threatens Miles, would you do something for me, Amy?"

Lady Bradford giggled, then clapped a mortified hand over her mouth to stop the girlish sound. She thought hard for a moment. "Well, I suppose that if you do help me save my son from harm, then I should do for you whatever you desire, shouldn't I?" she mused with a tipsy smile.

"I should think so. Have I your word on it, then?"

"If it would make you feel any better about it, Reggie, then perhaps we should draw up a contract." She giggled again.

"Splendid idea," he said, pulling a cotton napkin from the picnic basket. "I shall write it down here, and you will sign it. Good enough?" He pulled a quill and ink pot from a hidden compartment and proceeded to pen the agreement on the fabric. Then he held out the pen to Lady Bradford, who had vacated her side of the carriage and now sat next to him. A flicker of uncertainty passed over her beautiful features, but Reggie hurriedly poured a bit more Burgundy into her glass, urging her to drink.

You're an underhanded cad, Reggie, he told himself. But he had a promise to keep to Hawkins.

Couldn't have the poor fellow losing his position because of obeying the man he thought was to be his new master, now could he?

After taking another sip of wine Lady Bradford signed the napkin with a grand flourish and handed the pen back to Lord Stanfield. Then she promptly drooped against his shoulder, fast asleep. Lord Stanfield smiled to himself, blew on the ink until it was dry, and, after folding the napkin carefully and placing it in his pocket, draped an arm over her shoulder and joined her in dreamland.

They rolled into the yard of Bradford Hall in the wee hours of the morning. The crunching gravel roused the sleepers, and they looked at each other blearily.

"Oh, my head, Reggie!" groaned Lady Bradford. "I believe I overindulged in your fine Burgundy."

Lord Stanfield chuckled sympathetically. "Come along, my dear. Let us go inside and put you to bed. There will be plenty of time tomorrow to sort out whatever is amiss." He took her by the arm and helped her gently out of the carriage. They walked up the steps stiffly, feeling their years, and knocked loudly on the door. After several more minutes of knocking and waiting, the door finally swung open.

"'Oo the divil are 'ee?" snapped the woman who opened it.

The *woman?* Lady Bradford stared in surprise. "I beg your pardon?" she said haughtily, sweeping into the hall. "Where is Benson? Where is Lord Bradford? I demand to see my son at once!"

The strange woman's eyes narrowed. "If 'ee will wait in the paller, I'll get the missus." She scurried away.

Lord Stanfield and Lady Bradford looked at

each other in shocked silence. Then they walked toward the parlor as the rude maid had instructed.

Lady Westwood's maid raced to alert her mistress, whose expression sharpened angrily at the news of the visitors. Quickly she strode to her bureau, opened a drawer, and extracted the small derringer she had placed there. She dropped it into the pocket of her dressing gown and went downstairs. She could hear the visitors' voices as she approached the parlor.

"Just what in heaven do you think is going on, Reggie?" said the woman.

"I don't know, Amy. But I promise that we will get to the bottom of it."

Lady Westwood stepped into the room. Two faces turned toward her. "Welcome to Bradford Hall," she said sweetly. "I am afraid you have missed Lord Bradford, as he is on a brief trip to London, but I am his fiancée, Lady Westwood."

Lady Bradford jumped up from the sofa, her eyes wide. A shrewd glance told Lady Westwood all. The lady was Miles's mother, and she *knew*.

"Lady Westwood? The widow?" Lady Bradford said with blatant disbelief. "But Lady Westwood was nearly sixty and is—"

"That is quite enough, my lady," said Sabrina, calmly pulling the derringer from her pocket and aiming its deadly nose toward the elderly couple. "If you would be so kind as to come with me. Silently," she warned. She gestured toward the hall. Shocked but left with no choice, Lord Stanfield and Lady Bradford went in the direction indicated.

They were taken far upstairs and to a remote wing of the maids' quarters. In a tiny room with gabled ceilings and a low, narrow cot, the sourfaced maid reappeared to gag and bind them hand and foot under the direction of her mistress.

"Don't attempt anything stupid," said Lady

Westwood coldly. "I have killed once; I will not hesitate to kill again. I'd do away with you now, but I may need hostages later," she added blandly. Then the two women were gone, and the two prisoners huddled together on the mattress in the darkness.

Downstairs, Lady Westwood saw Sebastian Crowley, who had just returned to the Hall after his brief visit to London. "Ah, Sebastian. Good. I trust you had no trouble procuring a willing but still legitimate priest?"

"You wound me, Sabrina my love. Have I ever failed you?" he asked. "And now, even though I have not yet shaken the dust off my travels from my feet, there is something I hunger for even more urgently than food or drink."

Lady Westwood's lips turned up slightly as Sebastian took her by the hand and led her to her bedchamber. "Well now," she murmured huskily as the door closed behind them, "I cannot be so heartless as to let a starving man go hungry, can I?"

20

Miles peered intently into the mirror on his bureau. He looked impeccable, from the brand-new coat of black superfine to the stark white cravat tied in the Mathematical. His breeches were of charcoal wool, and his boots gleamed from the champagne polishing the footman had given them. He brushed a speck of lint off his sleeve and ran a monogrammed boar-bristle brush through his hair one final time.

Then he turned gravely to his valet, whose face registered naked concern. "I will bring her back safely, Benson."

"I hope so, sir. God keep you safe."

Miles moved from the bedchamber of his London town house and down the stairs.

The carriage that awaited him gleamed as brightly as his boots. It, too, was black, a shining, laquered town coach that was saved for special occasions requiring pomp and ceremony. On its door the Bradford crest shone in gold leaf. The two identical white stallions that drew it stamped impatiently, snorting with spirit and eager to be on their way. Miles nodded to the liveried tiger who held open the carriage door, then stepped inside and sat down on the padded leather seat.

Earlier that day, when Miss Pramble had burst in upon him with her tearful exclamations, he had been in his library at Bradford Hall, ruminating on his upcoming marriage to what had proven to be a she-wolf in sheep's clothing. Damn the woman! he had been thinking. No, damn him for falling for her trick! Miss Pramble's appearance in his private sanctuary had taken him completely by surprise.

"My lord! You must do something!" she had gasped, clearly distraught.

"For God's sake, woman, what on earth is the matter?" he had demanded, rising from his desk to help her to a chair by the immense fireplace. She was trembling.

"It's Jenny! She's gone away!"

For one horrible moment Miles was certain the girl had eloped with the despicable Mr. Crowley, who had disappeared shortly after seeing the future Lady Bradford back to the Hall, undoubtedly having gone to London to spread the tale of Miles's shame. Annoyance flashed over his features, and his mouth twisted into a wry smile.

"I fail to see what that has to do with me, Miss Pramble. Surely a woman eloping with her beloved is cause for celebration, not tears." His words brought the woman's head up with a snap.

"Elopement? What do you mean?"

"Come now, Miss Pramble. Have you not come to tell me of Miss Quince's departure with the estimable Mr. Crowley?" One eyebrow arched in sarcasm. "I realize you had hoped that I would wed Miss Quince, but can I help it if she prefers that ignoble fop?"

Miss Pramble's face darkened angrily, and she jumped to her feet. "My lord, Miss Quince has not eloped with that—that vagabond Mr. Crowley. Why, the dastard made off with every penny we

had!" Her eyes flashed. "Jenny's cousins, Lord and
Lady Merriweather, arrived only an hour ago, and
they have taken Jenny away with them. I can only
surmise it was under duress, although she did not
tell me so."

Miles's eyes widened, but then his face fell.
"Forgive me, Miss Pramble, but I fear there is little
I can do. I begged Jenny to marry me, and she
agreed, but then she saw something during our
ride she did not understand, and she probably
chose to leave Quince House posthaste. God
knows she had good cause."

His voice was raw with emotion, and his silver
eyes sparkled momentarily with what Miss
Pramble would have sworn were unshed tears. He
turned toward the window.

"I do not understand, my lord."

"No, why would you? Clearly Jenny did not tell
you what happened. To cut to the bottom of the
tale, I am to be wed to Lady Westwood very soon.
Suffice it to say that Jenny found the situation intolerable. But not, I assure you, as intolerable as I
find it myself."

Miss Pramble took a deep breath. She walked
forward and placed her hand on Lord Bradford's
arm hesitantly. "My lord. I hope you will forgive
me for what I am about to say. I do not know your
reasons for marrying Lady Westwood, but I do
know that Jenny loves you, probably even more
than she realizes herself. You must go after her. I
know that she would not have returned to London
with the Merriweathers of her own accord. Why
would she choose to be their whore, if you will
pardon my bluntness," she said boldly, "when she
loves you? I am certain that even if you must
marry Lady Westwood, Jenny would rather die
than lose you, even if it meant becoming your mistress. I know her. I raised her from the time she

was a little girl. And I know she would never have gone with her cousins if she had a choice. My lord," she said urgently, "I only hope you can reach her before it is too late, because if another man touches her before you do, she will never be able to look you in the eye again."

Miles stifled an agonized groan. He turned slowly, and they gazed searchingly at each other. Then, without another word, Miles strode from the library and instructed Benson to pack his bags.

He had arrived in London barely an hour ago. Upon his arrival he had sent a concise, polite note to the Merriweather household, informing them of his interest in their guest and the time of his up-coming visit. Now he settled back against the leather squabs, hoping the Merriweathers would wait until he got there to sacrifice Jenny's virginity. He took a deep breath and prayed, as he had done incessantly since leaving Bradford Hall, that he would not be too late.

The note from Lord Bradford was causing a flurry of excitement in the Merriweather house-hold—at least downstairs. Marybelle rushed around triumphantly, waving the heavy piece of parchment in the air, her eyes gleaming. "You see? What did I tell you, Augustus? The political high-and-mighties are already flocking to have a taste of our luscious little cousin." She shook her head. "Honestly. Even those rich lords in the House are not above taking it when it's free. And if we did not take advantage of their greedy lust, then some-one else would. Just look here! Miles Bradford is probably the most important person in our gov-ernment, excepting the Prince himself! What a coup!" she chortled.

Augustus simply nodded and took another sip of brandy.

She continued. "Now then, you must hurry upstairs and read the comments I wrote down for you. You must shine during this dinner, Augustus! I will not have your ineptitude in politics ruin your only opportunity to change your current unpopularity into a brilliant career. I have worked too hard to lose all now."

Her husband grunted his distaste. "I hate social playacting, Marybelle. You know that! Why, I'd never even have chosen to go into politics if you had not insisted."

His wife glared at him. "Don't even think of backing out now, Augustus. I have managed everything to this point. Your part is simple. I have instructed your valet to lay out the right clothes. All you need to do is bring up the subjects I have written down, take my cue during the conversation, and let the promise of after-dinner sweets mellow our illustrious guest. Do not fail me! Now go!" she snapped, removing the glass from his hand and pushing his heavy body toward the door.

Lady Merriweather hurried upstairs to the suite where she had installed Genevieve. She removed a heavy gold skeleton key from the folds of her ruby satin gown and unlocked the door. She stifled an annoyed oath as she heard the sobs coming from the dimly lit bed, its curtains obscuring the girl who lay upon it.

"Get up, Genevieve. We are going to have company tonight, and I cannot have you looking wan. You must look cheerful for our guest. Look at you!" she complained as Genevieve sat up, revealing her pale, tear-streaked face. "You look revolting. Come on. We can do something with your hair, and my maid will bring us some face paints to remedy the ravages of this ridiculous tantrum. Honestly. Is this how you repay me for rescuing

you from certain starvation?" She jerked
Genevieve from the bed, holding on to her elbow
with a steely grip, and thrust her into a chair at
the bureau.

"Marie!" Lady Merriweather shouted through
the open chamber door. "Bring my face paints at
once!"

The new maid scurried into the bedchamber.

"Do what you can with her. I want her looking
as appealing as possible, despite her silly tears."
Lady Merriweather turned and opened a drawer.

Genevieve's and the maid's eyes widened as
they saw what she held.

"When you have cleaned her up, put her in this.
I want her ready by nine. If you fail, Marie, you
will be out of my house without a reference." She
stalked from the room.

At half past seven the bell sounded in the front
of the house. The butler opened the door solemnly
and led the esteemed guest into the parlor, where
his hosts waited anxiously. "My Lord and Lady
Merriweather, Lord Bradford," the butler intoned,
reading from the card Miles had handed him. He
bowed and disappeared, closing the doors behind
him.

Lady Merriweather stood up, smiling brilliantly.
"My lord," she gushed. "How delightful to have
you dine with us. We are honored by your presence."

Miles bowed, finding it difficult to summon up
the polite nothings Society demanded. But there
wasn't a doubt in his mind that if he made a single mistake, they would see through his ruse, and
he would never be permitted to see Genevieve.
Therefore, he swallowed the bitter disgust that
rose like gall in his throat as Lady Merriweather
took him by the arm and led him toward a sofa.

"Aren't we, Augustus?" she demanded of her husband, who merely nodded and grunted an indecipherable greeting. She glanced at him meaningfully. "Would you like a brandy before we dine, my lord?" she asked Miles sweetly. "No? Well then, shall we go in? Come, Augustus!" Still clutching Lord Bradford possessively by the forearm, she ushered him into the dining room.

Dinner was a difficult affair for Miles, who found the desire to wrap his long, aristocratic fingers around his hostess's thick neck and squeeze growing with each passing moment. Lady Merriweather babbled nonstop, eliciting only an infrequent nod of agreement from her husband, who was stuffing food into his mouth, jowls shuddering, as if it were his last meal.

Marybelle's ruby satin gown echoed the purple veins in her cheeks, indicative, Miles thought, of an overfondness for food and drink, which she was hiding for his benefit. Pity her husband could not keep his indulgence from sight, too, he mused, watching as a piece of chicken slid from his host's fork and dropped unnoticed onto his white lace cravat.

Somehow Lord Bradford managed to respond to Lady Merriweather's snoopy, probing questions about his political views. At last she regarded him coyly over her last bite of trifle.

"My lord, is the trifle not to your liking? You have not eaten much. Perhaps it is too rich for you, and a different kind of dessert is more to your taste." She winked at him, and Miles savagely thrust aside the desire to plunge a butter knife into her fleshy bosom.

Instead he looked at her with practiced detachment. "Perhaps, my lady. What did you have in mind?"

"My young cousin, Genevieve Quince," Marybelle simpered, "has come in from the country. They have different ways in the country, you know. I'm sure she would love to . . . talk . . . with you if you are quite finished with your supper." She raised her thin eyebrows in question.

"That has possibilities. Where is the lady? Why did she not come down to dinner?"

"She has been napping—in preparation for a long evening." She chuckled lasciviously, winking again. "Perhaps you would be willing to go upstairs to visit her."

"But of course," he replied smoothly, placing his napkin beside his plate and rising. "Now?"

"Ah, my lord," Marybelle giggled, "you are so eager to please the young lady? Of course. Now will be fine. Just go up the stairs. Hers is the fourth room on the right. You will need this." She held out the gold key, and once again Miles had to thrust aside a burning desire to crush the breath from Lady Merriweather's throat.

"Thank you," he murmured calmly, pocketing the key. He nodded politely in Augustus's direction and walked indifferently from the room. Once out of sight of the Merriweathers, Miles took the stairs three at a time, inwardly cursing. At last he came to the indicated door and slid the key into the lock. It turned easily, as if recently oiled, and he pushed the door open slowly. He stepped into the room.

Only his lightning reflexes saved his life as a brass poker descended rapidly toward his skull. The girl holding it cried out in pain as his deft fingers wrapped around her wrist and squeezed until she dropped the weapon. To Genevieve's amazement, the man who had entered the dimly lit room began to chuckle.

"Well met, Miss Quince," he said with humor. "It is a good thing, is it not, that I am acquainted with your habit of clubbing your enemies? Otherwise I would even now be lying dead on your rug, and you, no doubt, would be waiting for the magistrate to take you to Newgate."

"Miles!" she cried, throwing her arms around his neck.

Lord Bradford coughed as the terrified girl nearly choked off his windpipe. "I take it you are happy to see me?" he laughed. He felt the arms abruptly release him, and Jenny stepped away. His smile vanished as he saw the sudden hatred in her eyes as she jumped to an incorrect conclusion.

"I might have known that you would be the first. You take a fiancée, even against her will, then you decide to forego buying me as your mistress and take me free instead," she said scathingly.

Miles stepped forward, only to stop as the girl backed up to avoid his advance. She had moved into the glow of the firelight, and he caught his breath at the vision she made. His groin tightened automatically.

She was clothed, if one could call it that, in the most diaphanous garment he, a renowned rake accustomed to seductive mistresses, had even seen. The nightgown crossed over one shoulder, Grecian style, and was caught around her slender waist with golden cord. The garment's fabric was white gauze, so sheer that he could easily see her long, shapely legs and the dark, rosy circles of her nipples, not to mention the darker triangle between her legs. Her red hair, coiled atop her head with more golden cords, gleamed in the firelight.

"Jenny," he said shakily, gazing at her all but naked body.

"Don't come another step closer, you—you roué. I would rather die than have you touch me!" She had backed up to the window and now stood pressed against the thin pane.

"Jenny, come away from the window," Miles demanded, forcing his eyes to her face. "I promise I have not come to ravage you. I want to help you escape."

"Help me escape? Don't make me laugh," she gasped with a low sob. She pressed closer to the window, which creaked a warning.

"I swear to you, Jenny. I will not touch you." He turned his back. "Get dressed."

Her bitter laugh surprised him. "I am dressed, my lord. This is now the only article of clothing I possess. Don't you like it? Marybelle evidently selected it especially for you."

Miles swallowed hard against his hatred for Jenny's cousins. He thought swiftly and at last turned back toward her, carefully keeping his eyes averted. "I will wait for you downstairs. Someone will bring you a gown."

Without waiting for her response, he walked with new purpose from her bedchamber.

Lady Merriweather looked up with surprised dismay as Lord Bradford strode into the parlor, where she and Augustus were engaged in a game of whist. "My lord! Is something wrong? Is the girl not all you expected? Oh, dear. Is she giving you trouble? If you will give me but a moment, I will go up and talk some sense into her."

An images of Lady Merriweather beating vulnerable Jenny rose in Miles's mind, and he clenched his fists. "No trouble at all, my lady. In fact, just the opposite. I find that your country cousin pleases me so much that I have decided to take her with me. Name your price, madam." He watched her with carefully masked emotions.

Worry was replaced with greed as she comprehended his meaning. "Why, my lord, I don't know. She is, after all, my cousin, not a slave. How could I sell her to you? And even if I could, she is excep-

tionally lovely and would no doubt bring an ex-
traordinary sum in one of the more reputable
houses of pleasure here in London."

Her eyes gleamed expectantly, and Miles ignored the now-familiar desire to murder her. "I
must have her, my lady. I will pay whatever you
ask. Anything."

"Anything, my lord?"

"You heard me. Now name your price before I
lose patience and retract my offer." He turned
away impatiently as if that were exactly what he
intended to do.

"Wait!" Marybelle cried. "There may be a way
we can do business, Lord Bradford." He turned
back toward her. "Perhaps you will be willing to
put out a few good words about my husband in
your political circles?" He nodded. "And I want
five thousand pounds for the girl." She held her
breath. To her delight, he did not even flinch at the
astronomical sum.

Immediately Lord Bradford drew a cheque-book
from his pocket, wrote her a draft, and thrust it
into her grasping, eager hands. "Now then, get her
dressed," he demanded. "If she is not inside my
carriage within fifteen minutes, I will cancel the
cheque." Miles walked sedately out of the house
and entered the carriage as if he had no more on
his mind than purchasing a new hunter from
Tatterstall's.

The room exploded into a flurry of activity.
Cousin Marybelle nearly killed herself running up
the stairs, her heart pounding in her ears. She burst
in on Genevieve. In one hand she carried the girl's
threadbare traveling gown, in the other the cheque
she would not release even for a moment. "Get
dressed! You're going for a little ride. You are very,
very lucky, my girl. That handsome gentleman has

decided to take you with him. He paid me *five thousand pounds!*"

Genevieve gasped. Was there nothing the man would not stoop to? Her comment about taking her for free must have goaded him into this action. "I won't! I won't go with him!" she cried in anguish.

Cousin Marybelle's smile vanished. "You will, Genevieve. Do I have to call Augustus to help you? He's had his eye on you for quite a while. Perhaps he would enjoy a little time with you before you are gone forever."

In truth, she had no intention of allowing this to happen; she did not want to lose the five thousand pounds. Without waiting for Genevieve's response she left the room, slamming the door.

Trembling, Genevieve began pulling the dress on over her head.

Miles watched as his tiger handed the pale girl into the carriage. She huddled in a corner, eyeing him balefully. He gave her a small smile. "Excuse me for a moment, Jenny. There is something I must do before we depart." He stepped out of the carriage, then, turned back. "Don't try to run away. You are my property now, you know." He grinned, pretending not to notice that she did not share his joke.

He closed the carriage door firmly and walked back up the steps. The butler, who had not yet left the doorway, bowed and stepped aside. Miles walked swiftly down the hall to the salon. Before the footman could open the doors, he kicked them wide with one booted foot, startling Jenny's cousins, who were busy toasting each other over glasses of sherry.

"Just one thing," Lord Bradford said as they jumped to their feet. "If either of you ever mention this little arrangement to anyone, I will personally see to it that you not only lose everything you own, but also that you are thrown into prison for kidnapping. Do you understand?"

His words were like shards of ice. The two frightened people nodded silently, absolutely certain that the furious, forbidding gentleman meant every word.

Miles smiled coldly and bowed with mock politeness. "Good. Good night, my lord, my lady." Then he was gone.

"Stop shivering, Augustus," snapped his wife, cursing that he was no match for a man like Lord Bradford, who clearly terrified him. For a moment she felt a stab of envy shoot through her as she watched Miles stride manfully down the hall. Genevieve did not deserve such a prize.

But, Marybelle thought, she was now a very, very rich woman, and Genevieve didn't really matter anyway. Give Lord Bradford a year, and his lordship would have discarded the chit. She felt a certain satisfaction as she imagined Genevieve selling her body in the streets to survive. Who knew but that the girl would not even return in hopes of repeating her good fortune and nabbing yet another rich protector? With a smile, Marybelle ogled the cheque still in her hand.

Miles jumped up into the carriage, and it jerked forward. Genevieve refused to look at him. "Contrary to your beliefs, I am not going to have my wicked way with you. I am taking you to my mother's house here in London," he said to her averted face. No response. At last he sighed and laid his head back against the seat.

Genevieve watched as his eyes closed. After a while, believing him to be asleep, she allowed the burning tears that had been demanding release for so long to roll down her cheeks unchecked, but she held back the gulping sobs that ripped at her chest so as not to awaken Lord Bradford.

Through half-closed eyes, Miles watched her. In another fifteen minutes the carriage rolled to a halt, and he roused himself to disembark. He held out his hand to Genevieve who refused to take it. With an impatient sigh he grasped her elbow and forcibly removed her from the vehicle. "If you prefer, Miss Quince, I would be happy to find an out-of-the-way inn and do exactly what you are expecting me to do."

At this Genevieve practically hurtled from the carriage, and Miles stifled a laugh. They walked up the stairs and knocked on the door. It was opened by Hawkins, his mother's butler.

"Lord Bradford!" the butler said in surprise. "You are supposed to be in the country!"

"Where is my mother?" Miles demanded. "I have brought her a guest."

The butler frowned worriedly. "She is not here, my lord. She had gone to see you, at Bradford Hall. It seemed most urgent." Concern creased his brow.

Miles drew a deep breath and turned back to Genevieve. "I cannot leave you here unchaperoned, Jenny. You will have to come to Bradford Hall with me." Then he frowned. "On second thought, perhaps it would be better if you stayed here. If it was ever found out you had traveled alone with me, you would be hopelessly compromised. No man would ever have you."

Genevieve looked at him. "No, my lord," she said hastily. "I will go with you. I have no intention of marrying. All I want to do is to return to Quince House and take up my business there. Miss Pramble must be terribly worried."

"Indeed she is," he replied. At her startled look, he quizzed, "How else do you think I knew where to find you? I'm not in the habit of racing to London at top speed just for the sport of it, you know," he said dryly. "Very well, Miss Quince, we shall go. Although I must say that your eagerness to share my company is most suggestive. Come along." And with that he unceremoniously bundled her back into the carriage.

The chit was too uppity by far, he thought. He had saved her virtue, and she rewarded him by insisting he was a villain, he harrumphed. And then they were flying through the night, each mile bringing them closer to Bradford Hall.

21

It was dawn by the time they reached their destination. Genevieve woke suddenly as the carriage lurched in and out of a pothole. Her head jerked upright, and she almost burst into tears of gladness at being home again.

The early-morning sun shone on the shallow lake of Quince House. And there, on its surface, several baby swans meandered hither and thither, diving into the water in search of bugs and soft plants, their stubby tails pointed skyward.

"Oh, look!" she cried to Miles, pointing at the cygnets.

He grinned. "Do you like them? I asked Benson to find them weeks ago. They must have been delivered in our absence. I seem to recall your having mentioned a desire for swans."

Genevieve quickly realized that she had yet another thing to be grateful to Lord Bradford for. She frowned, a little abashed. "Thank you," she said stiffly, looking down at her clasped hands. As she did so, she became aware of the threadbare state of her gown, and her hair hanging limply over her shoulders. Why she should have cared, she could not imagine, but she suddenly wished desperately that she looked more attractive.

As if he could read her mind, Miles smiled at her gently. "You look beautiful," he said softly. Then he turned away as the carriage pulled up the drive of Bradford Hall. "Damnation!" he said sharply. "Either my coachman forgot you were here, or he is under the same mistaken impression that *you* are: that I am abducting you. I specifically indicated that you were to be left at Quince House." The carriage rolled to a stop, and Lord Bradford jumped out, prepared to give the remiss servant a piece of his mind. The words, however, froze on his tongue.

Genevieve stared at him curiously through the open carriage door. His face was set and determined, almost grim. "What is it? What is wrong?" she called.

"Stay there, Jenny. Do not get out of the carriage," he commanded.

"But she must get out, Lord Bradford. Both of you must come into the house with me," said another masculine voice.

Genevieve stepped out and raised her eyes toward the voice. Sebastian Crowley, a snub nosed revolver in his hand smiled down at her from atop an unfamiliar roan stallion.

"Miss Quince. How pleasant to see you again."

"You!" she cried furiously. "Stealing my money wasn't good enough for you? What is this all about? Just what do you think you're doing?"

Sebastian stopped smiling. "I don't know what you're talking about. I didn't steal anything from you. Now then," he said softly to the tiger and coachman, "get down slowly, and don't either of you try to be hero."

The two men jumped to the ground. Dismounting, Sebastian tossed Miles a length of rope. "Tie them up, my lord." He watched as Miles obeyed. Now he pointed the revolver at Lord Bradford. "Inside. Now."

The trio walked into Bradford Hall. Lady Westwood was waiting for them in the hallway. She smiled triumphantly as she saw Lord Bradford and Genevieve.

"How convenient that both of you should be here," she said evilly. "That will save me having to track down Miss Quince. Good work, Sebastian. Bring them into the parlor." She turned away, her ebony satin gown rustling softly against the floor. She looked beautiful but deadly, a black widow spider awaiting her victims.

Genevieve's eyes sought Lord Bradford's, and he smiled down at her reassuringly. Then Sebastian Crowley pressed the revolver into his back, and Miles moved after Lady Westwood.

"You'll be pleased to know that we have special guests for our wedding, my lord," she said to Miles as they entered the parlor.

Genevieve gasped. At the other side of the room, hands tied behind their backs, an elderly lady and gentleman sat helplessly watching the spectacle. The man bowed slightly to Miles, smiling faintly. "My son!" cried the woman, attempting to rise.

The maid, Crenshaw, shoved her back down.

"Our wedding?" Lord Bradford repeated wryly, nodding pleasantly to his mother and Lord Stanfield. "Do you really think I should wed a woman who has her lover hold me at gunpoint? Come now, Sabrina. Exactly what is going on here? Why are my mother and Lord Stanfield forced to attend our marriage?"

Lady Westwood glared at him. "You men always think you control everything, don't you, my lord? Well, I have a surprise for you. This time, you are going to do exactly as I tell you. A priest is waiting to perform the wedding ceremony, and soon I will be rid of you." She sneered at him. "No more silly rides in the country. No more of your patronizing smiles. How sick I am of you, my lord."

Miles raised his eyebrows emotionlessly. "If my presence is so distasteful to you, then why on earth would you want to marry me, my lady?" he said blandly.

Lady Westwood laughed dryly. "Very good question, my lord. If you must know, the truth of the matter is, I am, sad to say, going to be a widow very soon after our marriage. Immediately after, in fact."

Genevieve stifled a cry. "You can't get away with this!" she said desperately.

"Oh, can't I, my little country mouse?" asked Lady Westwood hatefully, her ruby lips drawn back in a snarl. "You will soon see that I always do exactly what I plan to do. And I intend to become a very rich widow."

"You are forgetting something, I believe, Lady Westwood," Miles said calmly.

The woman turned toward him with a sneer. "And what might that be, my high and mighty lord?"

"Our marriage will not be legal without having had the banns read for three consecutive weeks, or without a special license. I have no license, and I do not recall hearing the banns read."

Lady Westwood laughed wickedly. Reaching into the pocket of her gown, she waved a bit of paper in his face. "Never fear, my love, that our union would not be all that is proper. I have a special license right here. Sebastian got it for us, didn't you, my love?" She beamed at her lover. Then, without a backward glance, she turned toward the door and walked out. In a few moments she returned, the priest Sebastian had brought her in tow.

The clergyman either did not notice anything unusual or did not care. He seemed too hard-pressed to keep his drink-fogged eyes open, much less notice that the entire wedding party was being held at gunpoint. He looked blearily at the young couple. Lady Westwood had taken Miles by the elbow and led him to the fireplace. The priest pulled a battered black book from his cassock.

"Get on with it!" Lady Westwood growled as he searched for the right ceremony.

The priest did not seem to hear her, but for a split second Genevieve could have sworn that he looked at Sebastian and *smiled*.

"Dearly beloved," he intoned drunkenly, swaying as he peered at his book, "We are gathered here today to join these two people in the bonds of holy matrimony . . ."

"Can't we skip all this nonsense?" interrupted Lady Westwood. "We want to be married before we both die of old age!"

The priest cast her a surprised stare, then leered tipsily at Lord Bradford, who remained silent, his lips white and tense. "An eager one you have here, my lord," he said with a lewd chuckle. "Of course, madam, if that is what you wish. Now let me see, how does it go?" He stared off into space for what seemed an eternity. "Ah, yes. Ahem. Dearly beloved, we are gathered here . . ."

Lady Westwood sighed with irritation as the priest took up where he had left off, peering carefully at the book before him through wire-rimmed glasses and mumbling eloquent words for at least another fifteen minutes before coming to the vital part.

Miles growled his vows through his teeth, his

bride's derringer nudging him in one kidney. Lady Westwood spat hers.

Then the priest looked up, pausing for effect. "I now pronounce you man and wife!"

"Finally," Lady Westwood sneered with satisfaction.

"You may kiss the bride," the priest instructed Miles.

Lord Bradford glared at him. "Go to hell!" he snapped, eyebrows drawn together like storm clouds.

The priest's mouth popped open.

Sebastian Crowley smiled good-naturedly and took the aged holy man by the arm, leading him toward the sideboard for a well-deserved glass of brandy.

"Very good," said Sabrina with a tight smile. "Now then, shall we all adjourn to the stables? I believe we have a bit of unfinished business to conduct. I would like to have everything taken care of before dinner. I vow, I am famished." She waved the group out of the house with her derringer.

"A fire, I think, my lord," Sabrina said to her newly acquired husband when they had reached the stables. "Grab one of those lanterns," she said, gesturing with her gun.

Lord Bradford complied, reaching for one of the oil lamps that hung from a low beam.

"I'd as soon shoot you all, but I wouldn't want to worry the neighbors," she said maliciously, herding them into a corner. "Light the lamp, dearest Miles."

"I would, my dear, but I have nothing with which to light it," he responded blandly.

Genevieve stared at him, amazed at his fearlessness in the face of death. Truly, he was the bravest, most wonderful man she had ever known.

"Then I suggest you find something quickly, or I will be forced to shoot your little friend," Sabrina replied congenially, turning her gun toward Genevieve.

Miles drew in a sharp breath and pulled a flint from one of the bags that hung against the wall. He struck it, and the lamp flared into life, filling the area with an eerie glow. From the stalls the horses whinnied nervously.

"Come, Sabrina," Miles said softly, trying a last tactic. "You'd just as well give me the gun and have done. You'll never get away with this." He extended a hand and walked toward her slowly, his thunder-gray eyes locked on her glittering green ones.

"Get back!" she cried, thrusting the barrel of the gun at him. "I *will* shoot you if I have to!"

Miles saw Sebastian Crowley closely but passively watching them in the shadows outside.

"You don't have the guts, my girl," he said, trying to keep her talking long enough to think of a way out of their dilemma.

"Oh, don't I?" she cried angrily. "I'll have you know that it won't be the first time I have killed! Just ask your dear mother there! She knows all about me."

Miles looked at Lady Bradford, who nodded nervously.

"It's true, Miles. She is not Lady Westwood. I do not know who she is. The real Lady Westwood was over sixty years of age. I ought to know, as we were at school together."

"What do you mean?" Miles said, looking at his mother's wan face incredulously.

"Lady Westwood was murdered in Hyde Park a little over a month ago, a fact I am sure this"—she searched for an appropriate word, but settled for a scathing intonation—"*woman* hoped you did not know. Her body was found, but her maidservant and companion had disappeared entirely. The real Lady Westwood had been leaving for a trip to France. Everything she had with her was gone, too. All her clothes, her carriage, her jewels ..." Her voice trailed off meaningfully. "I believe that your wife is the companion, Miss Bentley, while her maid is—was—Lady Westwood's maid."

Suddenly Miles remembered reading about the murder the night he had accosted Jenny in her bedchamber.

"Not quite correct, dear lady," said Miss Bentley with an evil grin. "The maid was killed as well, but apparently her body disappeared in the Thames where Crenshaw and I dumped it. Crenshaw was just one of the undermaids who also happened to hate that old bat Lady Westwood." She smiled maliciously, glancing at Genevieve. "Crenshaw is also a superb thief."

Genevieve's eyes flew to the woman, who stood slightly behind Miss Bentley. So *she* had stolen the money from Quince House!

Miss Bentley chuckled as she saw realization dawn in Genevieve's eyes. "Yes, Miss Quince. Crenshaw got such pleasure from it that I saw no reason to stop her."

"But why did you decide to masquerade as Lady Westwood? Surely you knew you would be discovered sooner or later," Miles said dubiously.

"When word of your love-lottery method of procuring a bride way out here in the country reached my mistress's ears, she passed it along to me. I was so tired of always being the servant, never the mistress, and I decided that the venture would be worth the risk. I never planned to continue portraying Lady Westwood for long. Only until I had inherited your estates. Then I planned to take the money and go to America. And now," she said with a pleased sigh, "I am going to do just that."

"I see," said Miles, thoughtfully, rubbing his chin. "And who, pray tell, is Mr. Crowley?"

"He is my lover, as you assumed. I met him in London just after the murders, and he readily agreed to help with my plan. He is going to accompany me to America, where we will be wed." She half-smiled. "But enough talk. Into the corner, my lords and ladies."

The captive group stepped back nervously as she waved her gun.

"Not so fast, my love," said Mr. Crowley from the doorway, grinning. Behind him, the priest, all traces of drunkenness vanished, watched the goings-on. "I am afraid I have some bad news for you. You see, I am not really named Sebastian Crowley."

Miss Bentley gasped, waving the gun nervously back and forth from the larger group to the two men. "Stop joking, Sebastian. It isn't amusing!"

"My name is really James Debenham. I'm from Bow Street."

Genevieve gasped.

"Sorry to put you to so much trouble, my lord," he said to Miles with a wry grin. "But it was gravely important that Miss Bentley completely believe I was on her side. We suspected she was our murderess when she and Crenshaw disappeared from Lady Westwood's estate without giving notice. Any servant hoping to find another position would have realized it would be nearly impossible without first obtaining a written reference from her employer or, as in this case, from her deceased employer's heir. But we had to have a spoken confession before witnesses before we could arrest her. Otherwise she'd probably have gotten off scott-free. Our courts don't like to sentence women to hang unless the evidence is fool-proof."

He turned slightly. "Ah, yes. Allow me to present my friend and partner, Mr. Hanlan, also a Runner. Naturally, he is not a real priest, nor was the special license a real one. If you had taken the time to examine it closely, my dear Miss Bentley, you would have noticed that it was not signed by either the archbishop or his representative, which it must needs be in order to be legal. Therefore, I am happy to inform you, Lord Bradford, that you are not truly married."

Genevieve was suddenly filled with indignation. "You mean you held a loaded revolver to Lord Bradford's back—and frightened the coachman and tiger—just to capture a criminal?"

"I'm sorry, Miss Quince, but this was a serious business. Besides, as for harassing Lord Bradford, perhaps we are now even for his slight with the horse." He smiled, and Miles returned the humorous glance. "And the coachman and tiger are quite well. I informed them of our plan a few minutes ago, when Hanlan and I released them."

"You have forgotten something, Mr. Debenham," Miss Bentley spat. "I still have my revolver, and I will not hesitate to shoot the first person who tries to stop me from leaving!" She backed up until she was nearly at the stable door.

Lord Bradford could see by her expression that she was calculating the distance to his abandoned carriage and did not see the coachman creeping up behind her, a log held in one meaty fist.

Mr. Debenham smiled. "No, my love. I assure you that I have forgotten nothing."

There was a sudden flurry of movement as the coachman brought his weapon down with a thump on Miss Bentley's head, followed by a

loud, unexpected explosion as the derringer dis-
charged.

The bullet grazed Miles's arm, spattering his coat
with blood, and the lantern he had been holding
crashed to the floor, flames instantly lapping at the
thickly scattered straw. In seconds the entire stable
was a blazing inferno. Someone screamed. Smoke
billowed. And the group stampeded toward the
open air.

It was only when Genevieve was standing outside the burning stable that she noticed Lord Bradford was not with them. "Miles!" she screamed,
struggling to break free from Mr. Debenham, who
held her firmly by the arm. "Miles! Where are
you?"

"Miss Quince," Mr. Debenham shouted over the
roaring flames, you cannot go in there! You'd be
burned alive!"

"But Miles is still inside! I have to find him!"
she sobbed, tears streaming down her cheeks.

There was a crumbling, echoing sound as the far
end of the stable collapsed, sending showers of
flame and sparks sailing up into the sky.

Genevieve moaned and turned her face into Mr.
Debenham's coat. She did not turn to watch the
horses stampede out of the burning building, and
thus she missed seeing the man now stumbling
outside, carrying the prostrate form of Miss
Bentley. He lowered his bundle to the ground.

"Is this how you mourn your beloved, then,
Miss Quince?" said a wry, humorous voice from
behind her.

Certain she was hallucinating, Genevieve was
afraid to turn around.

"I say, old fellow. How did you manage to steal
her away from me so quickly? I guess it's true
what they say: out of sight, out of mind."

Mr. Debenham laughed, and finally Genevieve

looked up. "Miles?" she whispered. She swayed unsteadily on her feet.

"Here now, Miss Quince," said Miles gruffly, tenderness welling up inside his chest. "I am the one who has been shot and who walked through fire to save the horses. Surely it is I who should be close to fainting!" And he did, in fact, crumple to the ground.

Genevieve cried out and dropped to his side. "Darling! Oh, my darling! You cannot die! I love you! Oh, please don't die, and I swear I will never do anything to anger you again!" she sobbed. "Anything you say will be law, my darling Miles! I will even become your mistress, if you still want me! Oh, Miles, Miles! Help me, Mr. Debenham!"

The Runner leaned to feel Lord Bradford's wrist.

Miles opened his silver eyes and winked at him. "You are my witness, sir," he said weakly before passing out again.

The detective grinned. "Lord Bradford has simply fainted from the heat and smoke and loss of blood, but his wound is not serious. Let's get him inside. Then, Miss Quince, you and I must take care of some business. I believe I owe you a substantial fee for my stay at your delightful inn."

22

Within a week Miles was feeling as good as new, although his mother had not yet allowed him out of bed. Now, as Lady Bradford dozed in the chair beside his bed, he slid the coverlet away, dressed, and crept from the room. He held his finger to his lips as he passed Benson, who, after whispering the news that Miss Bentley and Crenshaw were now incarcerated in Newgate Prison, grinned and pointed toward the double French doors leading out into the garden. Miles walked through them and out across the marble terrace.

Genevieve sat on a bench beneath a fragrant, low-hanging lilac watching goldfish flit here and there beneath the surface of a tiny ornamental pound. Her hair hung in soft, luminous waves, caught back with a simple blue bow.

Miles smiled as he approached, then paused, undetected, to watch his beloved for a few more moments. She raised her deep-blue eyes toward the sky, and he was astonished to see that they glistened with tears. He hesitated no longer. "Jenny, why are you crying?"

She jumped to her feet. "Miles! I mean my lord. I was not crying." He came a few steps closer, and her heart began to pound so hard that she was certain he must hear it.

" 'Miles' will do nicely, don't you think?" He gazed at her, hoping for a smile, but Genevieve said nothing, and simply looked down at the ground. Miles persisted. "I don't know if I was dazed with smoke, but it seemed to me—correct me if I am wrong—that, while I was lying on the ground at death's door, you practically insisted on becoming my mistress."

"Well, about that. I . . ."

"Now Jenny, I believe I even have a witness. Mr. Debenham was there, wasn't he? And he is a Runner, you know. He could throw you into prison if you don't keep your word."

Genevieve jerked her eyes up and glared at him. Miles laughed heartily, glad to see the tears vanish and the fiery glow return to her face.

"Lord Bradford, I refuse to be forced to—" But she did not get another word out, because Miles reached out an swept her into his arms. His mouth came down on hers, and it was not long before she was clinging to him and willing to do anything he asked.

"Now then, Miss Quince, are you ready to capitulate?" he challenged, breathing heavily.

She nodded helplessly, looking utterly dazed.

"Good. I don't want any argument. We will secure a special license and be married posthaste here at Bradford Hall. Afterward, we will travel through Europe. I thought we would visit France first—Cannes, Paris, then perhaps Italy and Rome."

"Married?" she cried with disbelief. "But—I—I thought—"

"Now, Miss Quince," he said with mock disapproval, "I simply must refuse to be your light-o'-love. After all, I have hopelessly compromised you any number of times. We *must* be married. If you care not for your reputation, then think of mine. Society would never forgive me!"

Genevieve's face fell, and she looked down at the ground once more. "Oh. If that is why you wish to marry me, I assure you, it is not necessary."

Miles chuckled and lifted her chin with one finger so that she was forced to look into his eyes. "You silly wench. Do you really think I would marry you if I did not want to? I love you, Jenny. I desire nothing so much in the world as that you become my wife."

He paused, gazing at her face as if memorizing it. "I learned a very important lesson when I almost lost you. I was a fool. A proud, stiff-necked fool. But no more. Nothing matters but that we be together. Nothing. No one's opinion. Now stop your ridiculous comments and kiss me, and devil take the Beau Monde!"

She capitulated gladly.

After a long time, they came up for air.

"I fear that if we do not go inside now, my dear, our marriage will be consummated before it is performed." Miles laughed, taking a deeply blushing Jenny by the arm and leading her toward the house. "Besides, we must give Mother the happy tidings."

They walked through the French doors to hear a worried feminine voice echoing through the house.

"Where could he have gone, Benson? I was sitting right there, and he simply disappeared!" Lady Bradford bustled into the parlor, which they had just entered, and sighed with relief. "There you are, Miles!" Behind her came Lord Stanfield. "We must talk, dear."

"Yes, Mother. We were just coming to look for you."

She ignored his comment and rushed on. "I suppose you know what you must do, Miles. I raised you to be an honorable man. You have compromised this young woman's reputation, and now that you are well enough to be up and about, you must marry her forthwith!" She scowled at Lord Bradford but looked secretly pleased, as if she couldn't have arranged matters any better on her own.

Miles laughed heartily. "Whatever you say, Mother."

Lady Bradford looked startled, but then her face lit up happily. "Quite so, my dear. I am glad you are finally seeing reason," she said with satisfaction.

"Speaking of which, Lady Bradford," came a voice from behind her, "I feel forced to bring up a certain matter of some importance. Another matter of honor and reason." Lady Bradford turned to look at Reginald, who cleared his throat and continued. "You apparently feel it vital that Miles marry Genevieve because they spent several hours together, at night, unchaperoned—is that correct?"

"Of course," she replied with a contented sigh.

Lord Stanfield grinned. "Well, then, dear lady, it would appear that we, too, must wed. For did we not spend several hours in just such a situation, and finish them in a bedroom?"

Lady Bradford's eyes widened. "Truly, Reggie, that is not the same thing! We—"

"I beg to differ with you, my lady. What would Society say if they knew you and I had shared a cot without benefit of wedlock? More important," he said smugly, drawing a small square of fabric from his breast pocket, "what would they say if

they knew you had welshed on a signed contract?" He flicked the napkin open with a flourish.

Miles watched the unfolding drama with twin-
kling eyes. "May I?" he asked, and Lord Stanfield
handed him the bit of cloth. "Well, Mother, it certainly appears to be in order. And this is your sig-
nature, is it not?"

She nodded, then drew an annoyed breath.
"Yes, but—"

"There is no *but* about it, Mother. As you said,
you raised me to be an honorable man. If *you* fail
to act honorably, who says I might not feel permitted to do likewise?"

Lord Stanfield beamed, and Lady Bradford shot
an irritated look at her son.

Miles continued. "So what of it, Stanfield? What
would you ask my mother in return for your services?"

Lord Stanfield hesitated. "That is something I
must discuss with your mother in private, if you
don't mind, Bradford," he said softly, his eyes
never leaving Lady Bradford's.

"Of course," said Miles understandingly. "Jenny
and I were just on our way to breakfast."
Genevieve smiled up at him as he led her from the
room.

Lord Stanfield looked steadily at Lady Bradford.
Her hands trembled as she plucked nervously at
the folds of her pale-green muslin morning dress.

"You know what I want, Amy."

"Yes."

"Well then?"

"Well, my lord, it would appear that I have no
choice."

Reginald sighed. "Nonsense, Amy. You can refuse me if you wish. I would never force you to do
anything." He pulled her gently into his arms. "I
love you, Amy. Always have. You know that."

Slowly Lady Bradford's arms wrapped around his neck, and she kissed him on the lips. When at last she raised her head, she gazed up at him adoringly. Reginald was stunned into silence.

Lady Bradford raised her eyebrows questioningly. "Well?"

"Well what?"

"Ask me, Reggie." She looked at him tenderly.

"Marry me, Amy," he said gruffly, his voice rough with emotion.

"I will. Oh, yes, Reggie. I will. I love you, too." And she pulled his lips back to hers.

23

S oon thereafter a double wedding was held in
the small chapel at Bradford Hall and an enormous banquet served. Miss Pramble, who had
been given charge over Quince House, insisted on
preparing some of her specialities for the army of
guests, many of whom were staying at the new
inn.

Because they were Jenny's only living relatives,
Miles had dutifully invited Lord and Lady
Merriweather, her cousins, to the ceremony. He
grinned as he watched them, satisfied at the bitter
disappointment on Marybelle's face. As usual, Augustus said next to nothing, for he was far more
interested in the brandy served after the ceremony
than in the happy occasion.

In all, it was a lovely wedding, with one bride
dressed in pristine white and the other in ice-blue.
The guests, including the solicitor Mr. Dobbins
and the Earl and Countess of Glenworthy, could
not help commenting on the need Lord Bradford
seemed to have to be touching his new wife at all
times. His fingers, complete with gleaming gold
band, never left her hand, her arm, or her slender
waist. When the newlyweds disappeared earlier

than was normally acceptable, people simply smiled and went on with their festivities.

Jenny had been shy about leaving the guests so abruptly. However, after pulling her into the cover of an enormous lilac and kissing her into submission, Miles finally succeeded in convincing her that she wanted the same thing as he. To preserve her maidenly sensibilities, he led her into Bradford Hall through the kitchen door so that no one would see them, and up the back staircase to the blue bedroom he had created just for her.

Jenny gasped at the exquisite chamber, and Miles felt a satisfied glow at seeing the proper woman in this place where she belonged. He leaned down and kissed her gently on the tip of her nose, and she gazed up at him, all the love in her heart reflected in her eyes.

"I am afraid I am dreaming," she whispered.

"If you are, I hope you never wake up," he said gently. Her full lips tempted him, and he lowered his face to hers to cover them in a sweet embrace.

She felt him smile against her mouth and looked at him with mock outrage. "What reason have you found to laugh at me this time?" she demanded.

"I was just thinking how adorable you look when you are not in control of a situation," he said softly. "And I cannot wait to see you in the morning when you wake up in fact, as well as name, as my wife."

Genevieve frowned and swatted him playfully. "I don't want to look adorable." She stood on tiptoe to boldly nibble on his earlobe. "I want to look so irresistible that you will always remember I am your wife."

"Oh, my dearest," Lord Bradford whispered passionately, his mouth caressing her lips, then wandering down her slender neck, "you are most definitely irresistible."

"I do love you, Miles," she said shakily, pulling him back to her mouth.

His tongue probed her, his teeth bit gently at her lips, until Genevieve felt as if her bones were melting. His hands were warm on her flesh, and she quivered to his touch. His fingers danced over the thin silk of her wedding gown, teasing, tempting, finally reaching her breasts and making her shudder as she felt her nipples harden and thrust against his fingertips. He shocked her still further by lowering his head and suckling them gently through the fabric, making wet places that were chilled by the evening breeze that flowed in through the open window. Genevieve gasped and arched her back, and one of his hands found the tiny pearl buttons that ran up the back of the gown. He released them. He did not remove the dress yet, but slid its hem up so that he could caress the soft, silky flesh of her thighs.

Genevieve thought she might die from all the startling new sensations ricocheting through her virginal body. His magic had her fairly writhing beneath his skillful hands. When she felt him lower the constricting garment over her shoulders, felt the warm breeze caress her bare breasts, she moaned with a curious mixture of pleasure and frustration. And then his mouth was on her naked nipple, his tongue and teeth driving her to utter distraction. She made to pull his head closer to her breast, but Miles backed away enough to finish undressing her.

Though she blushed furiously to stand naked in the light of his masculine gaze, he gently urged her backward and onto the bed, watching her as he began to remove his own clothing. When he was stripped of everything but his breeches, his fingers returned to her aching flesh. He touched and caressed her all over, all the while murmuring words of love. Then slowly, his fingers slid between her thighs. She gasped at the shocking intimacy, but he continued stroking and probing her until she was writhing and lifting her hips to meet his bold caress.

The ache in his groin was reaching urgent proportions, and Miles grasped Jenny's wrist with his other hand, pressing her hand to the rock-hard bulge in his breeches.

Genevieve gasped anew, but Miles looked deep into her sky-blue eyes, and she trustingly left her hand where he had put it. He closed his eyes, shuddering under her tentative touch, and she was flooded with a feeling of delicious power. Emboldened, she began removing her husband's breeches, sliding them down over his hips until he could kick them impatiently from his feet. She ran her hands down his thickly haired legs, glorying in the strength and fullness of his muscular body. Then, shyly, her hand made its way back up to the place where his body craved it most. She wrapped her fingers around the long, warm shaft and instinctively began to move them up and down in slow strokes until Miles grabbed her hand and pulled it away. She looked up at him, alarmed that she had done something wrong.

"It's all right, darling," he whispered, kissing her gently. "You simply please me too well."

"Oh, Miles," she said passionately. "I never knew anything could feel like this. Please don't stop, my love. Make me your wife!"

Lord Bradford groaned and moved atop her, clasping her shoulders with his strong hands. "God, Jenny, you are so beautiful," he murmured. "Your skin is like sweet cream, and your hair—your hair is like a sunset, gold touched with scarlet." Parting her legs with his knees, he positioned himself to enter her.

Genevieve's eyes widened at the feel of his warm bluntness insistently probing her most intimate parts. Miles laughed softly, gazing into her eyes, and longing washing over her in a huge wave. She arched her hips, and her lips parted, her pink tongue peeping out to moisten her mouth.

Miles gritted his teeth at her innocent action, which nearly unmanned him before he even entered her. He pushed softly, placing the tip of his engorged manhood within. God, she was so warm, so silky, so tight. He longed to thrust himself into her but held back when he bumped into her maidenhead. He paused to reassure her. "I am honored to be your first, sweet wife. I could not have dreamed for more. This will hurt, my love, but be brave and it will only last a moment. Then I promise you it will be very, very good."

Genevieve gazed at him, tense. Then she nodded briefly, her teeth clenched.

Lord Bradford took a deep breath, then thrust deeply into her velvet softness. Once inside he held completely still so that he would not lose control.

Genevieve cried out and closed her eyes at the pain, but she was pinned beneath his powerful body. At last the stinging pain subsided, leaving her feeling full and possessed. Slowly she opened her eyes to look at her husband.

When she did, Lord Bradford felt a wave of fire wash over him. For Jenny smiled with all the seductive power of a woman loved. He began moving smoothly within her, fitting perfectly like hand in glove. Jenny's eyes glazed over as she caught the rhythm and began to move with him. They were one, and together they sailed to the stars, where there was nothing but glorious, dazzling heat and the music of the universe. In a surge of passion Jenny thrust her hips wildly against his, and Lord Bradford felt his control evaporate.

"Oh, yes, Miles!" she cried, clutching his shoulders and biting his neck.

"My love, I cannot hold back," he gasped. "I want you to come with me, darling. Fly to the moon with me, my love! Now!" With a lunge, he sank deep within her, crying out his ecstasy. His seed erupted in a fiery gush, searching for that tiny part within her with which it could join to make a new life.

Powerful tremors engulfed Genevieve and tossed her about like a leaf in a hurricane. She clung frantically to her husband. A voice she did not recognize as her own cried out in ecstasy.

At long last she stopped thrashing. Her cries of pleasure slowed to a soft whimper.

Miles held her close. Her face was buried in the side of his neck, and he gently rolled off her until they lay side by side, exhausted but happy. In a few moments her deep breathing indicated that she slept, and with a contented smile her lord settled down beside her, unable to take his eyes from her face until he, too, slept at last.

Epilogue

Exactly six months after happily missing the entire London Season, and after taking care of some pressing business—expressly that of sending Madame Mimi Devereux her *congé* along with a large sum of money and a grateful note thanking her for her services, which he would no longer require—Miles sat in his library at Bradford Hall reminiscing on the past half year. Shaking his head in wonder, he stood, left his sanctuary, and closed the door behind him. He climbed the grand staircase and entered his bedchamber.

He smiled as he saw his beautiful wife soaking languorously in a large copper tub, one slender leg hanging lazily over its edge, her back toward the door. Her cinnamon hair was piled in a mass of curls on the top of her head.

"Francine? Is that you? Would you hand me my towel, please?" She did not turn, believing the intruder to be her new maid.

"No, wife," Lord Bradford replied, coming forward. He placed his hands on her damp shoulders, then lowered them to caress her bare, wet breasts. "It is not Francine. It is not Miss Pramble. It is not Jasper. It is not Aunt Hester. We are completely alone. And as for your towel, I don't think you will be needing it just yet."

He began to remove his clothing, and Genevieve felt a delicious, familiar warmth between her legs. She waited until he stepped into the water opposite her, then gave a tug on his ankles and had the satisfaction of watching him sit down rapidly with an undignified splash.

"Wretch!" he cried, seizing her bare thighs. "I can see I am going to have to teach you who is master!" He pulled her down under the water, and she emerged bedraggled and sputtering. But before her fiery temper could take hold, he leaned to silence her outcry with a moist, steamy kiss.

The two lovers drew back and gazed at each other with sudden desire. Then Genevieve moved to straddle his legs and perch on his lap, cradling his manhood between her thighs. She kissed him deeply, her pink tongue darting in and out of his mouth.

Miles gave a delighted laugh and pulled her so close that her erect nipples grazed his hairy chest.

"I think, my lord, that there is no question of who is master here," Genevieve breathed contentedly.

"So you finally admit that I am in complete and utter control?" he said smugly.

Rather than offering him one of her pert retorts, Genevieve suddenly blushed and looked away from her husband.

"Is something amiss, wife?" Lord Bradford asked with a frown.

"I am not certain, my lord, if you will think it amiss or not."

"What is it, my darling?"

"Only that you seem to take great pleasure in my body, my lord, and I am not certain if you will for much longer." Genevieve caught her lower lip between her teeth.

Lord Bradford smiled at her gently, thinking her simply modest and insecure. "You are the most beautiful woman in the world. Your body pleases me immensely. It is exquisite. How could I ever find anything wrong with it?" He reached to trace her nipples with one finger.

Genevieve drew in a sharp breath, then burst out, "Oh, my love, I fear that you will not want to touch me any longer when my belly begins to swell, as I have reason to believe it soon will." She turned her head away in embarrassment.

Lord Bradford let out a whoop of joy. Catching Genevieve's in his arms, he pulled her on top of him, sending bathwater sloshing over the rim of the tub.

"You are with child? Oh, Jenny! How could I not be happy to have you swell with my seed?" He paused, looking at her with concern. "Dearest, never worry that I shall find you other than delightful. I only hope that you are pleased."

When she did not turn toward him, Lord Bradford placed his forefinger beneath her chin and raised her face to his. Her eyes remained lowered. "Jenny?"

Her lashes rose at last, and Miles's heart caught in his throat as he saw that her eyes were filled with sparkling tears. Then she smiled, and he laughed with relief.

"Oh, yes, my lord, I am honored to bear your child. I am only weeping from happiness. I do confess to having quite a desire for a little Lord Miles who looks just like his father. And if this babe does not fulfill my wish, I fear I may make demands upon you to mend the situation, again and again, until the young fellow makes his appearance!"

Her husband's eyes darkened with passion. "Only if you give me a dozen little ladies who will grow up to be beautiful, teasing hoydens just like their mother," he said tenderly, lowering his head to kiss her again.

Suddenly he drew back and grinned broadly. "You know, my best friend, Tony Ashleigh, sent me a missive just this morning to tell me his wife is at last breeding."

Genevieve smiled. "What happy news!"

"It's positively delightful news!" he boomed. "Just as I planned," he announced smugly. "Our children will play together and when they are of age, wed each other." He looked very pleased with himself, proud of his mastery of every situation.

Genevieve giggled. "I see nothing amiss in your wish that our children be playmates, but do you not think that their genders—and their desires— might dictate their mates?"

Lord Bradford looked downcast. "Mmm. I suppose you are, as usual, correct, my dearest wife."

"However, I am most certain that any child of yours will be irresistible," she cajoled him. "And, as I suggested, we can always keep trying until we get the sexes right." She smiled seductively, and his crossness instantly fled.

Then he gazed at her, suddenly serious. "My darling, I worship you. Can you ever possibly love me as much?"

Genevieve answered him with a butterfly-soft kiss, her lips barely touching his, until her husband groaned with passionate frustration and sought to show her who was master once more. And then there was no more talk for a very, very long time.

Avon *Regency* Romance

Kasey Michaels

THE CHAOTIC MISS CRISPINO
76300-1/$3.99 US/$4.99 Can

THE DUBIOUS MISS DALRYMPLE
89908-6/$2.95 US/$3.50 Can

THE HAUNTED MISS HAMPSHIRE
76301-X/$3.99 US/$4.99 Can

THE WAGERED MISS WINSLOW
76302-8/$3.99 US/$4.99 Can

Loretta Chase

THE ENGLISH WITCH 70660-1/$2.95 US/$3.50 Can
ISABELLA 70597-4/$2.95 US/$3.95 Can
KNAVES' WAGER 71363-2/$3.95 US/$4.95 Can
THE SANDALWOOD PRINCESS
71455-8/$3.99 US/$4.99 Can

THE VISCOUNT VAGABOND
70836-1/$2.95 US/$3.50 Can

Jo Beverley

EMILY AND THE DARK ANGEL
71555-4/$3.99 US/$4.99 Can

THE STANFORTH SECRETS
71438-8/$3.99 US/$4.99 C